The Art
of the Break

The Art
of the Break

MARY WIMMER

THE UNIVERSITY OF WISCONSIN PRESS

Publication of this book has been made possible, in part, through support from the Brittingham Trust.

The University of Wisconsin Press
728 State Street, Suite 443
Madison, Wisconsin 53706
uwpress.wisc.edu

Gray's Inn House, 127 Clerkenwell Road
London EC1R 5DB, United Kingdom
eurospanbookstore.com

Printed in the United States of America
This book may be available in a digital edition.

Library of Congress Cataloging-in-Publication Data

Names: Wimmer, Mary B., author.
Title: The art of the break / Mary Wimmer.
Description: Madison, Wisconsin : The University of Wisconsin Press, [2022]
Identifiers: LCCN 2022008288 | ISBN 9780299339746 (paperback)
Subjects: LCSH: Cheesemakers—Wisconsin—Fiction. | LCGFT: Fiction. | Novels.
Classification: LCC PS3623.I5886 A88 2022 | DDC 813/.6—dc23/eng/20220413
LC record available at https://lccn.loc.gov/2022008288

For
MY FAMILY

The Art
of the Break

Chapter 1

Unable to sleep, Charlie spent the early morning hours making a batch of cheddar in her kitchen using fresh milk from a farm just thirty miles west of her home in Milwaukee. Cheesemaking calmed her and cast her into a state of creative concentration so even her growing worries about Dad diminished some. She put the last cheese form under a press, wiped down the counter with a mixture of bleach and water, and mulled over the truth she'd been ruminating on—he wasn't well. She could tell from their phone call last night: how he'd paused for long seconds, searching for words; how he'd called her Ria, her long-dead sister; how he'd gone on about buying new cheesemaking equipment he could not afford. Then from left field, he brought up goat cheese and how it was going to be the next new thing and how they should buy goats.

"Really? You hate goats," she'd reminded him. "The bucks are aggressive and stinky, and they pee everywhere during rutting season." Could it be dementia? she'd wondered. Maybe a stroke, or one of those ministrokes?

As she towel-dried the clean pots and utensils, Lucy appeared in the doorway, sleepy in her pink pajamas, yawning and rubbing her eyes. Time for *Captain Kangaroo*? How was it already 9 a.m.? Charlie was late for work at the cheese market. Shoot. She shifted into gear. "Watch your shows in the kitchen. Dad's sleeping." She kissed Lucy's cheek, still warm from sleep, rushed into the bathroom, brushed on mascara, rubbed Carmex on her lips, and called out to Rick to wake up. He didn't respond. He was passed out on the couch with the TV on. Again. They'd stopped sleeping together months ago, years after she'd started seriously thinking about taking Lucy back home to Falls River. On good days, Charlie told herself they should stay together for their daughter. On bad days, she knew better. She stayed because Rick needed her.

She stood next to the couch and studied him. His breathing was phlegmy and loud, an effect of smoking a pack a day. On TV, a local reporter mused about how the Brewers could move into first place if they beat Boston at home today. This meant there would soon be tailgaters at the nearby stadium parking lot, with the smell of cooking brats and hamburgers drifting over to their neighborhood.

She traced Rick's mouth with her eyes. It was almost feminine, with lips that curved upward in the corners. The scar from a hockey game in high school bisected his chin. Long, auburn hair with gold flecks clung to his head, and his thick eyelashes skirted his cheeks. He was handsome even as he slept off another night of drinking. His good looks were what she'd noticed first, when they'd met seven years earlier at the Milwaukee Cheese Market, where she worked. Six weeks later, he told her he loved her on the beach at Lake Michigan near the marina, sailboats ethereal in the light from a full moon. She shook off the nostalgia that tethered her to him. Why not just leave? She could go up to Falls River, see Dad, and talk to him about moving back home and working in the cheese factory again.

"Please get up," she said. When he didn't respond to her voice, she moved closer to him, shaking his shoulder. "Come on. I have to work."

He opened his eyes, looked at her for a second, then closed them, mumbling something inaudible as he turned on his side, his back to her now, asleep again. She sighed as she looked at the pots she used for making cheese on the kitchen counter next to the sink, smelled bleach, and heard the calming voice of Captain Kangaroo and the clink of Lucy's spoon on her cereal bowl. She thought of how her mother would do the same thing—turn her back to her, as if sleep was all she could abide. Charlie recognized the feelings of intense loneliness she'd carried as a child. She felt them as she pulled on jeans and a T-shirt, gave her hair a quick brush, and told Lucy to get dressed. She'd bring Lucy to work today. Rick was still drunk.

～

At the cheese market, Charlie massaged a wedge of cheese, caressing it like a worry stone. The soft muslin fabric evoked thoughts of Dad—how he'd taught her that clothbound cheese, not covered in wax or plastic, allowed for a unique mingling of bacteria, moisture, and air that gave it an earthy, savory taste. She relaxed into the daydream of Dad's lessons in cheesemaking, telling herself he was fine. Her daydreams and the predict-able routines of working at the cheese market were especially welcome after her sleepless night, though Lucy didn't seem fazed. She was coloring and chatting with customers.

Charlie plunged her T-shaped tester into the cheese and pulled out a sample the circumference of a number 2 pencil. Handing half to a woman customer and keeping half for herself, she broke her piece in two, notic-ing how easily it separated; breathed in the smell of it, pungent and earthy; and felt the consistency, just on the verge of crumbly. The taste was complex, at the same time tart and sweet; smooth, with characteristic nutty undertones, leaving a lingering salty zing on the bottom back of her tongue. It was a satisfying wave of flavor. It had depth and what Dad called a "gorgeous zest."

Another customer, wearing a Green Bay Packers jersey, asked her for a sample, then a pair of twins about Lucy's age in Brewers gear put their hands out. They wore Hank Aaron's number 44 jersey. She smiled at the boys and handed them some cheddar samples. "Are you guys going to the baseball game today to see Hank?" She knew he was back playing for the Brewers this season; the whole town was excited. Heck, Charlie was excited, though she didn't have time to attend many games even with the ballpark right down the block from their home.

"Yes! Hammerin' Hank is back!" one of the boys proclaimed. They popped the cheese into their mouths, then wiped their hands on their shorts before disappearing into the crowd of shoppers.

The cheese market was busy today, July 3, filled with parents and kids who'd tomorrow decorate their bike handles with streamers and use clothespins to fix playing cards to their wheel spokes for neighborhood parades. Kids were excited for nighttime fireworks and parents carried the relief that followed a long, cold spring after an even longer, darker winter in Wisconsin. With such long and dark winters, an epidemic of chronic melancholy ensued here each year, producing an alarming num-ber of alcoholics.

The Packers fan was talking to her. "Kind of sharp, but it's good."

"So good." The woman customer was clutching her purse to her chest in the way some suburbanites do downtown. Wearing pearls and pumps, she was the 1950s version of women who worked in the home: a house-wife. It was a narrow path Charlie did not want to follow. It's the 1970s, for

crying out loud. Time to lose the pumps and pearls. Put on some hip hug-
gers and stop it with the curlers at night, the girdles, the mind-numbing
housework. You don't have to do that anymore. She knew her anger was
misplaced, that she harbored the belief her mother had felt trapped by
the constrictions put on women. She softened her thoughts and smiled at
the purse woman, grateful to have been born at a later time, feeling fortunate that the owner of the cheese market, Oscar Warner, respected her
and took her under his wing, teaching her about Vermont and European
cheese and the intricacies of being a cheesemonger. A cheesemonger. She
liked the sound of it. It gave her a comforting connection with her mom,
who'd sold cheese at her parents' shop in London near Piccadilly Circus
before she met Dad, fell in love, and immigrated to the United States, what
people called an English war bride.

"It's an English cheddar from Somerset," Charlie told them.

"I'll take two pounds," the woman said.

"Give me one," the Packers guy chimed in, helping himself to more
samples Charlie had placed on the counter. He was making a meal of it,
and she tried to hide her amusement. She liked selling cheese, turning
people on to the vast variety of tastes from Wisconsin cheddars to French
camembert and brie. Still, she'd worked here long enough and was ready
to get back to the vat, and back to making cheese.

Positioning the block under the cutting wire, she lopped off a one-
pound wedge, then a two pounder, before wrapping and tucking the re-
mainder into the cooler.

"Charlotte, phone call." Wyatt, her coworker, yelled, even though he
was standing just eight feet away from her. He was her age, early thirties,
tall and thin with shaggy hair and wire-rimmed glasses. They'd been lab
partners at the University of Wisconsin–Madison. These days, Wyatt was
working on a master's degree in journalism at Marquette University, having decided he liked writing about science more than being a scientist.

Charlie left the cheese on the cutting board, irked by the interruption.
Rick probably needed something. He was always looking for something
he'd misplaced, or asking her to bring home food because he was too
hungover to go to the grocery store.

"What about my cheese?" the purse woman called out.

"He'll help you." Charlie nodded at Wyatt, who had already taken over
at the cutting board.

Lucy, perched on a high stool next to the phone, was drawing pictures of goats. Charlie circled her arm around her and grabbed the phone off the wall hook.

"This is Charlie."

"It's Uncle Jack." In all the years she'd worked here, Uncle Jack had never called the store. A weird tingling ran up the skin on her arms.

"Your dad's had a heart attack. He's in the hospital."

Chapter 2

"Oh jeez, how bad is it?" Charlie rubbed Lucy's back.

Uncle Jack's words came through the fits and starts of a crackling connection.

"Doc Cooper says his heart is badly damaged. He talks a little bit, but mostly sleeps."

"Damaged?" With the bad connection, she could barely hear him. Had he said heart damage? Charlie thought of her sister, Ria, in a hospital room twenty years earlier, encased in an iron lung. She covered her free ear so she could hear better.

"He's hooked up to all sorts of machines," Uncle Jack said. "Can you come up?"

"Of course." Charlie's heart pounded fast, but she took a deep breath and calculated how long it would take to go home, talk to Rick, pack, and drive north to Falls River.

"I can be there in four hours." She should have gone up there a few days ago. "What happened? Was he alone?"

"Yeah, he was making cheese," Uncle Jack said. "I found him lying on the floor next to the vat. I knew he hadn't been feeling too good, so I was checking on him. Must have happened right before I got there."

"Making cheese," she repeated. "That figures." He was doing what he loved.

"See you soon. Drive safe," Uncle Jack said. "We're at St. James, room one-nineteen."

Wyatt had abandoned his customers and stood next to her.

"Dad's had a heart attack."

"Oh my gosh, you need to go." Wyatt wrapped her in a bear hug. "Don't worry about us. You go. Take care of your dad." She heard the midwestern kindness. Having grown up on a farm in western Wisconsin milking cows,

8

Wyatt had five brothers and treated her like the sister he never had. Tears welled up in her eyes. He was always so nice.

"Thanks, Wyatt."

"Lucy, we need to go." How much should she tell her? "Grandpa's sick."

Lucy looked up at Charlie under a veil of blonde hair falling across her face. Her sweet little girl.

"Okay, Mom."

Charlie took off her apron and grabbed her purse from under the counter, and they headed out the front door, crossing the cobblestones on Third Street. She held Lucy's hand, and the two started running on the uneven stones, past a popular German restaurant and Turner Hall, a gymnasium and meeting place built by German socialists in the late nineteenth century. Two blocks south of Turner Hall, they hopped into her Volkswagen Bug, which, earlier that morning, she had parked in a garbage-strewn lot next to an abandoned building. Milwaukee had a blighted feeling in places. Many people had moved west to the suburbs, choosing wide roads and nondescript strip malls over brick and stone buildings constructed by stone masons and other artisans during the previous century. These old buildings were what Charlie loved about the city—what she would miss if she moved back to her hometown. She drove west on Wisconsin Avenue, the main downtown street, with empty storefronts and fast-food wrappers pushed around the sidewalks and gutters by the wind.

Charlie thought again about her plan to leave, to take Lucy up north for good so she could experience clear air, clean rivers, giant pine forests, and friends and family she loved. She could take Lucy away from a father who was falling apart.

She trembled, close to tears thinking about her dad in the hospital. Should Lucy see her grandfather hooked up to machines? She was only five years old. Because of what had happened to her sister, Ria, when she was a young girl, Charlie worried about Lucy all the time. She felt the old, familiar dread yanking her back under, strong as a river current. And she'd been barely treading water lately. In just ten minutes, they neared home, and Charlie could smell meat cooking on the grills of tailgaters gathered in the parking lots around the stadium. She turned onto their street and was surrounded by two-story wood-sided duplexes painted white or shades of gray or tan with distinguishing features like porch size, or an American flag flying out front. Some had gardens nurturing fledgling tomato plants and some had fences, but all were built so close together that Charlie heard her neighbors' toilets flush on summer evenings when the windows were open.

Throbbing behind her eyes felt like the start of a headache and her side hurt from running. Charlie peeked over at Lucy. She was staring at her. They smiled at each other.

"Is Grandpa going to be okay?" she asked.

"We'll see, honey." Charlie reached for Lucy's small hand and held it. "Uncle Jack said he's pretty sick."

"I'm going to give him these goat pictures," she said. "I already made two." She held up drawings of Billy goats and kids beside a house that looked like the old farmhouse Dad lived in.

Halfway down the block, Charlie parallel parked in front of their place, and they climbed the stairs to the upper level. Even though the second-floor duplex was a rental, it still felt like home with its beat-up wood floors and small kitchen cluttered with the pots and utensils she used to make cheese. The landlord was happy to let them paint the rooms when they'd moved in five years earlier, gold and blue to complement the colorful braided rugs and L-shaped green couch in front of the brick fireplace. The closed door to the small guest bedroom meant Rick had migrated to the bed in there. Drawings of animals, Lucy's creations from the night before, were strewn across the floor.

"Come here." Charlie led Lucy to the couch. "Listen." She paused, smoothing her daughter's hair away from her eyes. "Grandpa's had what they call a heart attack."

Lucy thought for a moment and leaned closer, her green eyes growing wide. "Can he talk? Mr. Jones, the janitor at my school, was attacked and when he came back, he couldn't talk very well. His face looked like it was melting. Like this." She demonstrated, drawing the left side of her mouth downward. "Remember he cleaned up my puke that time in kindergarten?" She paused and gripped Charlie's hands with her little ones. "Can Grandpa talk, Mom?" she asked again.

"Yes, I think Grandpa can talk." Charlie cupped Lucy's cheek, absently wiping a smudge of crayon off her nose with her thumb. "We need to drive up and see him." Her desire to get on the road intensified, but she needed to help Lucy understand what was happening.

"Is he going to die, Mom?" Tears appeared. Lucy adored Dad. He had taught her how to make cheese. Together they had watched the milk heat and thicken in large vats, checking the temperature every so often. Lucy had helped Dad fold the cheese, squeezing out the curd from the whey. She had listened to his pronouncements, "Listen to the whey; it will tell you what it needs."

"I don't know. His heart is having trouble pumping blood to his body." Is he going to die? Charlie wondered. "Pack your paper and crayons, and you can make him more drawings on the drive up north. Hurry. And throw some clothes in your little suitcase." Charlie wrapped Lucy in her arms for a quick hug.

"I'll leave Daddy's picture by his door, okay, Mom?" She retrieved a drawing on plain manilla paper from the bag of supplies Charlie had tossed on the counter and carefully set it on the floor by Rick's door. She'd drawn cows and rainbows in a thought box above a picture of Rick sleeping. His eyes were closed, and a smile covered his face like a wish.

Opening the door to Rick's bedroom released a pungent mix of odors—cigarettes, stale beer, and food. Always food. Smells from the kitchen where he worked clung to his clothes. Today he reeked of fish from last night's Friday fish fry. Life as a cook meant late nights, but drinking with his coworkers after work meant Rick slept until midafternoon if left to it.

With his head resting on his pillow, his body hugged into a fetal position, he looked vulnerable, less guarded. When his eyes were open, they were pale green. Charlie was adept at watching his face for signs he was unhappy, like she'd done with Mom after Ria had died. Was his sigh just a sigh or was he sinking into a dark whorl of anger and self-castigation? But talk about it? Nah, a man wouldn't, couldn't; that's not how he'd grown up, with a dad who worked the factory at Allis-Chalmers and a sweet, stay-at-home mom who adored him. His dad built big machinery, was a union steward, and belonged to the Knights of Columbus. He was also an alcoholic and spent most nights at the bar.

"My dad drank every night and he lived 'til seventy-something," Rick would say, one of the few references he'd make involving his father.

"But he died of liver failure," she'd remind him.

He'd just walk away.

She quietly closed his door, went into her room, pulled out her suitcase, and packed enough clothes for at least a month, then helped Lucy pack clothes, books, and toys. She lugged their suitcases into the kitchen and composed a note.

Charlie paused, uncertain what to do. She'd never just left him like this. Her instincts had always been to stay—to stand by him and try to help him with his nightmares and the flashbacks that seemed to appear out of nowhere. The message she left on the kitchen counter was short and to the point and said nothing about coming back.

Dad had a heart attack.

Lucy and I went to Falls River.

Chapter 3

On the drive up north, grim storm clouds threatened rain, but they made it to Falls River without seeing a drop. At the hospital, Uncle Jack met them outside Dad's room. Eight years younger than Dad, Uncle Jack wore a black felt cowboy hat over his shoulder-length blond hair and smiled easy and often.

"Hey, my favorite kindergartener." He scooped up Lucy into his arms.

"First grade." Lucy corrected him with an eye roll.

"That's what I meant." He put his free arm around Charlie's shoulders. "He's in there. You go in, and I'll take Lucy to the candy machine." Uncle Jack volunteered on the town fire department, was a master carpenter, and helped Dad at the factory. Charlie often teased him about being a renaissance man.

"Larry and Walter just left," he said.

"Darn." She wished they would have stayed. She could use their support. They were Dad's best friends.

"They'll be back." Uncle Jack squeezed her shoulder, then swung Lucy down to the floor.

"Let's go find you some of your favorite candy. Starburst, right?"

"Nope."

"Smarties?"

"Nope."

"Bottle Caps?"

"My friend Nathan likes those. But nope." She shook her head. "I like Laffy Taffy, how 'bout you?"

"I like anything chocolate."

Dad was lying, eyes closed, on the hospital bed in the center of the room. He looked pale, small, diminished under the white, cotton hospital blanket. She thought of Lucy's question, *Is he going to die?*

A troubled sadness found her. The last time they were together, they'd sat on the bench down by the Fox River the morning before she left and talked about Ria. Then surprisingly, the conversation had turned to Mom. He'd pointed to the river and said, "She's out there." He said he could feel her. His steel-blue eyes held a certainty that surprised her, especially since she and her father often talked about Ria but never about Mom.

"Evelyn?" Dad's eyes were wide open now, but he was not present. He moved his head back and forth on the pillow. Did he think she was Mom?

"Dad, it's me, Charlie." She rubbed his shoulder. He felt so thin.

"Charlotte." He looked at her hard eyed, as if seeing a disturbing memory. "I should have helped that boy." He was talking louder now.

"What boy?" Dad closed his eyes again and a tear released and traveled down the side of his face. He thrashed his body around the bed, agitated, mumbling something that she was barely able to make out.

"I should have helped him."

Was he talking about John, her childhood friend? John was the only boy she could think of who'd been around the cheese factory a lot. But why would Dad have regrets about John? It didn't make sense. John, who she'd always thought of as her first love, had gone to college at the University of Chicago, earned his teaching degree, and taught in Chicago Public Schools. The last she heard, he'd moved to De Pere, not far from here, and was teaching high school in Green Bay.

"It's okay, Dad," she whispered. "Don't worry." She sat with him for a while, thinking about what he'd said. A boy who he regretted not helping. His breathing was so shallow, his mouth open, his color off. He looked like he was fading away.

Uncle Jack stepped into the room. "Lucy has a good supply of candy, and she's being entertained by the nurse."

"He called me Evelyn."

"You do look a lot like her."

She thought of Mom, her brown hair, her high cheekbones. "I always thought I look more like Dad."

She had Dad's blond hair, blue eyes, and a smattering of freckles across her nose and cheeks. She'd been called beautiful but never thought of herself as such.

"You have his coloring, but you've got your mom's smile. Her face."

"He said something about not helping some boy. He got really agitated."

"Not sure what that's about." Uncle Jack stooped low, so he was eye to eye with Dad. "Karl, you okay? What can we do for you?"

Dad didn't answer. He just slept on, his mouth open. Uncle Jack stood up, and Charlie pulled Dad's blanket up to his chin. She looked at Uncle Jack and wondered if Dad was talking about Uncle Jack when he was young. *That boy*, he'd said. On second thought, he wouldn't call Uncle Jack 'that boy.' Because he was so much older, he'd always looked after him. But mostly, they looked after each other. Their parents had emigrated from Germany as a young couple, and became dairy farmers in Sheboygan, a community on Lake Michigan, north of Milwaukee. Grandpa Mayer died of a heart attack before Charlie was born, but she remembered Grandma as a sweet woman who spoke a mix of English and German; who had curly white hair she wore in a bun on top of her head; who gave her root beer and cinnamon hard candy; and who taught her how to milk a cow and how to make cheese in the kitchen. Charlie moved closer, sat in the chair next to the bed, and picked up Dad's hand. It felt burning hot.

"He's on fire."

"They've been using a cold cloth on his forehead."

She found a cloth and ran it under the tap in the bathroom. Placing it on Dad's forehead, Charlie cupped her hands on either side of his face.

"Dad, I'm here." Tears fell down her cheeks as she understood how sick he was now.

He stirred, moving his legs, then opening his eyes.

"Charlie." His piercing blue eyes, now the color of a bright sky at noon, focused on her for a second. "The natural. You know when to call a clean break."

Charlie smiled at Dad's reference to cheesemaking. A clean break was called when the milk coagulated to a critical point, when it reached the consistency of early congealed Jell-O. Cheesemakers dipped two fingers in the coagulated milk mixture. If the curd broke off clean—a clean break—the mix was ready to proceed to the next step in the process, cutting the curd.

"You taught me that."

Dad didn't register her comment. His gaze shifted to the window in the direction of the river across the street.

"Evelyn." His eyes widened slightly, then he laughed, still looking past Charlie's shoulder through the window to the river. Did he see her out there?

They heard only the beep of the heart monitor.

"I love you, Dad," she whispered, knowing that, like the river current, he was moving faster now, away from her. Take his hand, Mom, please, Charlie thought, hold it tight.

"He knows," Uncle Jack said.

Charlie leaned over; placed her arms behind her dad, hugging him as best she could; and whispered, "I heard you were making cheese. Was it the white cheddar? I was making that white cheddar this morning too. We need to finish that recipe. Come on. I don't think I can do it without you." She rested her head on his shoulder, wishing he'd say something.

In the hallway, they spoke to Doc Cooper. They'd known him forever. He'd treated Ria when she was sick with polio, and he'd helped them navigate all the horror surrounding Mom's death.

"I'm sorry," he said, holding Charlie's hand, which felt weird but comforting, nonetheless. "His heart isn't able to pump like it needs to. This heart attack was massive, and his heart is badly damaged. His body is filling up with fluid, and the medication we're giving him isn't helping."

"You can't operate?" Charlie asked. There had to be something they could do.

"I wish we could." Doc Cooper let go of her hand and folded his arms across his chest. "But it's not an option. There's just too much damage."

"So we need to . . ." She left it there, looking past him at Lucy drawing with a pen on a tablet at the nurses' station. "What do we need to do?"

"We'll keep him comfortable," Doc Cooper said. "See what the next few hours bring."

Charlie was having trouble wrapping her head around this. "He did seem confused lately when I talked to him on the phone."

"He may have been experiencing signs of dementia possibly caused by cerebrovascular disease."

It was a lot to take in, but it made sense. Charlie looked at Uncle Jack. "So?"

"You sit with him for a while," Uncle Jack said. "I'll take Lucy over to Booths Landing for something to eat. We'll bring you back some food." He checked his watch. "It's almost seven o'clock. It's getting late."

Before they left, Charlie brought Lucy into the room, and her daughter placed her small hand on Dad's shoulder, stood on her tiptoes, leaned in, and kissed him on the cheek. "Sleep tight, Grandpa." She eyed the monitor tracking Dad's heartbeat for a few seconds, then turned and walked dutifully into the hallway with Uncle Jack.

Charlie sat with Dad for the next two hours and watched him sleep. Uncle Jack brought her a hamburger, which she consumed even though she wasn't hungry. She was grateful Uncle Jack had dropped off Lucy to stay the night with his wife, Karen, at their home.

Shortly after midnight, Dad took his last breath. He died without having opened his eyes since earlier in the day, but there was something otherworldly in his expression. He had a slight smile on his face, or did Charlie just imagine it? Was Mom with him? Could he see her?

She hoped so.

Chapter 4

Charlie finally left the hospital around 2 a.m. and drove through town toward home. She headed past Booths Landing, Saint James church, Pawlowski's Polish bakery, the public elementary school Charlie attended for nine years, the Piggly Wiggly, and a smattering of businesses that had been here since she was a kid—Marty's auto shop, Joe's Barber, and the hardware store. She passed the new Falls River Food Co-op, run by a group of farmers that included Charlie's good friends Jenny and Pete. Housed in an old, red brick building, it had been a millwork when she was a kid. The town was small, but just five miles north was one of the state universities, bringing a steady stream of college students and commerce, and more university people were buying up land here, building homes and small farms, revitalizing what was once primarily a farming community with a few paper mills.

Charlie felt numb. Dad was gone, yet everything reminded her of him. Just outside of town there was the old Raines Sawmill and next to it, the sign that said Raines Dairy—Dad's milk supplier. The sign turned Charlie's stomach knot tighter. Casper Raines had been in her class at school, and he was, as Dad's friend Larry liked to say, a world-class a-hole.

Charlie checked her rearview mirror and saw Uncle Jack was following at a respectable distance in his red pickup truck. This comforted her. Occasionally, she could see the glow of his joint and the stream of smoke from his window in the streetlights. His house was not far from where she grew up, where she was now headed.

Her body ached because she hadn't slept in so long, and she was relieved when she turned onto Falls Road, which ran parallel to the Fox River. Charlie's shoulders relaxed, and she snuck glances at the river. From what she could tell in the half-moon light, it looked calm. Rick had once asked her how she could stand to look at it. His question irritated her. How could he have asked? The river was the heart of their town.

When they were kids, they played on the banks of the river—she, Jenny, Pete, John, and Faye, Pete's sister, who, a couple of months ago, moved up to Alaska to work on the oil pipeline. With buckets and bare hands, they'd catch frogs and turtles in the marshes.

In high school, they partied in fishing boats, and in college, she and Jenny sat by the river, drinking beer and talking about the stars, music, and their dreams for the future. So when Rick asked how she could stand to look at it, she'd just smiled and shook her head and knew. Having lost her mother in the river, she couldn't stand not to. She'd spent a lifetime wondering what it would have been like to have a mother for more than ten years. Here, she felt closer to her than anywhere else.

On Cricket Road, Charlie turned left, just a few yards to go.

Charlie turned into their driveway and parked the car in front of the old two-story farmhouse. Dad had always insisted on painting it white. Now, from the light of her headlights, she noticed he'd planted a pot of red geraniums next to the wicker couch and rocking chairs Mom bought years ago.

On the porch, Charlie stared at the fat June bugs that had managed to get themselves stuck on their backs like always. She'd researched this phenomenon in seventh grade and learned how bugs use the moon to navigate, how, tricked by the glow of porch lights, their exhausted legs relaxed and they rolled on their backs to die. She gently tipped them over with the toe of her sandal.

Charlie walked through the musty-smelling living room and into the kitchen, where Dad's morning coffee cup sat next to the sink. Best Dad Ever, it proclaimed. It was a gift she'd given him back in grade school. She winced, not wanting to deal with anything else, so she curled up on the twin bed in her old room next to the kitchen. It had a view of the river, with Charlie's collection of river rocks lined up on shelves Dad and Uncle Jack had built for Charlie after Ria died. They'd used wormy wood: maple, with indentations of bug squiggles. Charlie stared at the indentations she'd spent hours studying when she was a kid. Like then, she pondered the kind of insects that had left their marks there—weevil worms, beetle larvae, and the like. She didn't expect to fall asleep but closed her eyes and was soon overcome with a potent dose of weary sadness. She wept until sleep came like a gift.

Chapter 5

Charlie looked into Lucy's green eyes, which were so much like Rick's.

"Mom? Wake up." She was yelling, and her wide eyes told Charlie her daughter was worried. Charlie struggled to wake up and, for a second, she forgot about Dad dying. As the events of last night flooded into her consciousness, she pulled her thoughts together and focused on Lucy. She needed to tell her.

"Hi, pumpkin." Charlie smiled at her, sat up, and pulled her into a hug. She was soft and smelled of fresh air and pine cones.

Sure enough, over Lucy's shoulder Charlie spotted several pine cones lined up on the shelves next to the river rocks.

Lucy hopped onto the bed and launched into a commentary. "The corn is not knee high. It's way taller, Mom."

"I noticed."

"But it's supposed to be knee high by the fourth of July, and today is the fourth of July."

"Sometimes when there's a lot of rain, it grows taller."

"Can we have a barbecue?" She chomped on a piece of taffy, and Charlie worried about her teeth. Uncle Jack and Karen must have fed her breakfast with taffy for dessert. They spoiled her.

"I don't know, honey." Charlie knew Uncle Jack and Karen had not told Lucy about Dad dying. She dreaded it, so she listened to her prattle on while she got up and walked into the kitchen. Lucy followed.

"Can I have sparklers? I won't run with them."

"We can try to find some." There was no sign of Uncle Jack and Karen. They must be over at the factory, allowing her some alone time with Lucy. She reached for her hand and led her to the kitchen table so they could sit down, took a deep breath, and started. "Lucy, I have to tell you something important."

"About Grandpa, right?" Lucy scrunched up her face into a question mark.

"Honey, Grandpa died last night. It was really late and that's why I waited to tell you this morning."

Tears formed quickly and spilled onto Lucy's cheeks. "Why, Mom? I loved him so much."

"His heart was just too weak," Charlie told her. "When the heart is not working right, it can't pump blood to the body to keep it alive. It happens to some people when they get really old." It was heartbreaking to have to tell her, and Charlie began to cry. Again. So many tears. She'd read somewhere it's okay to show your sadness to kids when someone dies, so she let her tears fall unchecked.

"Is he in heaven?"

"I think so."

"What's it like?"

Charlie gazed around the kitchen at the oak cabinets and large pine table. The familiar scent of Dad's pipe tobacco lingered here, along with a musty old farmhouse smell. Sadness crept over her like a wave pulling her under. "Let me think—green fields of grass, corn, lots of wildflowers, rainbows, cows, a fast-moving river, and trees. Lots of trees."

"Like Falls River," Lucy said.

"And he'll be with Jesus, and your grandma Evelyn and Ria and his parents."

"Heaven is crowded, Mom."

"With angels, you bet."

This seemed to satisfy Lucy. She jumped off Charlie's lap as the front door slammed and Uncle Jack walked into the kitchen.

"Uncle Jack, Grandpa died." Head tilted back, she reached for his hand.

"I know, we're all sad," Uncle Jack said. "Your Mom wanted to tell you. That's why we waited." He pulled something from his pocket and squatted low so they were eye level. "Check out this stone I found down by the river near my house. I've been saving it for you."

"Thank you." Lucy examined the rock, rubbed smooth by the glaciers and river current, shaped into the form of a heart. She kissed it and stuck it in her pocket.

"Come on," he said. "Let's get you some curds."

They followed the Lannon stone path through the pine trees to the renovated barn where Morgan Cheese was made. Uncle Jack pushed open the door, and Charlie recalled Dad doing the same thing on a Saturday morning, just a few days before Mom died.

"Charlie, I know you're worried about your mom. She's going to go to Mayo Clinic over in Rochester, where she can get some help."

"For her sadness?"

"Charlie," Uncle Jack was saying now. "Are you okay?"

"I'm all right." She shrugged off the memory and tried to focus.

They walked into the small store that fronted the cheese factory. In a refrigerated case were rows of Morgan Cheese—his signature cheddars. What Dad lacked in variety, he made up for in quality.

"Hey," Charlie greeted Karen, a tall woman with long black hair and a warm smile. She wore jeans, a white embroidered shirt, and a beaded necklace she'd made herself in the style of her Menominee heritage.

"So sorry about your dad." She came around the counter and hugged Charlie. The jingling of her silver bracelets was the sound of high school, of evenings playing cards at her kitchen table listening to songs by Woody Guthrie, Johnny Cash, and Elvis.

"It's so good to see you." Charlie relaxed into Karen's strong arms. "Thanks for taking Lucy last night."

"Anytime. We love her so much."

"And here you go, young lady, fresh cheese curds." Uncle Jack handed Lucy a bag of curds. She selected one and bit into it with an audible squeak.

Charlie and Karen walked arm in arm over to the far side of the store and stepped into the factory, where two new stainless-steel vats for culling milk into curds stood. "Strange not to see Dad in there wearing his white lab coat, checking the vats, writing in his notebook."

Charlie felt Karen squeeze her hand. "It's not the same without him."

"I can feel him here." Charlie never knew the factory without her dad. As a kid, she'd worked alongside him at the two old vats he'd purchased from Switzerland after the war. She'd watched, listened, and learned: how to determine the correct proportion of rennet, the enzyme that allows milk to curdle; how to test for lactic acid levels; how to be patient, allowing the milk to coagulate; and how to call a clean break. She'd loved growing up at the cheese factory, a hub of activity with people in and out of the place—Dad's friends Larry and Walter, Uncle Jack, Karen, locals and tourists who visited to buy cheese and watched them perform the physical, slightly mysterious alchemy of cheesemaking. By age six, Charlie was helping salt the curds, then pressing them into forms, prepping the curds for the aging cellar. This was when bacteria secreted enzymes, infusing the cheese with flavor, affecting color, taste, and texture during the long, silent aging process.

You can't hear it or see it, but you need to trust it's happening, Dad had told her.

"His spirit is strong here," Karen said. "You know he was working on that new recipe when he died. But he hadn't made cheese in a while. Then he got up early yesterday, drove to that farm over near Fremont, picked up some milk, and started working on a batch."

Charlie nodded, surprised that just yesterday morning he'd been well enough to drive to a farm and pick up milk, then start making cheese. She saw him standing at the vat, falling onto the floor. She cringed at the image.

"He was so excited to be working with you on the white cheddar," Karen said. "It really kept him going, talking to you on the phone, your visits."

"Kept me going, too," Charlie said. Collaborating long distance by phone, they were developing new recipes, most recently the English-style white cheddar. The English style was more pungent, had more tang, than the milder cheddars Dad usually made. Unfortunately, it had been four months since Charlie had been able to get up north to see Dad. It had been almost a year since Dad made the last batch of white cheddar. She walked over to the vat and ran her hand over the stainless-steel rim. In it was a sour-scented mix of abandoned milk, ruined.

"I'll clean up." Karen's eyes were deep brown, almost black. She was nurturing in a no-nonsense way that conveyed an inner strength. "I'm here for you. Whatever you need."

Charlie nodded and knelt down on the cold, hard cement floor right where Dad must have fallen. She saw his black Wellington rubber boots next to her small ones and heard his voice: *The secret to making good cheese, Charlie, is good milk. Good milk, good cheese.* He knew someday she'd be alone at the vat like this. It was why he was always teaching. Always guiding her. Always demonstrating his love by including her and by the including, showing her she was worthy. Her father had imbued her with his wisdom and acumen, laying the foundation for her to carry on without him. She was now the memory holder and within her DNA were schemes of ancestral knowledge. She was her father's daughter. Scientist and artist. It was her turn. The irony of her wanting to be independent and make her own way struck her. Without Rick, yes. But without Dad wasn't how she'd imagined it. Anxiety crept up on her like a bully, threatening her confidence.

She stood up, wiped tears from her cheeks, and started humming to shake off the anxiety before it paralyzed her.

"Is that Johnny Cash?" Karen asked. "'Ring of Fire,' right?"

"Yeah, Dad loved that song." Charlie grinned at a memory of Dad humming the song as he cut curds. It was when she was in college and had come home to help with production, which he'd ramped up to help pay for her tuition.

She placed her hands on her hips and surveyed the two new vats. "When did the new equipment get here?"

"About three months ago."

"I didn't think he could afford it," Charlie said.

"I didn't either," Karen said. "Surprised me."

"At least he was doing what he loved," Charlie said. "New vats, new milk supplier. He was busy."

"He had a hard time getting over the bad milk incident," Karen said. "But last week, out of the blue, he said he was ready to move on."

Several months ago, Dad had stopped making cheese after what he called "the bad milk incident" involving his longtime milk supplier, Raines Dairy. He'd been cryptic about it in their telephone conversations. "We had an incident with Raines, bad milk, I'll tell you about it later."

"I wish I'd visited more," Charlie said. "I could tell he wasn't well."

"You've got your hands full," Karen said. "It can't be easy." Karen and Uncle Jack knew about Rick, how he was getting worse and the toll it was taking on her and Lucy.

"I have to go over to the funeral home." She wasn't looking forward to this. Funeral homes held bad memories from Mom's and Ria's deaths. "I'll just clean up and change."

Karen looked at her with concern and kindness. "You go with Uncle Jack," she said. "I'll watch Lucy."

Charlie let herself out the back door into the woods she'd played in as a young girl. These were old trees—hardwoods like red oak, white oak, sugar maple, aspen, and birch. Peppered in with the hardwoods were soft-woods—spruce, cedar, and tall pines. The woods were a cool haven in the summer and a buffer from biting wind during winter deep freezes when arctic air plunged south from Canada and parked itself in Wisconsin. Somewhere above, a cardinal sang happily, trilling into the quiet. Charlie scanned the foliage, trying to locate the bird. A movement on the ground twenty yards out caught her eye. It was probably a deer. Dad helped cull the herd each year, but they multiplied fast, and families traveled up the river basin, the females leading, with the bucks lagging behind in relative safety. Walking lightly so as not to startle whatever it was, Charlie followed the movement.

As she got closer to the sounds, she saw it was a man standing there, amid the trees. She stopped. Shoot. Was it? It looked like Casper Raines. He seemed to be studying the trees, measuring, then writing in a notebook. Yup, it was him—he was heavier, his hair was longer now, but otherwise he had the same greased-back dirty-blond hair. She moved toward him slowly but stopped twenty feet away, careful to keep a good distance between them. Raines was the last person she wanted to see. Ahead a robin watched her from a sugar maple. She steadied her eyes on the bird's burnt-orange breast, breathing in the thick summer air, deciding if she should confront Casper. When she looked back for him, he was gone.

Chapter 6

Six days later, Larry played taps on a beat-up bugle at the graveside service. He wore his army pins on what looked like a new suit jacket. It was the first time Charlie had seen him in one. Dad's other good friend, Walter, stood next to Larry, similarly dressed, though he always wore suits. Lucy stood next to Charlie with her hand over her heart. Charlie clutched the folded flag Larry and Walter had presented to her in honor of Dad's service. Father Bokowski invited them to drop a handful of dirt on the casket, and she thought of how they'd planted a vegetable garden every spring and how Dad had taught her how to turn the soil and fold in the compost—coffee grounds, banana peels, eggshells—they'd collected through the long winter. She would study this compost under her microscope, marking the passing of time by the richness of the decay.

Charlie smiled at all Dad's friends and people who'd come from town to show their respects. All the while, a chorus of should-haves chanted a dreary dirge in her head. She should have visited more often, should have helped more with the business in the past few years, should have left Rick and moved back home.

After Dad's burial, a lunch was served in the church basement: ham and rolls, potato salad, wild rice, and homemade pies made by Karen and her friends.

At Charlie's table, Larry turned to her and began speaking in a low voice. "You know, your dad told me all about the new cheese." He spoke from the corner of his mouth, barely moving his lips. "Karl was sure he was onto something big. Said he'd bet within a year he'd have a prize winner. Called it his opus. 'What the hell is that?' I asked him. He said, "Wait 'til you taste it, ya hick.'"

Charlie chuckled at Larry's hush-hush talk. He was such a character, and she loved him for it. "We were going back and forth with it, testing recipes," Charlie said. "I'd make variations of it in the kitchen at home. Dad made the sellable batches at the factory."

Larry looked over both shoulders and leaned in so close she could smell the coffee on his breath. "It meant a lot to him. Working with you like that on that recipe."

"It was a white cheddar," Charlie said. "An English-style cheddar in honor of Mom. The kind she'd talk about, that they made at the family farm in England, before the war."

"Shush." Larry's eyes were wide. "You don't know who's listening."

She looked around their table. No one was listening. Lucy stood next to Uncle Jack, who was teaching her how to flip coins. Karen was deep in conversation with Jenny. Walter, who probably was listening, though he couldn't hear too well, was seriously involved in eating a piece of home-made pecan pie.

"Nobody's listening, Larry," she assured him.

"It's why he bought all that new equipment," Walter said, without taking his eyes off a piece of pie navigating toward his mouth. "To make the new recipe."

"Why he bought all that? For cripes' sake, Walter, he bought that equipment for Charlie," Larry said.

"What?" Charlie tried to wrap her head around what he'd said. "Dad bought it for me?"

"He was hopin' you'd come back. Karl told us about Rick," Larry said, dropping his voice volume again on the last part.

"You weren't supposed to mention Rick. Didn't we agree?" Walter looked pained but kept working on his pie.

Charlie let this sink in. She had told Dad about Rick, just not how bad it had gotten recently.

"So the whole town knows?" Charlie felt her cheeks get hot.

"Not the whole town, just me and Walter. 'Course, Jack knows."

"And Karen," Walter said between bites.

"Karen probably told John." Larry was still talking out of the corner of his mouth.

"John knows?" Charlie hadn't seen John Stone since they went camping in college on the Brule River up in Nicolet National Forest. Karen had told her he was now canoeing in the Boundary Waters for two weeks with a group of high school students.

Walter nodded. "Yup, and Jenny knows. She probably told her husband, Pete."

"Walter, don't ya think Charlie was the one who told Jenny? We got phones now, old man." He was right. Charlie had talked to Jenny, her closest friend from high school, several times over the past few months. About Rick's moods. About how she wanted to leave him.

"Stop, you two." They were still bickering. They hadn't changed, and the fact that they hadn't was somehow reassuring with everything else that was changing. She'd never told them, but when she was a kid, after Ria died, she imagined herself as Dorothy from *The Wizard of Oz*. Walter, with his round face and soft belly, was the Cowardly Lion, and Larry, because he was hyper and skinny, was her Scarecrow. Uncle Jack was left with being the Tin Man, but it fit him because he was so loyal and caring. Charlie loved these guys.

"Mom." Lucy stood in front of her, holding onto Uncle Jack's hand. "Watch this."

Uncle Jack flipped a penny into the air. It did several spins before landing in Lucy's palms. She closed one fist around it. "Heads or tails?"

"Heads," Charlie told her.

She slowly opened her fist.

"Tails, you lose," she shouted.

"Dang it." Charlie smiled at Lucy. "Bad luck."

"If it weren't for bad luck, you'd have no luck at all," Uncle Jack quipped.

"So true." She pulled Lucy onto her lap. "Except for Lucy. She makes up for it."

"I'm tired, Mom."

"So am I, sweetie."

Karen joined them and smoothed Lucy's hair back from her face as Lucy tilted her head back to smile at her. They'd become close in the past few days, playing cards in the store at the cheese factory, making baskets and jewelry, collecting stones by the river.

"I'll take her home so she can rest," Karen said. "This is winding down."

"I'll come with you." Uncle Jack took Lucy's hand in his as she scooted off Charlie's lap.

Charlie walked over to where Larry was chatting with the women who had organized the lunch. She hugged and thanked them. A smart-dressed woman approached her. It was Mrs. Vandercook, one of Mom's old friends.

"Dear, please come visit me over in Westfield." She touched her hand to her hair pulled back in a French twist.

"I will do that." Charlie hugged her, smelling lavender. The smell triggered a memory of Mrs. Vandercook and Mom having tea. Mom was laughing at something her friend said. Charlie had loved Mom's laugh. It was such a rare sound.

"Larry, you stay out of trouble," Charlie told him, giving him a kiss on the cheek.

"That don't sound like too much fun." He hugged her. "How about some sheepshead one of these Sundays?"

"You got it."

Jenny joined her. "Let's go over to Booths Landing," she said. "I told Pete we need a little time together."

They walked across the street to the restaurant. Perched on top of the hill above the river, it exuded Northwoods cozy with knotty pine walls, a stone fireplace, and a jukebox now playing "Angel from Montgomery," a John Prine tune about a woman stuck in a bad marriage.

"So what exactly did Rick say about why he couldn't come?" Jenny folded her hands on her pregnant belly.

"When I called him and told him about Dad, he really seemed upset." Rick had respected Dad, calling him "The Scientist." "But he said he had to work."

"Like they couldn't do without him for a few nights."

"Honestly, I'm relieved he didn't come up." Charlie took a swig of beer. "I think he's seeing one of the regular customers. Her name's Kathy." She rubbed her eyes and thought of how this should be humiliating, but she just felt numb.

"Asshole." Jenny flipped her long, ginger-colored hair off her shoulder. "Now maybe you'll move back home."

Jenny had never left Falls River. She commuted to Stevens Point for college and worked in the canning factory on weekends, and after graduation, she married Pete. They bought a farm and grew mostly corn but dabbled in everything from cows to chickens and pigs. From their huge garden, they harvested and canned jams, pickles, and spaghetti sauce. From their bees, they made honey they sold at the co-op, and they made small batches of kitchen cheese from some Guernseys they'd bought at an auction. Jenny being up here was another good reason to move back.

"I've been thinking about it a lot. Lucy has seen so much. Rick's getting worse. I don't know how he keeps that job."

"I don't trust him."

"You and me both."

Charlie was suddenly desperate to change the subject. "Do you remember how we used to help my dad and Larry at the cheese factory?"

"Your dad was cool." Jenny winced and rubbed her side. "He actually talked to me, not like other adults who just ignored us."

"He was kind of obsessed with making cheese," Charlie said.

"True, he'd mostly talk about cheese," Jenny said. "He was like this cool cheese scientist with his white jacket, his round, wire-rimmed glasses, that pocket protector he always wore. He loved you so much. You really should get that factory up and running again."

Charlie exhaled, looked out the picture window at the stars in the sky, and bent lower to find the North Star, using the Big Dipper as her guide. "I don't know."

"Shit, what's not to know? You're good. Stop doubting yourself all the time."

"Do I?" There it was: the brightest star in the sky.

"I rest my case." Jenny laughed.

"Funny. I just wonder if I can do it without him."

"Use those notebooks he was always writing stuff in. You got those, right?" Jenny raised her eyebrows with the question.

"I've been looking for them."

"You can't find them?"

"Yeah, it's weird."

Jenny winced again. "This one is feisty. Always kicking me. Feel it."

Charlie placed her hand on Jenny's belly, felt a kick, and smiled. Tap-tap. It was oddly intimate. But women had been doing this forever. It was the circle of life. Dad was gone and soon a new baby would be in their lives. It was a bittersweet, cosmic mystery. Charlie had grown up Catholic but hadn't gone to church much lately; she wasn't so sure she believed what she'd been taught about life after death—heaven, hell, purgatory, babies in limbo. Sure, she'd kept the faith when talking to Lucy about Dad being in heaven. But does anyone really know? When Mom died, she'd clung to the belief she'd see her again, but now Mom felt far away. Even her memories of Mom were so few and faded that she had to fight to hold on to them.

"Guess what?" Jenny asked. Then, before Charlie could answer, she replied, "John's back."

Charlie knew Jenny would bring him up. He'd spent several years in Falls River during elementary and junior high school, then moved to Madison for high school. "I heard. Karen told me he got a job in Green Bay teaching. He was always smart."

"And good looking." Jenny smiled. "I saw him last month. He came into the co-op."

Charlie didn't tell Jenny how much she'd thought about John over the years. Especially during hard times. Especially lately.

"I heard he's up in the Boundary Waters," Jenny said. "Coming back this week."

"He loved to canoe."

"Yup." She raised her eyebrows. "Didn't you guys hook up in college?"

"I'm still trying to figure out if that was real or just a dream," Charlie said.

"Oh, it was real."

"Just so long ago."

When would she see him? It was sure to happen soon. Did he still wear his hair long? Did he still have that gentle way about him? She'd often thought about the college summer they'd gone from being friends to making love in the back of his pickup truck, under the Northern Lights. Was he seeing someone now? She'd heard he was living with a woman in Chicago before he moved back up north.

"Not that long ago," Jenny said.

"Camping was fun," Charlie said, dodging the subject because she didn't want to admit how much she still cared about him. "And I miss water skiing."

"You were fearless on those skis," Jenny said.

She *had* been fearless then. Getting up on one ski behind Pete's boat at his family's lake house near Minocqua, she'd traveled outside the wake, hovered, then dug in the rear end of her ski to carve rooster tails behind her before she traversed the wake again and did the same trick on the other side. She'd give Pete a thumb's-up signal to go faster for the thrill of careening through the water and the wind. "Fearless is not a word I'd use to describe myself now."

"What are you afraid of?" Jenny asked.

Charlie thought for a second about her question. "The big one is leaving Rick."

"Oh, honey, that should be easy. You should have left him years ago." Jenny lifted up her long hair to cool off her neck.

"Easy for you to say, married to Saint Peter," Charlie said.

Jenny leaned in. "Remember, you weren't even going to marry Rick." She said his name with a hard *k*, an indication of her mistrust.

Jenny was right. Less than a year after she'd met him, she'd found out she was pregnant, and by then she'd begun to have misgivings about him. It wasn't his nightmares about the war. She could understand that. She knew no one came back from Vietnam unchanged. She'd tried her best to help him and to calm him. But his drinking was enough to make her pause. When she found out about the other woman he was seeing, she left him for a couple of weeks but ended up back with him. She did love him. It was a wild love: slightly dangerous; addictive. Lucy was conceived during that time, during a night of makeup sex, after Rick promised she was the only one who really mattered to him.

When Charlie found out she was pregnant, Jenny came to Milwaukee to help. She knew of a place in Chicago where you could get an abortion. Pete's sister Faye had gone there a while back.

∼

Whenever Charlie heard blues music, she thought of that night in Chicago with Jenny, who was in her blues phase after having spent a few days in Memphis with Pete on their way down to Florida. She and Jenny had driven to Chicago from Milwaukee in Jenny's truck and checked in at the Blackstone, an aging hotel whose fading luster only added to its charm. They walked over to Kingston Mines, a new blues bar with a dark interior, packed that night to see Koko Taylor, a local favorite. Her songs were about bad luck and heartbreak, about endurance, not in spite of being a woman but because of being a woman. Until that moment, Charlie hadn't fully processed what was happening. It was 1969 and women had declared themselves liberated, but in so many ways, life was still the same. Like many, she'd been taught that having sex before marriage was a sin, and sexual revolution or not, single, pregnant women were stigmatized. She had a college friend who'd gone to live with relatives in Vermont for the duration of her pregnancy and one who spent her pregnancy in a special home for unmarried mothers. Lordy, even though her dad was pretty cool, she couldn't tell him about it—he'd be so disappointed in her. She considered her options. Her dreams of being a research scientist had morphed into a plan to eventually go back and work with Dad, maybe taking over the factory when he retired. She hadn't even known Rick for a full year, and marrying him hadn't been a serious consideration on her radar. Getting an abortion or giving up the baby for adoption seemed inevitable. But that night she'd paused—really thought about what it meant and examined feelings she hadn't fully explored. During the long, slow riffs of guitar and veracious vocals, Charlie felt a clarity about what she should do.

After the blues show, they'd walked across the street from the Blackstone and sat on a bench in Grant Park, facing the lake. It was warm for January, and there were plenty of folks out for a stroll. Strings of Christmas lights in the trees gave the place a festive feeling, providing a sharp contrast to Charlie's introspective mood.

"You're quiet," Jenny said.

"This isn't for me," she told Jenny.

"Having second thoughts?" Jenny asked.

"Yes." Before they left Milwaukee, she'd thought of the embryo inside her as just a mass of cells, but now she saw further into the future. "What if this is a little girl? What if she's got blonde hair like Ria? What if she's the best thing that ever happened to me?" She already felt better, relieved at having made her decision.

"I didn't think you would do it," Jenny said.

"I'm pretty sure I'll be bad at mothering," Charlie said, admitting one of her biggest concerns. "Just look at my own mom."

"Your mom."

Charlie held her breath as Jenny paused. Her mom had always been somewhat of an enigma, and she was thirsty for any insights about her.

"So pretty," Jenny continued. "You know, my parents always thought there was something about the war that . . . troubled her."

Charlie nodded. "Her brother died." She had studied the pictures of Mom and her brother, Edward, together on the family farm in Somerset. They'd seemed close.

"Oh yeah, I remember," she said. "Edward. That must have been hard. Maybe that affected her in a way Rick is affected. What do they call it?

Combat stress, something like that. Anyway, you'll be a good mom is what I'm trying to say."

"Thanks," Charlie said, but she still wasn't convinced.

They sat in silence for a few moments, the triangle of moonlight reflecting off the steadfast lake and looking like a postcard or an advertisement. Come to Chicago, figure out what the heck you're going to do with your life. Marry Rick? It was the elephant in the room.

"You're right, the war did something to Rick," Charlie said. "Sometimes it scares me. I honestly wouldn't have so many reservations about marrying him if it wasn't for his drinking, which I know he does to help him forget Vietnam, which he never talks about."

"Do you love him?"

Charlie thought about how Rick sang silly love songs to her, how they hiked in the woods near Lake Michigan and then had picnics on the beach, how they spent hours in the kitchen talking while he created amazing meals. He always seemed so happy when he was cooking, and she loved that about him.

"I do love him."

"And you think he'll want to get married?"

"I think so. He talks about it. A lot." Sometimes she wondered why he talked about it so much, like he was desperate to start a family, as if it would solve everything.

"I'll talk to him about going to the VA for some help," she said.

"Okay." Jenny nodded slowly, reached up her arm, wrapped it around Charlie's shoulder, and pulled her in close.

Charlie knew Jenny was hiding her reservations about Rick. But what else could she do? Later that night, she'd called and thanked the woman from the underground network of women who called themselves "Jane." It was a lifeline for so many women, with abortion illegal. She apologized for wasting their time and told her she would not keep her scheduled appointment.

"Don't apologize. You take care now, honey. Call us if you need us," was all she said.

~

Jenny grabbed Charlie's hand on the table. "It was meant to be. That's what I think. I can't imagine you without Lucy."

"I can't either," Charlie said.

Later, they stopped at the food co-op. Above the door was a brightly hand-painted sign that announced, "Falls River Food Co-op, All Are Welcome."

"Nice sign, kind of folksy," Charlie said. "You're a regular Sam Drucker." They often joked about the television shows they'd watched growing up— *The Beverly Hillbillies* and *Green Acres*, goofy shows with goofy characters like Sam Drucker, the balding owner of the general store in the fictional town of Hooterville.

"Did you know Sam Drucker not only operated the general store; he ran the town newspaper and post office?" Jenny asked.

"He wasn't a real person," Charlie said. "You know that, right?"

"I know way too much about him," Jenny said.

Inside the co-op, the air smelled like spices, sweet basil, and earthy roots. There were bins stocked with nuts, potatoes, flour, oats, next to a sitting area with tables and two comfy chairs. Seed catalogs were scattered on an antique sideboard.

"It's really nice. I want to just hang out here."

"Please do. We bought the whole building. We're renovating, building apartments upstairs. College students are looking for places to rent. It's a good market."

Charlie gathered some items and placed them on the counter to purchase. The refrigerated case next to the cash register contained several varieties of cheese, and she spotted some of Dad's. Morgan Cheese—the name was in red with an image of a black cow placed below the lettering. Charlie's eyes filled with tears as she thought back to the day she'd shown Dad the drawing she'd done in art class and he'd told her it was good enough for their logo. "It's really good, Charlie. Let's use it," he'd said. She felt proud he'd validated her artwork, especially because, during those high school years, she'd gone through periods of grief. Dad had helped her though those times. He'd kept her busy at the factory. He'd boosted her confidence with compliments about her artwork and cheesemaking acumen.

Charlie wished they could work side by side together again in the cheese factory, one more time. She should have insisted Dad see the doctor. This guilt was all too familiar. She'd felt it after Ria died. Questions had swirled around her nine-year-old brain, questions she'd never shared with anyone.

If she hadn't taken Ria to the playground that day, would she have gotten sick? Would Mom have sunk into the depression that overwhelmed her? Charlie was mired in the hot pain of loss and self-recriminations. What was happening here? She'd never felt so much anxiety, not even after Ria died. Or Mom, for that matter.

"You okay?"

Jenny came around the counter and put her arm around Charlie. Charlie rested her head on Jenny's shoulder, steering clear of her belly, but Jenny pulled her closer into the soft cushion of her body.

"I'm worried about you."

"They're all gone now," Charlie whispered.

"You've had it rough. Rougher than most."

"I want to stay here. But I'm afraid of what Rick will do if we stay."

"I'm here for you whatever you decide, Char."

"I know you are."

Chapter 7

When Charlie returned to Dad's house, Lucy was in bed and Karen was sleeping on the couch. Pulling a blanket over Karen, Charlie felt an urgent need to go over to the factory to look for the cheese recipes, to dig into Dad's accounting ledgers. The kitchen table was piled with leftovers—pie, rolls, brownies. The refrigerator was the same: stocked full of ham, potato salad, beans, and watermelon. She grabbed a beer and walked over to the factory.

It was eerily quiet. The only noise was the steady hum of the cheese coolers. She stood next to the new stainless-steel vats and wondered again how Dad had afforded them. In her memories, she and Dad were at the two old vats they'd used for twenty years—vats constructed of wooden exterior frames and stainless-steel interior pans. She could still feel the thrill of calling a clean break for the first time. It was just after Ria died.

~

The vat was filled with milk. Charlie watched as Uncle Jack turned on the agitator and Dad added the rennet to help with the process of curdling. "Now we let it drop." He swept his arms over the mixture like an orchestra conductor signaling musicians. Charlie knew the whey would rise as the curd formed, but like countless Saturdays, Dad explained the process.

"See how the body builds? You can't let it set for too long."

Charlie peered into the vat to watch the whey rise and mingle on the ever-shifting surface.

Time passed. This is when Dad got really serious. Checking his black notebook and the clock, he paced back and forth, then periodically stopped and studied the milk as it gelled to just the right consistency.

"See if you can tell if it's ready." Dad's request surprised Charlie. He'd never let her test the curd. She suspected he was trying to help her forget

Ria for a moment, forget how Mom just slept all the time. She studied the mixture, imagining Ria at her side. *Ria,* she instructed, *you have to know when to call a clean break. Here, like this.* Slowly, Charlie curled her index and pointer fingers and dipped them backhanded into the mixture. It was warm and felt alive on her skin, alive with the process of transformation to what it would later become. She talked to Ria in her mind.

Ria, you can be whatever you want to be.

I wanna work at a carnival.

Okay.

What do you want to be, Charlie?

I want to be a cheesemaker like Dad.

Me too, Charlie.

Then pay attention. When you call a clean break, you wait 'til the mixture becomes like Jell-O, just as it starts getting firm, just at the point that the curd breaks clean from the mixture.

Charlie held her breath as she felt the curd slip off her fingers and watched it fall back into the vat: A clean break.

"I think it's ready," Charlie said, stifling her excitement, wanting to appear serious, a real cheesemaker.

"Lemme see." Dad had an intent look on his face as he dipped his fingers into the mixture. He turned and looked at Charlie; the corners of his blue eyes crinkled behind wire-rimmed glasses as a slow-moving smile formed on his handsome face. "I think you're right."

She grinned, pleased she'd been correct when she'd "called it."

"You're a natural, Charlie."

~

As she inspected the new vats, Charlie thought about what Walter and Larry had said at the funeral. Knowing how unhappy she was in Milwaukee, Dad had bought this equipment for her, so she could come back to the cheese factory and work with him. She walked over to Dad's rolltop desk and pulled open the lower drawer, where he kept the most recent ledgers. She knew the rest of the books were housed in the filing cabinets next to his desk, records beginning in 1946 when he'd started Morgan Cheese after returning from the war in Europe. She opened the ledger containing accounts from the past year, releasing the familiar woody-orange spice of his pipe tobacco. Tears formed as she remembered how he'd smoke his pipe, always tucking it into the right corner of his mouth, puffing two or three times, then blowing out twirls of smoke.

The most recent entry showed Dad had used the new milk supplier from over by Fremont for the last milk order, the one he'd been working on when he died. He'd been excited about the new dairy even though Raines Dairy had been his supplier for almost thirty years. It was strange that he'd used a new supplier after all this time. Charlie knew Old Man Raines was living in a nursing home because of dementia, but Casper had taken over the business. Prior to the new milk supplier's entry, which was marked "paid," the last two milk deliveries from Raines Dairy were marked "unpaid."

It took her almost an hour to page through and study all of Dad's ledger entries back to 1960, but she was able to confirm they'd all been marked "paid." Curious, she paged through the ledgers from the early 1950s and late 1940s. All paid. She stopped when she noticed nearly an entire year marked "unpaid." The unpaid dates started in March 1956, not long after Mom died, and ended in December 1956. Charlie sat back in the old, wood swivel chair and rubbed her neck, sore from bending over the brittle pages. What had happened? From his records, she knew the milk was delivered, and she remembered Dad was making cheese back then. True, it was around the time some of the batches had been ruined from phage, the attack virus that killed starter culture bacteria. But he was still making cheese. Why didn't he pay the milk bills?

Tired of spinning her wheels about the question, she got up and walked over to the stairs that led to the aging cellar. It was time to taste the white cheddar—even though she hadn't found anything to help her figure out how Dad had afforded the new equipment, or even loan documents for the expensive vats. Maybe the paperwork for the loan was in the house somewhere.

Charlie heard noises outside. She paused. It was definitely noises—rustling, like someone walking in the leaves and underbrush. Who would be out there in the woods? She went over to the window and peered into the darkness. Nothing. She opened the door and walked outside.

"Who's out there?"

Inside, from the other side of the factory, she heard another sound, the factory door opening. Jeez Louise. It was Grand Central around here. Her nerves were shot.

Karen walked into the office. She was carrying two cans of beer.

"You scared the crap out of me," Charlie told her. She could feel her heart steady and slow.

"Sorry about that. Just wanted to see how you're doing." Karen handed her a beer. "Want to check out the cheese?"

"Yes, I've been dying to." Charlie shook off the uneasy feeling she had about someone lurking outside.

"Your dad was really excited about that new recipe you guys were working on. As you know, over the past several years, he made about twelve different batches and rejected every batch but the last one. Said you guys finally nailed it and he was gearing up to put it in production using milk from the new dairy in Fremont."

"Wouldn't that be something?" Charlie felt a tinge of excitement. He'd told her the batch was good, but could it really be the *good enough* one? That's what he'd always called a cheese good enough to wear the Morgan label. She'd have to taste it and decide for herself.

Wooden stairs led down to the aging cellar, where humidity levels and temperature were closely monitored. Pine shelves Uncle Jack had built lined the walls, filled with blocks of cheese placed in neat rows. The room was cool, and Charlie shook off the chill, or maybe it was the lack of Dad's presence that sent shivers through her. She was glad Karen was with her. She backtracked to the last recipe in her mind; it must have been the one they'd finished twelve months ago.

"Here it is." Karen stopped in front of a shelf with neatly stacked cheese covered in wax.

Eagerly, Charlie grabbed a tester from the shelf, reached out for the nearest block, cored the center with her tester, pulled up the cheese, and placed it in the palm of her hand. The white cheddar was slightly oily to her touch. She examined it for texture by rubbing it between her thumb and finger, then brought it to her nose. It smelled earthy, fresh. Finally, she tasted it. First she tasted a tart tease of cheddar with a hint of salt, then a blast of flavor tang on the back of her tongue.

From that blast of flavor, she knew it was special. But it wasn't only the taste: it was the feel of it, the smell, the look. It was the kind of cheese that made people want more. It's what she and Dad had been going for all those months, trying and testing and tasting, and talking over the phone. It was a Wisconsin version of a white English cheddar.

"I love it," she said to Karen with a slow smile. "It's a bit more crumbly and sharper than Dad's usual cheddar." She thought of the phrase Dad used when he was happy with a batch of cheese. "It's close to perfect."

"Your dad's highest praise," Karen said.

"It's what we were going for, an English cheddar from Somerset. The kind Mom had talked about. Oscar, the owner of the Milwaukee Cheese Market, ordered something similar after a trip to London cheese shops and Somerset factories a while back." Charlie thought of the last time she was at the cheese market, selling the Somerset cheddar to the purse woman and the guy in the Packers jersey. "How much do we have?"

"About two hundred pounds."

"Do you have the recipe?" Charlie asked. "I've been looking for his notebooks."

"I've been looking all over for them too."

"So, where are they?"

"Last time I saw them was the day before his heart attack, lying right on his desk. When I looked for them after I got back from the hospital the next day, they were gone."

Chapter 8

"Why's the water going so fast?" Lucy asked questions in rapid succession, sometimes before Charlie could finish the answer.

"It's the current. It moves the water in the direction of Lake Michigan from Lake Winnebago up through Appleton and Green Bay and out into Lake Michigan."

"Why?" Lucy picked up a stone and tossed it into the river. They watched it disappear.

Charlie contemplated her question. Does she mean why does the river run? Here was an existential question too deep for this early in the morning. She likely means what *makes* the river run. A memory from science class in junior high presented itself. "It has to do with gravity. Gravity is a force that pulls things to it." Their walk in the backyard by the river had turned into a science lesson.

"What about the fish?" Lucy asked, searching for more stones, her bent head a mass of curls.

"They can either go with the current or swim against it, I guess."

"Wouldn't that be hard?"

"Not for some fish. Some can swim against the current—like salmon and sturgeon—and the females swim upstream to lay their eggs. They're strong."

Charlie's thoughts shifted to her younger self using all her strength to lift herself up on one ski behind Pete's boat, careening across the wake so low to the water she'd reached down and touched the surface with the tips of her fingers. What had Jenny called her the other day? Fearless? She felt more feckless than fearless.

"Really strong," Charlie repeated, trying to focus on Lucy. Lately, she'd been so distracted, thoughts came and went, riding a train of worries. Where to start? The cheese factory? The house? Things needed to be organized and cleaned. She needed to locate the white cheddar recipe. She had to get a handle on Dad's financial situation. She and Uncle Jack were planning to drive over to Appleton to meet with Walter tomorrow, which was a start. He'd been Dad's attorney since forever.

Lucy placed her hands on her hips and tilted her head. "My teacher says be strong if someone is being mean. Tell them to stop it and just walk away."

"Good advice," Charlie told her daughter.

Just walk away. Could she do it? Leave Rick? He'd never liked it up here. She heard his voice: *There's nothing to do up there.*

For Charlie, though, being here the past few days—even with Dad dying and the funeral—felt right. Perhaps because she was away from Rick, not having to worry about his unpredictable moods and his drinking. Perhaps it was being around old friends and family and fresh air. Whatever it was, she was feeling more like herself.

At the edge of the river in the shallow calm, Lucy settled on her haunches and dipped her hand into the water, pulled out a stone, studied it, then tucked it into her pocket. "Mom, can I go help Karen make baskets?" She stood and looked up at Charlie, and there was Ria's face, clear as day: In the way Lucy tilted her head when she asked a question. In the way she asked so many questions. They were so much alike, like a part of Ria resided in Lucy through familial DNA instructions. Or, their souls were mingled, creating the sensation of having been here before. Charlie had felt that way about Lucy from the day she was born. Lucy was a sweet, old soul.

"Mom?"

Charlie nodded. "Sure."

"I love you."

"I love you too, pumpkin," Charlie whispered, and she watched Lucy run to the house, where Karen was on the porch, making a basket out of sweetgrass. They waved to each other.

Hearing the hum of a motor, Charlie turned back toward the river. A small fishing boat approached. The driver maneuvered the boat up to their rickety wood pier ten yards from where she stood, on the south end of their property. As he came closer, she could see his hair was long, pulled back in a ponytail at the base of his neck. He waved as he pulled the boat alongside the pier. It was John.

"Hey." John cut the motor, gathered up a rope from the bow of the boat, and tossed it to Charlie like they'd done many times as kids and again during the one college summer they'd spent time together.

"Hey." Charlie caught the rope and tied it to the pier post. "You're back?"

"Yeah, I've been here a few months," he answered. "Sorry about your dad."

"Thanks." Suddenly, she felt nervous, which was weird: it was just John. But he looked so good. The planes of his face had become more angular, as if he'd settled into a more handsome version of his younger self. Charlie recalled the last time they'd been together: the kiss, his hands on her back, her legs wrapped around him. At the memory, her cheeks grew hot. She pushed her hair back from her face, hoping she hadn't turned all red and blotchy.

John was fiddling with the boat key in the ignition, thankfully not looking at her. His hair fell forward to cover his face. He smoothed it behind his ear, a gesture she'd seen him make a hundred times growing up. He'd always had long hair, which gave kids like Casper an excuse to tease him. They'd bully him about his hair and his weight.

"You look good," Charlie said.

"What?" The way he looked at her expectantly took her back to the good times they'd had: studying together, riding bikes, hiking in the woods, sitting around the campfire on winter nights, the northern sky crowded with stars.

"Nothing."

It wasn't just his face that looked good. In his red plaid shirt and jeans with holes in the knees, he looked fit. Reflexively, she pulled in her stomach and tugged her blouse lower over her shorts. John finally got the key out of the starter and stuck it in his pocket.

"Nothing, huh?" He hopped off the boat. "You been up to the cove? We could take a ride up there."

"Sure."

He looked past her shoulder and grinned. "Hey, Karen."

"Hey, John." She walked up to them, holding Lucy's hand, and stood next to Charlie. "Don't be a stranger. Come over for dinner tomorrow? We're having a belated Fourth of July party."

"Sounds good," he said. "And who is this?"

Lucy was studying John and the boat.

"I'm Lucy," she said.

"It's good to meet you, Lucy." John extended his hand to her. "I'm John."

"It's nice to meet you." Lucy said the words she'd been taught, placing her small hand into John's.

"Do you like horses?" John said. "Maybe someday your mom can bring you up to the reservation. My friend has a horse."

"Can I?" she asked Charlie.

John smiled, and the dimple she remembered appeared on his left cheek. Charlie nodded.

"You two go take a ride," Karen said. "I'll make Lucy lunch. We need to finish making that basket. John, I want to hear all about that canoe trip."

"I got some good stories."

"Tomorrow then."

"I'll bring the beer."

Karen reached for Lucy's hand. Charlie and John watched them walk back to the house, Lucy asking about the baskets. "Can I make my own?"

"She's a beautiful little girl," John said.

Charlie turned to him with a bundle of emotions—anxious to hear what he'd been up to the past few years, attracted to him in a way that made her feel shy, excited to get out on the water with him like old times, and comforted by his strong presence. He'd always been a solid anchor for her when waters got rough.

Chapter 9

Out on the river, they rode in silence. It felt good to feel the wind, to see familiar sights along the shore: the smokestacks of the paper mill, fields of corn ripening in the hot sun, cows grazing in the distance. Just before the cove, the river narrowed and John slowed, then turned off the engine. He swiveled his captain's chair to face Charlie, who sat riding shotgun on a similar chair. Rather than look at him, she shifted her gaze past his shoulder to an old bur oak near the riverbank. This anxiety was strange. Growing up, they had been so comfortable together; they'd talked about everything.

"You went on a wilderness trip?" she asked him.

"I took a group of high school students up to the Boundary Waters," John said.

"You're teaching?"

"Yup, at the high school in Green Bay," John said. "History and current events."

"Karen told me Grandma Stone died. I'm sorry."

"A couple years ago."

"Grandma Stone. Man, I loved talking to her." She had been maternal toward Charlie, giving her the female attention she craved. "She'd take us birdwatching with those old binoculars, searching for hawks and loons out on the lake."

"She taught us how to make a loon call." John placed his hands together and blew gently between his thumb knuckles.

Charlie did the same. "Whenever I see a loon, I think of her." They tapped the maple trees for syrup in the spring with her and ice fished in the winter. Charlie showed Grandma Stone slides of cheese mold under the microscope, and she told Charlie it looked like the surface of the moon, proving the moon really was made of cheese, a sentiment that caused them both to laugh out loud.

"I miss her." John's gaze settled on Charlie. He'd always done that—really looked at her with a serious, earnest expression as if she was the most important thing in the universe. "So, how are you? And I want the truth."

"There's just so much to sort out." She noticed fine lines on either side of his mouth that hadn't been there before. "Dad dying." She shook her head. "I can't believe he's gone." A tear came quick and ran down her face. She brushed it away with the back of her hand. "You should have seen him in the hospital. I think he saw my mom. He looked out the window and laughed."

"I've heard of things like that happening," John said. "Like a vision."

"Like she was waiting there for him," Charlie said.

"I'm really sorry I couldn't be at the funeral."

"You missed ham and rolls at the church." Charlie leaned back in the chair and looked up at the sky. "Larry being Larry, talking about the new cheese recipe Dad was working on, highly top secret. Jenny and I had beers afterward. Well, just me. She's pregnant." She eased into the comfortable way they'd talked as kids, telling each other everything; always rehashing what happened, the people, the places; discussing in detail small things like the cookies at Pawlowski's Polish bakery, the old fox that ambled through town, the wolves howling in the woods, and the way the moon had looked the night before.

"Last time I saw Larry was about two months ago over at Booths Landing. We had a drink together. He got pissed off about something, what was it?" John stood up, stretching his arms out like he was holding the earth. "He's always worked up about something."

Bellows of geese interrupted them as they flew overhead. Charlie considered how they'd be migrating south in a few months, to avoid the biting cold of Wisconsin winter. It got so cold up here. The days were long and the nights quiet, snow piles like icebergs along the side of the road. She considered how she would be migrating the opposite direction if she moved back. She really loved those winter nights, sitting in front of the fireplace for hours.

John snapped his fingers and pointed at her.

"Casper, that's who he was pissed at."

"Really?" Her stomach tightened. "I saw him on our land the other day."

"Casper?" John sat down, started the engine, and turned the boat toward shore. "What was he doing?"

"I don't know; just walking around. I didn't talk to him."

"Strange." John slowed and turned into what they called the cove but was really just a bit of shore carved into the riverbank. It formed a quiet spot where they'd sit and watch the turtles climb on logs felled from storms. Here, they'd birdwatch, study dragonflies flitting nervously, and fish with worms for bluegill and perch.

"Something's going on with Raines Dairy. Dad stopped using them. I looked at the ledgers and found out he owes them money from way back. I'll find out more when I meet with Walter."

"He's got no right being on your land."

"It is kind of creepy." Two snapping turtles on the turtle log sat motionless, quietly ignoring them.

"So why was Larry pissed off at Casper?" she asked. Larry had a long history of conflicts of one sort or another with the Raines family going back to Old Man Raines, Casper's father, when Larry had worked for him at the sawmill, cutting logs.

"I heard him say something about money and trees," John said. "Said something like, 'You ain't getting no trees and you might just not get your money either.' Then he called Casper a crook."

"You think he was sizing up the trees that day I saw him?" she asked. "Does he think he's going to get them if we don't pay?" Even as she said it, it seemed far-fetched. It was money owed from twenty years earlier.

"Could be."

Twenty years earlier. So many of Charlie's memories lived there—in the spaces around and between Ria and Mom's deaths. One of them was a bizarre incident involving raccoon hunting with Larry. It was a memory she and John shared.

⌒

Shortly after Ria died, Charlie and John were riding around on their bikes in her driveway doing stunts on homemade ramps. It was an early November afternoon and most of the leaves were off the trees. Everything was fading into dull gray, and a foggy mist had parked itself on the woods and near the river.

They stopped when Larry drove up in his truck.

"Where's your dad?"

"He went to Appleton, needed something," Charlie said. John jumped his bike off a ramp they'd built out of plywood.

"Your mom here?"

"She's sleeping." She didn't want to think about Mom just then. All she did was sleep. Even John asked if she was okay that morning when he first came over.

"She okay?" Larry asked.

"Ask her." Charlie cupped her hand to her mouth, quickly realizing she shouldn't have said it, but Larry didn't seem angry. He just looked at her like he was sorry for her. Like how all the adults in town looked at her these days.

"You kids wanna go raccoon hunting?"

John stopped his bike short, so the back tire slid sideways, a trick they'd both spent hours perfecting that summer. "Sure," he said. "I have to call my grandma."

"Okay." Charlie considered whether to tell Mom as she got off her bike and leaned it against a ramp.

John hopped off his bike and ran toward the house with Charlie.

"Get your boots on," Larry called.

When they came back to the truck, Larry was pulling out his .22 rifle from a case on the flatbed. He let his tired-looking hound out of the front cab. Buster never barked, and Charlie couldn't imagine he'd be much help raccoon hunting.

"We're going up by the bend in the river, over by that marshy area," Larry told them.

Charlie knew the place, a mile into the woods where the raccoons were plentiful because of the proximity to the marsh with its grasses, shrubs, cottonwoods, and plenty of box elders. The trees grew like weeds and were prone to losing their limbs to high winds, which raccoons used to their advantage, building dens in the rotted-out hollows.

"We'll go past the old sawmill," Larry said. "Lots of places for them to hide there."

"Did he say sawmill?" Charlie whispered to John.

"Yeah."

"Larry, are we going to the old mill?" she asked.

"Best place to hunt 'em."

"I'm not supposed to go there, my dad said."

"We ain't going on the property."

Charlie considered this, then shrugged. "Okay." Technically if they weren't on the property, they weren't at the mill.

"Listen." Larry was all business. "Pretty soon I'll let Buster here loose." Buster looked around all droopy eyed, like he didn't have a clue. "When he finds one, he'll chase 'em up a tree. You kids just watch. He'll smell 'em out and chase 'em. When he's treed 'em, you'll hear short, sharp barks." Charlie was skeptical but didn't say anything. Buster didn't seem to know how to bark, much less chase anything.

"Okay," they said in unison.

Charlie trained her eyes on Buster's skinny butt as they walked further into the woods toward the old mill, cautious, stepping lightly on the leaves covering the forest floor, trying not to make noise. Larry wore heavy black boots. John had on rubber-soled sneakers, and she wore her knee-high Wellingtons. Charlie knew not to go ahead of Larry. Never walk ahead of a man with a rifle, Dad had told her on the two occasions he'd taken her grouse hunting. One of those times, he let her get a shot off into the river just to know how it felt to shoot a gun. She'd held steady and felt proud to take part in what Dad and his friends did nearly every weekend during each hunting season: deer, pheasant, grouse, and duck—they did it all. Except Dad said raccoon hunting was a waste of time. But Larry liked to sell the hides to a guy in Rosholt who made hats out of them.

As Charlie trudged on, she thought of how Mom had looked that morning: tired, blurry-eyed, slow moving, empty of life like a sad shadow. Charlie missed her old mom. She missed their walks in these woods with Ria.

Charlie was following closely behind John and nearly bumped into him when he stopped. Up ahead of Larry, Buster stood at alert. He was transformed, with his muscles tensed and his chest puffed out. With a low growl, he sprung forward, running fast through the trees, letting out long bellows, "arruuu, arruuu."

"You kids stay behind me now." Larry picked up his pace. John and Charlie looked at each other and grinned before they started trotting to keep up.

"This is cool," John whispered.

"Hear it?" she asked. Buster was barking now. "He must have found one."

They followed the sound of Buster's short, sharp barks twenty yards ahead to a gnarly box elder. Larry was there with his rifle aimed up at a fat raccoon on the branches above them.

"You kids stay way back there now," Larry admonished again as he took aim, right between the eyes. Charlie braced for the sound of a gunshot. It snapped like a firecracker and echoed in the forest. Larry must have hit the raccoon because it toppled off its perch, bouncing off other branches as it made its way to the ground with a thud in the mud and long grass. Buster sniffed the dead raccoon, then came over to Charlie and plopped down with a groan as if to say, my work is done here.

It didn't take long for Larry to stuff the animal into a burlap sack.

"Come on, yous guys." They headed back the way they'd come and within a few yards, heard shouting.

"Hold up." Larry held up his arm and they stopped.

"Somebody's yelling," John said out of the corner of his mouth in a quiet voice.

"Get down low," Larry said, staring in the direction of the shouts. They tiptoed, bent over like a bunch of ducks.

Without their feet rustling up leaves, they could hear what was being said.

"You good-for-nothing little shithead, Casper, I said get that firewood cut." John and Charlie looked at each other and mouthed *Casper*.

"The ax broke, I told you." Casper's voice was full of fear.

"Old Man Raines got him by the neck," John whispered.

"Where?"

"Just beyond the fence there."

Charlie oriented her eyes in the worsening fog to where he pointed and could make out the old man. He shoved Casper up against a tree in the yard, dusted with rusted-out truck parts. On the other side of the yard was an old trailer and next to it, a wood-sided building that was the abandoned sawmill. Charlie gasped when Old Man Raines hauled off and hit Casper in the face with the back of his hand. Casper's neck snapped back, and his head hit the tree. It hurt to watch, and Charlie feared for his life. Casper stumbled forward but didn't fall. He put his hand to his face.

"Stop." Casper's voice was high-pitched and pleading.

"You piss your pants, boy?" Old Man Raines laughed.

"Old man's drunk," Larry said. "Wait here."

Larry set the burlap bag with the dead raccoon inside on the path next to them. Charlie studied it, half-expecting it to start moving. Buster settled himself between her and the bag. She scratched his neck.

"What's he doing?" she asked.

"I don't know. Larry's kind of crazy. Once, at Booths Landing, he punched a guy in the nose because the guy was drunk and was gonna drive."

"Hey, you fellas seen a dog run by here?" Larry asked. Old Man Raines looked over at Larry. Casper rubbed his head and started backing away until Charlie couldn't see him anymore. She realized then that Larry was trying to help Casper. Not that she liked Casper, but she was glad. His dad scared her.

"Larry. What the hell, you lost your dog?"

"Nah, just misplaced him," Larry quipped.

Old Man Raines ambled over to Larry, his big belly sticking out from his plaid coat that wouldn't have zipped if he'd tried. He walked unsteady and with a limp. The men began talking, but Charlie couldn't hear what they were saying.

"Old Man Raines is a mean drunk," John said.

Charlie considered this. She had it rough, her mom sick and sister gone, but she'd never been mistreated by anyone like what she'd just witnessed.

~

"Remember what you said about Old Man Raines the day we saw him hit Casper?" Charlie didn't wait for John to answer. "You said alcohol changes people. Makes them unrecognizable."

"I saw plenty of it at college. Hell, Chicago has a huge drinking culture. I used to hang out at the bars on Rush Street. That just got old after a while."

"Rick's been drinking a lot." Saying it out loud was hard.

John didn't seem surprised. "Some of these guys who come back from Vietnam have a real hard time. Think about it. What they went through. I was lucky I was a full-time student. Really lucky."

"He can get help at the VA, but he refused to go. I ended up going to therapy myself." It felt good to finally talk about it.

"It's so hard," she said, realizing how exhausted she was. Placing her hand in the river, she studied how the water shifted over her fingers. The green color became clear droplets when she raised her hand above the surface. "Funny how you can be in a city, surrounded by tons of people, and still feel alone." There were just two people she'd considered friends in Milwaukee—Wyatt and Langston, her downstairs neighbor, though she only knew Langston because of Rick. When Lucy was younger, Charlie would take her to the park or on walks and would watch groups of other moms and their kids and wonder how they'd met, what they had in common, what they talked about.

"City's not all it's cracked up to be. People can be really cold." John turned on the motor. His mood had changed to anger. It was an abrupt change. She'd never seen him so closed off.

What happened in Chicago? she wondered. Why did he move back here? Did it have to do with a woman? She was afraid to ask. Anyway, the motor was loud, and he seemed so distant.

They rode back home in silence. When he dropped her off and they said good-bye, he didn't mention getting together again. She didn't either.

~

Charlie had first really gotten to know John at the falls in 1955, a few months after Ria died when she was nine years old. Her friends had stopped coming over, their parents terrified polio was contagious. Who could blame them? Polio had been making people sick since the turn of the century with a surge in cases in the early 1950s. Nobody knew for sure how polio spread. It was only later that they learned it was from contaminated water, feces, that sort of thing. Mom and Dad kept her home from school in September, afraid she'd get sick and die too. Even so, they didn't keep much of an eye on her. Dad was busy at the cheese factory, and Mom was too tired to pay much attention. That left her with long hours to herself.

One morning, she'd hiked along the river to her favorite spot, where she liked to sit on the smooth, flat rocks on the edge of the falls. Perched on the rocks, she sketched a stand of white birch, attempting to capture shadows the trees made on the forest floor littered with leaves.

She saw him then. John Stone was walking through the forest. His long hair fell to his shoulders and his face already hinted at the man he would become, with a square jaw and thick dark lashes. He was a tad overweight, with full cheeks and a belly hanging over his jeans. He looked up at her perched above him.

"Hey, Charlie."

His smile was quick, and he didn't seem surprised to see her.

"Hey." Her heart beat a little faster. Not having talked to many people in the past weeks, she was out of practice conversing with kids her age. But John was always nice to her. He had moved to Falls River the past spring from the Menominee Reservation. They'd sat next to each other that May and she knew he was smart because he aced most tests and talked a lot during class discussions.

"Mind if I sit?" he asked, and he sat down before she could answer.

"You haven't been at school," John said. "What've you been doing?"

"Oh, this, that, and the other thing," she said. Nothing, she thought to herself, except chores, taking care of Mom, helping Dad at the factory.

"So, what's this?" John asked, nodding toward her sketchbook. "That or the other thing?"

"I just like to draw." She was surprised at how easy it was to talk to him.

"It's nice. I like the way you did the shadows." John pulled out a pocketknife and began to whittle a stick with short, fast cuts. "I can't draw."

"I'm surprised you're not afraid to be around me," she said. "Aren't you afraid you'll get sick?"

"Nope." He stopped whittling and looked at her, his gaze steady, without pity. "You okay? I went to Ria's funeral."

"Thanks for coming." She purposely sidestepped his question.

"I know what it's like. My mom left when I was three. Went back to Chicago. I don't even know why. My dad died from cancer last year. It's why we moved here." John stared at the water falling over the river rocks. "That and my grandma said I need to get a good education."

"Bet you miss them," Charlie said.

She looked up at the clear blue sky where cirrus clouds swirled and formed a playful mosaic. She imagined Ria, her arms flung wide, her face turned up to the heavens.

Why are the clouds so spread out?

They're called cirrus clouds. That's just how they look.

They look like cotton candy being pulled apart.

That's 'cause the angels like to eat cotton candy.

For real?

It's what I believe.

"Bet you miss your sister," John said. Had she said something out loud about Ria? Was she going nuts?

"Sometimes." She missed her so bad it hurt.

"Most people got the vaccine now," John said. "Some people in town are saying they don't trust it. Won't let their kids take it." He tossed the stick he had been whittling into the river. It was quickly scooped up by the current. "They're stupid."

They sat in silence and she sketched an image in the clouds above the birch trees: a young girl, her hair a mix and swirl of cirrus clouds.

Nearby, a mourning dove cooed a gentle, melancholy note, over and over as if yearning for something or searching for something she'd lost. Charlie found it sad yet somehow soothing.

"My grandma says mourning doves bring hope," John said.

She looked at him and considered how she'd found a new friend.

For the first time in a long time, she didn't feel so alone.

Chapter 10

Uncle Jack, Karen, John, Lucy, and Charlie sat around the campfire listening to John's stories about canoeing with twelve high school students in the Minnesota Boundary Waters. John was relaxed, laughing about overturned canoes, lost toilet paper, and bears, with none of the uncharacteristic anger he'd shown the day before at the end of their boat ride.

"This would be a great time for a song," Lucy announced. "Come on, Mom, you like to sing." Lucy's body was nearly blocked by a black acoustic guitar she held out to Charlie with both hands.

"In the shower or with you. Not in front of people."

Lucy handed Charlie the guitar. "We're not people, Mom. We're family."

"Okay. As long as you're not people." Charlie settled the guitar on her lap.

"We're from outer space," Lucy whispered, then spun around, flailing her arms in a well-practiced impression of the robot from *Lost in Space*, a favorite show she watched in reruns.

"Danger, Will Robinson, danger, danger, danger," Lucy said, spinning her way onto Karen's lap.

"You look like an alien with orange lips, Miss Robot." Karen pulled a napkin from her pocket and wiped the Cheetos dust off Lucy's lips.

The guitar was old, its fretboard covered with nicks left over from someone else's fingertips. Karen had picked it up from a musician she'd dated years ago, before Uncle Jack. They were celebrating the Fourth tonight since they'd spent the real Fourth sadly making funeral arrangements. It was fitting that Dad had died in the early hours on the Fourth of July. He was proud to be a second-generation American and often spoke of his parents' traveling here through Ellis Island, then living in Brooklyn for a short time. They'd finally settled in Wisconsin like scads of other German immigrants.

Charlie tuned the guitar and started strumming a Joni Mitchell song, "Both Sides Now," a song she'd taught herself during long nights when Rick worked late at the restaurant and she was home with Lucy.

On Karen's lap, Lucy stared at the fire and the ever-changing shapes the flames created flitting off the wood. This tune was a lullaby Charlie would sing after she'd tucked her into bed. As usual, Lucy soon closed her eyes.

John came back from behind the garage with a pile of wood. He placed a couple logs into the fire, poked it a few times with a stick, then settled into his chair. She could tell from his smile and how he nodded his head a few times that he approved of her rendition of the melancholy song. Or so she hoped.

Charlie concentrated on the words, studied his expression, and picked through the cords. She really loved this song. She always got lost in the introspective lyrics about love, life, clouds, about not letting people know how much you care. When she played the final cord, he raised his eyebrows.

"Nice," he said. "You play guitar now?"

"I know a few songs," Charlie told him, relieved he was back to his old even-tempered self.

The temperature had dipped below seventy, cool for July, and the fire felt good. Earlier, they'd had a cookout with brats and hot dogs, roasted marshmallows on the fire, and hiked through the woods, where Lucy spotted a mother and fawn walking in the ferns. At nightfall, Lucy had finally gotten her sparklers, twirling them around in circles to make traces of fire in the air just as Charlie and her friends had done when they were young. Her dad would cook brats for everyone on a small charcoal grill near the house, while John, Jenny, and Charlie used rocks to snap rolls of caps on the hard surface of the driveway. Afterward, Uncle Jack and Larry lit off firecrackers. One year, Charlie taught Ria how to hold a sparkler, and her eyes lit up from the fire stick she held between her fingers like a jewel.

Now they were at Uncle Jack and Karen's home, not far from Dad's place, an old stone house built by a logging tycoon when logging made some men rich. One of the bedrooms was a studio where Karen made her baskets and jewelry. Uncle Jack spent a lot of time in the stone shed next to the house, where he did woodworking: crafting benches from cherry wood, pine tables he sold to farmers, and bookcases he sold for cheap to college students. Each summer, he and Karen traveled around Wisconsin to flea markets and small art fairs, selling wood pieces and baskets they'd made during the long winters. Last year, they'd gone down to Key West, so they'd concentrated on baskets, which Karen sold on commission at an art shop there.

Charlie stopped playing and leaned the guitar against her Adirondack chair. She studied Lucy, who looked so serene with her eyes closed and Karen's arms wrapped around her. Surrounding them, tall pine trees stood like bodyguards, the sound of the river rushing fast a distant hum.

"We need to tell you about what happened with Raines." Karen's voice was quiet even though it was doubtful Lucy would wake up—when she slept, she slept deep, sometimes snoring but rarely waking during the night.

"I'll get some more beers." Uncle Jack walked over to a cooler.

"I wanted things to quiet down a little before telling you this," Karen said.

Charlie braced for bad news, knowing this had to involve the cheese factory.

"A while back, Raines Dairy got in some trouble," Karen said, carefully repositioning Lucy under her arm.

"Casper Raines in trouble, now why doesn't that surprise me?" Charlie said as Uncle Jack handed her a beer.

"Shouldn't." He half-smiled.

"About a year ago, he put Old Man Raines in the nursing home. He has dementia," Karen said. "You knew that?"

"I'd heard."

"After Casper took over at the dairy, the first few month's deliveries were fine. We had no complaints," Karen explained. "I guess it was about two months in, and we started having problems with the milk."

"It wouldn't coagulate right; the curds weren't forming like they should," Uncle Jack explained.

"Didn't take long. After two bad batches, we began to suspect Casper was watering down the milk," Karen said. "So we tested it."

"Turned out we were right," Uncle Jack said.

"We stopped paying him." Karen smoothed Lucy's hair away from her face. "Your dad went to see Casper and told him he knew the milk was bad."

"So it started happening shortly after Old Man Raines went to the nursing home?" Charlie asked.

"Yup." Karen nodded.

"Old Man Raines was a curmudgeon and a drinker, but his milk was good thanks to Larry and your dad," Uncle Jack said. Charlie knew the story: after the war, Larry and Dad had helped Old Man Raines set up the dairy.

"Your dad refused to pay Casper for the bad milk," Karen said. "He filed a complaint."

"He could lose his license to sell milk or get a fine," Uncle Jack said. "Could get both."

"It doesn't explain how much money Casper claims your Dad owes him. He's going around town talking about it," Karen said. "That debt accrued back in the 1950s, for crying out loud."

"Yeah, I noticed there was about a year of unpaid milk bills. It was after Mom died," Charlie said.

"Your dad and Old Man Raines seemed to have some kind of loyalty to each other. Why, I don't know," Karen said. "Anyway, he never asked for the money."

The whole scenario made Charlie uneasy. Karen rarely got rattled, and she seemed worried.

"I can't prove it, but I think Casper's been doing stuff." Karen took a sip of beer.

"What?" John sat forward in his chair, his face lit up by the flames of the campfire.

"What's going on?" Charlie felt uneasy. If Casper was bold enough to try to sell bad milk, what else was he capable of now that he was threatened with going broke?

"I can't be sure it was him, but about six weeks ago, I came into the cheese factory and someone had unplugged the cooler. It was a weekend. The cheese had sat there in the heat for three days or so. It was ruined. Couple hundred dollars' worth."

"That's so messed up," Charlie said. "Did you talk to him about it?"

Karen looked down at Lucy, who had opened her eyes and was staring at the fire again. "I had no proof. All I can say is just be on your guard."

"About what?" Lucy asked.

"About making sure the cheese coolers are plugged in," Karen told her. "Now how about you and I go inside and you can lie down on the couch?"

"I'll give you a ride," Uncle Jack said as he lifted Lucy from Karen's lap.

Lucy snuggled into his shoulder. "Bye, Mom." She waved, happy and content.

After the others went inside, John and Charlie sat talking by the fire. He told her about the old house he'd bought in De Pere close to the high school where he worked in Green Bay. They discussed how much an alarm system would cost to set up at the factory, how they could install deadbolts and spotlights instead of an expensive system that she could not afford. Then John changed the subject.

"Hey, I just wanted to say I'm sorry for the other day on the boat. I was embarrassed and didn't want to tell you about what happened in Chicago."

"You seemed upset." Charlie poked the fire with a stick and watched the sparks fly and settle. "So what happened?"

"It was shitty. Kate, the woman I was seeing, decided she liked my roommate better."

"Oh, man, you don't deserve that."

"I was starting to wonder if I do. Like what's wrong with me?" John laughed, but she could tell he still hurt. She could tell by the expression in his eyes, how he squinted a little. It was what he'd always done when they were kids.

"Nothing." She said it to herself, but he heard her because he was looking right at her. "There's nothing wrong with you," she repeated.

"Thanks for saying that. I was really busy teaching at a high school in Chicago. Anyway, one night, we go to a party at her friends' house in Evanston. On the way back to Chicago, she tells me she's in love with Dave."

"What did you do?" Charlie asked. It was so weird that he'd gone through the same sort of betrayal she'd suffered through with Rick. She understood his anger. She knew how humiliated he must feel.

"Well, we got back, and I walked around the city just thinking. I guess I kind of suspected, but hearing it made it real. I remember standing on the bridge, looking at the Chicago River, wondering, What the hell am I doing here anyway? Sure, my mom and her new family were there. We'd spend time together. But she had her own life. Why not just go back to Wisconsin, teach, help out at the reservation? Chicago just seemed cold and damp and too much concrete. Too much everything."

"So you moved back up." Charlie watched him toss another piece of wood into the fire, noticing how at home he seemed here. "It's hard to imagine you in Chicago anyway."

"It makes more sense to be up here. I got the job in Green Bay. I take kids up to the Boundary Waters. Honestly, what happened was shitty, but it got me back up here." He bent down next to the fire and softly blew oxygen into the embers, coxing flames to ignite the small pieces of kindling he'd added. "Anyway, I thought I should tell you. Now she's calling me, saying she's sorry. Pretty crazy, hey?"

"She wants to get back together?"

"I guess so. I'm not sure." John looked at her, expecting a response. *No, you should not get back together*, she wanted to tell him. *Not with someone like that, who would drop you for your roommate. Not when I'm right here wanting to be with you.* But how could she when she still hadn't cut ties with Rick?

John needed to cut his own ties.

Chapter 11

The next morning, with Lucy and Karen gone to fields outside of town to gather grass for making baskets, Uncle Jack and Charlie drove over to Walter's office in Appleton. It was early and a light fog had settled on the fields of wildflowers—red clover, phlox, and ethereal white Queen Anne's Lace. The possibility of John getting back with Kate was unsettling. Other worries mingled in the rumination feedback loop of Charlie's brain. She worried about Casper lurking around the factory and the financial quagmire she'd found herself in. She missed Dad more than ever. And there was Rick. She'd tried calling him several times last night, but he hadn't answered. She'd always been worried about Rick hurting himself, and now, without being there to check on him, her worries intensified. Next to her, Uncle Jack was subdued and quiet. She could sense his curiosity about her silence. He began drumming his fingers on the steering wheel.

"I have a feeling this meeting is not going to be good," Uncle Jack finally said. "Your dad wasn't making much money at the factory. The past few years have been tough for everyone up here with the recession. I just hope there's some money left for you and Lucy."

"I knew things weren't good," she said. The recession had hit everyone, especially farmers, and high inflation was brutal on the dairy industry. "Plus, this stuff with Raines is disturbing."

"Raines won't give up. He's hurting for money just like everyone else—shit, farmers are holding auctions; seems like every week there's another one." The skin on his knuckles was tight as he gripped the steering wheel.

"Don't worry about me. I can handle him," Charlie said with more conviction than she felt.

"You shouldn't have to deal with all this bullshit." He sighed, then gestured to the radio. "Mind?"

"'Course not."

"I was going to call you about this Casper stuff." He found a station playing the Rolling Stones. "But I didn't want to bother you. Knew you have a lot on your plate."

"An understatement," she muttered, rubbing her neck. Suddenly it was hard to breathe.

"You okay?" Uncle Jack glanced over at her a few times.

"I don't feel so good." Her blood pulsed. There was a pounding in her ears. She couldn't think.

"Let's get you some air." He pulled over and stopped on the wide gravel shoulder next to a field of corn basking in the morning sun. She opened the passenger door and ran between the rows of corn, stopping after a few yards, bending over with her hands on her knees. It was the weight of Rick's illness, the space where her father had been, an image of Lucy's small face. Breathe. Remember to breathe. *They're anxiety attacks*, the VA had counselor told her. *Just breathe.*

She closed her hand around the soft silk of a corn husk and uttered an awkward, half yelp, half scream to stop this feeling of fading, like she was going to pass out. She watched ants crawling around in the dirt, their fine legs like strands of hair. The family *Formicidae*. She let one crawl onto her finger. Uncle Jack's boots appeared in front of her.

She stood up. Her feeling of being on the verge of dying had passed. *Just breathe.* "Everything is so screwed up."

He studied her, eyes narrowing.

"What's happening, Charlie?" His voice was quiet.

"Rick's getting worse." She focused on Uncle Jack's hands, which showed many nicks and callouses from a life of sanding wood and pounding nails.

"Sure seems like it. So, what do you want to do?"

"What I want is to start over," she said. "Honestly, I'd like to make cheese."

The corn stalks were stoic, the wind gently moving their tassels and leaves. She smelled the soil, could almost feel the sweet corn growing slowly, like children. She ran her hand through her hair. Talking about it was a relief.

"Being here has been so good for Lucy. For both of us." She looked at Uncle Jack, eyes so like Dad's, just deeper set and a darker shade of blue. "Lucy loves you guys. I can see she's getting closer to you and Karen. I want to stay here. I really do. But shit, how am I going to make a living?

I've been thinking about getting the cheese factory up and running again."
After she said it, she held her breath. Saying it out loud felt like a risk she
needed to take. She watched a smile appear on Uncle Jack's face.

"You were always good at it."

Relieved to hear Uncle Jack supported her idea, Charlie suddenly felt
energized. "I'm itching to get back to the vats."

"Let's try to make that happen."

"Think there's a chance?" she asked.

"Sure. But it's not going to be easy."

"I know."

"Come on." Uncle Jack put his arm around her. "Let's go talk to Walter."

"Talking to Walter is always good." She kicked a stone across the dirt.

"All right then."

They hopped back into the truck and drove into Appleton, listening to
John Prine tunes with the windows down, munching on cheese curds and
pistachios, and sharing bittersweet memories of Dad.

Chapter 12

Downtown Appleton was anchored by the Fox River with a thriving downtown main street lined with diners, small shops, and offices. They pulled in front of a red brick building near the river and headed up a cement walk that was bowed and cracked in several places from the aggressive roots of a large maple tree. The porch had seen better days, with chipped and crumbling cement around the edges. A rusted metal glider with faded floral cushions and a spindly geranium plant inhabited the far end, where an ashtray with a half-smoked cigar in it sat on a tree stump, evidence that Walter had been there.

They entered a waiting room on the first floor and saw more evidence of Walter—leather chairs and *Field and Stream* magazines scattered on an Early American–style coffee table. Watercolors of geese flying over steamy marshes hung on wood-paneled walls.

"Come in, come in," a voice called from an office on the far side of the waiting room.

Walter sat at a large desk behind several piles of legal folders. He stood up with some effort and came around to give Charlie a hug.

"So good to see you," he said. "You and Lucy holding up okay?" Walter had walked with a limp ever since she met him. Now he leaned on a wooden cane. The war had left him with a bum leg. Dad always said that was why Walter had gone to law school on the GI bill instead of farming.

"Uncle Jack and Karen are taking good care of us."

They sat down in two old courtroom chairs across from Walter, and he opened a legal file on his desk.

"Better be." Walter smiled at Uncle Jack. "Hello, Jack. Are you behaving yourself?"

"Of course not." Uncle Jack crossed one long, thin, jean-clad leg over the other.

"I'll cut to the chase." Walter pulled out papers from the file, including Dad's will.

"The factory, house, and land are heavily mortgaged. There are bills. Outstanding money left to pay on the new factory equipment—this here loan from the bank." Walter handed Charlie some papers. Sure enough, the loan was for the vats, a cheese press, and various other cheesemaking equipment.

"So that's how he got the new vats," she said. Mystery solved.

"Leveraged the assets for that. The factory, the house—they aren't worth much. But the land with all those old trees. That's your biggest asset," Walter said. He caressed the stack of papers. "Your dad's estate is deep in the hole. I'm sorry, Charlie."

"How could Dad have let this happen? He'd always been so careful with money." A new dress for Christmas and Easter, that was it. Plastic bags worn inside her old rubber boots, so her feet would stay dry in the snow. Secondhand sweaters from the church. They didn't have much, but she'd never felt poor. Dad ran a solid business, but they weren't rich. He prided himself on paying his bills on time.

"The recession was hard on him, and that run-in with Casper about the bad milk put him behind. He told me all about it. Plus buying that equipment," Walter said.

"A Bermuda Triangle of events," Uncle Jack added. "He wasn't making much cheese to sell in the last year, just working on that white cheddar. His magnum opus."

"He was, how should I say this . . . a little obsessed with the white cheddar," Walter said.

"Please don't tell me he bought some goats," Charlie said. "He said goats were the next new thing. Goat cheese was going to be big."

"He did go on about goats." Uncle Jack laughed.

"No goats," Walter said. "Least not that I'm aware of."

"I think he was slipping," Uncle Jack said. "He'd repeat himself a lot."

"True. There was this time he called me three times one evening," Walter said. "It was on a Sunday. He didn't remember we'd already talked, so we recycled the whole last conversation."

"He'd do that but then the next minute he'd seem just fine," Uncle Jack said. "Guess it was worse than I thought."

"There's more." Walter picked up an envelope. "I just got this. Casper Raines is suing the estate." He took out some papers and passed them to Charlie.

She read the words at the top: Summons and Complaint. Her heart raced. "A lawsuit," she read out loud, "has been filed in circuit court seeking a judgment for payment of past due receivables to Raines Dairy." Skimming the rest of the letter, she took in the details. Raines Dairy, specifically Casper, was suing Morgan Cheese.

Shit. She checked the date: July 3, the day of Dad's heart attack.

"I'm sorry, Charlie," Walter said. "Farmers are hurting up here. Milk prices are so low that families can't earn a living. Everyone's affected. There's been barn sales, lots of foreclosures. Dairy farmers take a hit, and it's like a domino effect. Cheese prices fall. I don't need to tell you that. Raines is probably in the red, without his dad, after the bad milk shenanigans. He's clearly desperate."

Her head was spinning. They'd been through some bad times, and she knew what loss felt like. But a lawsuit. This was new territory. Her plan to reopen the factory was getting more complicated.

Walter rubbed his chin. "It's your decision, but I'd suggest you sell everything to pay off the debt."

Charlie's heart sank at hearing his advice. There had to be some way. "How can he sue? I checked the books. This debt is twenty years old."

"As long as there were open books since then, he can still sue."

"Well, sure there were. We used Raines Dairy up until Casper tried to sell us that bad milk," Uncle Jack said.

Charlie looked out the small, dirt-crusted window at a pair of black birds perched in a pine tree. They squawked, fluttered their wings dismissively, and flew away. A heavy burden settled itself in the space between her shoulders.

"Is there any way to save the factory?"

"You'll need to talk to the bank, extend your credit on the equipment loan." Walter rubbed his chin. "We'll have to go to court. Show the judge you got a plan."

"But I don't have a plan."

"Figure one out." Walter shook his head, raised his eyebrows. "'Course they don't normally loan to women." He turned to Uncle Jack.

"He left you his guns, Jack. I'm sorry there's not more for the family."

Chapter 13

Charlie spent the next morning taking inventory in the cheese store at the factory. Handling the squares of cheese and lumpy bags of curds made her feel achingly nostalgic. Stocking the cooler had been her job for as long as her memory allowed, her first job at the factory. Feeling the hunks of cheese now was like touching Dad's hand because she imagined he'd been the last one to stock the cooler. She thought about her meeting with Walter. It was worse than she'd imagined, and what she'd imagined was pretty bad. Forging ahead with her plan to reopen the factory, she'd made an appointment to meet with the loan officer two days from now. She hoped she could get more time on the equipment loan, maybe a business loan for start-up costs. First, she had to deal with Rick.

She needed to call him. She was stalling, wondering what to say. Should she tell him she'd like to stay here? She needed to discuss her plan to enroll Lucy in school at Falls River Elementary. In some ways, it would be easier on the phone than in person. On the other hand, it seemed cruel. Did he deserve more?

At one time, Charlie would have thought yes.

They'd met for the first time in front of a cheese cooler like this. Charlie was restocking the Morgan Cheese cooler section at the cheese market in Milwaukee the summer after graduating from college.

A cute guy in an army jacket and jeans stood in front of the cooler. His wavy blond hair had hints of auburn and fell just past his collar. She was amused by the way he carefully studied the cheese labels, up close like he was reading a book.

"Man, there's so many choices. How do you pick one?"

Charlie looked around the area to see who he was talking to. No one.

"We got smoked cheddar, sharp cheddar, mild cheddar." He ran his hand over each one. She continued stocking the cheese, watching him from the corner of her eye, listening. "We got five-year, ten-year. This one's older than my guitar." Still talking to no one.

"Can I help?" she asked.

He turned slowly toward her and smiled. His teeth were unusually white, his eyes green, a light shade of moss.

"I'm sure you could."

"About the cheddar." He was so sexy, it was hard to take her eyes off him. "What are you looking for?" Charlie tried to sound casual and not stare.

"I think I just found it." He stepped closer to her.

"Did you really just say that?" He was kind of corny but cute.

"Yes, I did." He grinned, nodded, and went back to studying the cheese. "I'm a cook. I'm looking for a good cheddar for grilled cheese."

Charlie reached for the Morgan two-year aged.

"This one's good. It melts nicely, has a full-bodied flavor." Close to him, she could see curly hairs on his upper chest, and what looked like dog tags. A vet. He had a few freckles on his nose, and his beard was a multi-colored mix of red, brown, and blond. Her instant attraction to him was unnerving, exciting. He reached out for the cheese, and their hands touched. Charlie knew her cheeks were flushed.

He snapped his fingers and pointed at her. "Hey, do you want to come over to the restaurant later, help me with this recipe? You seem to know a lot about cheese."

It turned out he worked at a German restaurant in West Allis. She met him there after work and Rick gave her a tour of the place, which was empty, closed because it was Monday. The dining room was covered in murals painted in the 1930s by a German artist named Peter Gries.

"My dad's parents came here from Bavaria, Germany, near Switzerland," Charlie said. "They came through Ellis Island."

"We get a lot of immigrants in here—Germans, Austrians, Polish. Got a group of World War II buddies come here on Mondays. They play sheepshead, drink beer."

"Sounds like our house in Falls River, every other Sunday growing up."

"Check out this one." He stopped in front of a mural depicting a group of wild boars in the woods. "This one reminds me of Vietnam. Guess because I saw some wild boars over there."

"How long were you there?" Strange, even though she'd gone to UW–Madison, where she'd seen a lot of veterans on State Street, she didn't know many vets, only the brother of a friend and a guy who worked at the cheese market. Her gut reaction was negative because she knew guys coming back from Vietnam carried the war with them. Who wouldn't? The news stories were horrific. She put her feelings aside because Rick was so dang hot and he was interested in cheese and cooking, which she found sweet.

"Two years." Rick leaned on one of the wood tables and lit a cigarette. "See his eyes here, this one." He pointed to the huge wild hog in the center of the painting. "He's got that hunted look." He didn't elaborate.

Charlie examined the expression on the animal, a mix of fear and threat. Ominous. It scared her, thinking of what Rick must had seen over there. She searched her brain for something to say.

"I've never hunted wild pigs, but I've hunted plenty of deer, raccoons," she said. "Raccoons always looked just plain terrified. Like they knew. We'd shoot them right between the eyes." Yikes, maybe she shouldn't have said that. She held her breath and was relieved when Rick laughed.

"Wait, you went raccoon hunting?"

"Sure, once in a while." She shrugged. "Mostly we made cheese. My dad has a cheese factory, Morgan Cheese. You bought some."

"You sold me your dad's cheese. Isn't that a conflict of interest?"

"Maybe."

Wandering around the restaurant's empty dining room, examining the murals, Charlie told Rick about Falls River, making cheese, moving to Madison to study biochemistry.

"Why biochem?"

Charlie thought for a moment. She'd never been asked this question. "I like to see how things work at a microscopic level, how everything changes, transforms, forms new life, how things decay and die."

Rick closed his eyes and for a moment he seemed miles away. She thought of some of the stories she'd read about what happened to the soldiers in Vietnam—the napalm, Agent Orange, fighting in jungles. The killing. They were so young. She studied his face and imagined what he'd looked like as a boy, his long lashes brushing the tops of his cheeks. He opened his eyes but did not smile. "I've seen way too much of that." He blinked as if trying to get rid of an image, then abruptly banged the table with his right palm. "Let's make that grilled cheese."

They went into the kitchen. "My grandmother made the best grilled cheese. Grandma Sobczak. She was from Poland." Rick pulled out a cast iron frying pan, placing it on the stove. He began expertly slicing a loaf of bread. "She always used Oscypek, a smoked cheese. She'd send me to get it at this little Polish store near our house on the south side. That store's gone now."

"I could get that for you. I'll check it out." She was relieved he seemed calmer now. Maybe cooking was his go-to, where he immersed himself in the work and was able to stave off bad feelings.

"Grandma always said it was the cheese that made the difference. 'Course she made her own bread. I use her bread recipe too."

This guy was a baker and a cook. Nice. Plus, he was totally sexy, especially in the kitchen. She watched him monitor the frying pan, turning the sandwiches, toasting them until they were crispy and bronze with cheese oozing from the sides.

He looked up and saw her staring at him. "What?"

"You seem so happy doing this."

"I guess I am. All those days I spent in the kitchen, helping my grandma, listening to her stories about Poland and the war."

"My grandma had stories too. About dairy farming in Bavaria, then hard times, a farm crisis."

They ate the sandwiches with pickles and beer while seated on high stools at the butcher block counter. "Now that is a grilled cheese sandwich," Rick said.

"Award winning."

"That's high praise from a real cheesemonger." He used his beer bottle as a microphone. "I want to thank the academy, Morgan Cheese, Charlie, my grandmother, and, oh yeah, Charlie's dad, who I hope one day to meet."

"You'd have to go to Falls River, and I'm not sure you'd like it there."

"Try me."

Later, they went to Rick's apartment, a small one-bedroom not far from the restaurant. He played guitar and sang Bob Dylan tunes—"You Ain't Goin' Nowhere" and "Tonight I'll Be Staying Here with You." When he sang, he looked at her the whole time, and she felt like she was on fire, seduced by his voice and rocked with an ache she hadn't felt since John, with whom she'd lost touch after he went on a semester-long trip to study in North Dakota. After John left, she'd had a series of unsatisfying short relationships and drunk one-night stands that left her feeling dull-headed. So when the song ended, and Rick whispered the words that started them on a path together for the next seven years, she was all in.

"I've been looking for you for a while now, Charlie."

He leaned in real slow. Keeping his eyes on her, he kissed her. She felt thrilled, like she was on the edge of a cliff, prepared to jump, with no care about how or where she'd land. She fell for him and with him. Hard.

Eight months later, after the eye-opening trip to Chicago with Jenny, Rick was enthusiastic when she'd told him she was pregnant. He'd even proposed on one knee, at dinner in the restaurant where he worked. The room full of customers had erupted in cheers when she'd said yes. They got married at the church in Falls River with Jenny as her maid of honor and Langston, Rick's army buddy, as best man. Afterward, they threw a big party at Booths Landing, then honeymooned in the Apostle Islands, hiking and sleeping in a tent. They kept it simple. It was a happy time.

Now, Charlie dialed their home number using the phone on Dad's desk in the factory. Rick answered on the second ring.

"Hey, when are you coming back?" He sounded tired.

Charlie leaned into the desk, her hand on the smooth wood, worn from so many years of use. She could hear Rick breathing.

"Say something." He sounded vulnerable.

"I'm not sure what to say."

Rick took a drag on something, a joint or a cigarette, could have been either. "Please come back, Charlie."

Tears of frustration formed in her eyes. She stared at the empty vats surrounded by ghosts—Dad, her younger self, Mom carrying Ria on her hip. She felt herself pulled into a spiral of unhappiness whenever she thought about going back to Milwaukee.

"I feel like crap. I want to kill myself," Rick said.

Charlie got scared whenever he said stuff like this. It wasn't the first time. "I'm sorry you feel that way. You can call the VA, talk to someone." It was what her therapist told her to say, to keep repeating, when Rick talked about hurting himself. She had also advised calling the police.

"Just come home, babe. That's all I need."

"Don't start getting all down on yourself. Promise me that." This was a joyless dance—Rick tanking downward into depression, her trying to yank him back up.

"I'll try. I'll feel better when I see you."

"I'll come down tomorrow." Charlie wiped tears off her face. She needed to see him for herself. If she saw him, she could figure out how to leave him. People got divorced all the time. Why was it so hard for her to just do it? She wished he would get help.

After she hung up, she realized with ambivalence he hadn't even asked about Lucy. Or, for that matter, about how Charlie was doing. Not surprising. He'd always been so wrapped up in his own problems he couldn't seem to see that she and Lucy were there, right in front of him.

Chapter 14

"Hey, babe." Rick leaned forward to kiss her mouth. She turned her cheek, and he awkwardly kissed her ear.

"That's how you want to play this?" He smoothed back his hair, wet from the shower. "I guess I deserve that."

"I'm not playing." She searched for words to describe her feelings. "I'm just a little overwhelmed."

"Let's start over." He stood with his hands on his hips. "Welcome home. I hope you're hungry."

He stepped over to the stove. "I'm making eggs scrambled with cheese, the way you like them."

"Landslide," a new Fleetwood Mac song, was playing on the stereo. Clean dishes were drying on the rack next to the sink. Newspapers in the living room were piled on the ottoman, neatly stacked, and the rug revealed tracks. He'd actually vacuumed.

"No Lucy?"

"She's with Karen and Uncle Jack." Charlie put down her purse, grabbed the mail from the front table, and sat on the stool at the kitchen counter, watching Rick stir milk into the eggs. He was wearing cut-off jean shorts and a plain V-neck blue T-shirt, but no shoes. She felt wary. He was turning on the charm.

"There's coffee." He spooned eggs onto two plates, poured two cups of coffee, and sat down next to her. Buttered toast and some strawberries were arranged on a large plate, the one etched with wildflowers they'd bought in Door County years ago. Having gotten up early to make the drive back to Milwaukee, Charlie was hungry. She tasted the eggs—cheesy eggs, Lucy called them. Rick had taught Lucy how to crack eggs into a pan, pour in the milk, stir, and sprinkle the cheese into the mixture. Lucy loved the rare attention from Rick, wanted so badly to please him. She beamed when he complimented her. Rick was patient and funny with Lucy during these times, pretending they ran a restaurant, with Charlie playing the role of regular customer. They'd had some happy times. It wasn't all bad.

"How are you doing?" she asked. "You seem better."

"I'm fine." He sat down on the stool next to her. His hair was longer now, curling in neat waves as it dried. His curls always seemed tame compared to her wild ones. She stared at his face. His eyes were red-rimmed, bloodshot, with dark circles underneath.

He wasn't fine.

"I'm really trying here." A tear slipped out of the corner of his left eye. "I miss you guys so bad." He put his fork down and wiped his face with the back of his hand.

Charlie's instinct was to comfort him. She reached out and placed her hand on his shoulder. He leaned into her, burying his face in her neck. The smell of his shampoo was familiar. She felt his upper arm muscles tense.

"Please, don't tell me you're leaving me," he whispered.

Was she? Charlie felt a familiar attraction to him. She reigned it in with memories of his infidelities, forcing herself to say what she had come to tell him. "I want to move up there. I want to reopen the cheese factory. I want to enroll Lucy at the elementary school I attended."

"Okay, I'll move there with you." He sat up and smiled. "Work in a supper club. Anything."

Surprised at his offer, she laughed. "Ha, you at a supper club. I can't see it."

"Come on, Charlie," he said. "We're so good together."

She moved away from him on her stool and took a sip of coffee. "Are we?"

"We were."

He looked at her, the eggs on his plate getting cold. The smell of bacon was still strong. She felt so sad. Talk. Always talk. He was going to get help, going to stop drinking. It was all just talk.

"Years ago, we talked about moving up there," she said. "Remember your plan to open a restaurant? Morgan Cheese House." Her instinct was to mollify him and try not to upset him. It was a habit she'd honed after living through bouts of his depression: walking on eggshells.

"Morgan Cheese Haus, not house, *haus*, in honor of your dad. We could still do that. *Up nort dair.*"

Charlie swallowed a forkful of eggs and took a bite off a piece of toast. Rick was always talking in that way, what he called an *up-nort accent*. She'd found it funny at first but soon realized he sounded too much like Larry and a lot of the people she'd grown up with and loved. Soon she stopped laughing when he said things like "up nort dair" or "yous guys." Irritated, Charlie considered the array of feelings she'd had since she arrived. This was a familiar roller coaster.

She needed to buy herself some time. "I'm going to use the bathroom."

The air in the bathroom was still steamy, and the floor was wet. He'd always managed to soak the floor when he took a shower. She looked at herself in the mirror. Haggard was the word that came to mind. Dark circles shined under her eyes, with a crop of new wrinkles on her forehead. She splashed water on her face, blew her nose, and sat on the toilet. As she went to toss the tissue into the wastebasket, something caught her eye. Under some tissue was a bright-pink piece of material. It looked like underwear. Charlie nudged the tissue aside and stared at what was underneath: pink lace underwear with blood on it. What the hell? It didn't take more than a few seconds to understand: Rick must have had a woman over here. She wasn't surprised, just angry at herself for being even a smidge tempted by him earlier.

How could she let that happen? Was she so needy that she'd settle for any little crumb of affection offered? Hadn't she told herself she didn't want to be treated like this anymore? A new resolve girded her actions as she blew her nose again, washed her hands, and ran her fingers through her hair. Buck up, she told herself in the mirror, turning her head left, then right, examining her face. She didn't look so bad. She thought of Larry. Stop dithering, he'd say to Uncle Jack in a game of blackjack or when Walter tried to choose between whiskey or beer. *Stop dithering.*

Rick was still sitting at the kitchen counter when she came out of the bathroom.

"So, what's up with the underwear in the wastebasket?"

He looked down at his empty plate and set his fork next to it.

"You weren't supposed to see that."

"No?" There was a time when she wouldn't have said anything. Those days when she was so afraid of losing him, so scared, so very young, she'd accept it as just the way things were.

"It's nothing. You were gone. I was lonely. Please, Charlie, I was stupid."

His earnestness was real. At this moment. But it never lasted long. He just did what he wanted. "I agree. It was stupid." She grabbed the mail from the counter, sorted what was hers, stuffed it in her purse, and walked to the door. "In a way, I'm glad." She tried to open the door, pulled hard, but it was stuck. It always did that. So many things in this house were broken. "Makes it easier for me to leave you here." She yanked the door again and banged her elbow into the wall when it swung open. "Ouch." Rick stood there, his head tilted sideways, as if he was trying to figure out what was happening.

"Please don't go."

She stopped fumbling with the door. "You know how you repeat over and over 'I'm sorry' when you're having a nightmare?"

"You told me."

"It makes me cry. But, and this is so weird, you never say it to me. Even just now."

"You just don't understand." His voice was strained, his gaze focused on the past, thousands of miles away. "You never did."

She was so tired. "I know."

Chapter 15

Charlie started getting sleepy three miles outside of Falls River, so she pulled into a gas station near the fairgrounds, where the carnies were setting up the rides for the county fair held every third week in July. Sipping her black gas station coffee that tasted too good for gas station coffee, she stood in the parking lot next to Dad's truck and gazed over the midway, grateful to be back up north breathing in the country air, albeit dusty now from the dirt riled up underneath all the trucks ferrying rides and animals into the fairground. What a relief to be away from Rick again. She felt physically lighter. The sting of betrayal had eased with each highway mile, as the forest became taller, denser with more birch, pine, and aspen trees than grew in the city.

It was warm, in the upper eighties, even though the sun was already behind the trees bordering the fairgrounds, where the carnival rides were scattered like huge toys. Charlie watched the workers setting up a Ferris wheel. The fun house, with its red-and-white barrel entrance and leering clown faces painted on the side of what was essentially a trailer, was already set up next to a small roller coaster, red and yellow bumper cars, and several carnie games. Workers were testing the merry-go-round and the horses rode riderless, up and down in a lonely performance to the iconic sounds of organ music.

She thought of the days in Milwaukee when she'd taken Lucy to the zoo, holding onto her perched happily on top of her favorite white stallion on the merry-go-round. She remembered that those hours spent mothering were long. Though she was grateful to Rick for doing a lot of the cooking, she'd get angry about having to shoulder the bulk of the child-rearing plus taking care of the house. Most of all, she remembered how alone she'd felt. Maybe if she'd had more women friends, it would have been different.

They went to the zoo once a week because she and Lucy both loved the animals, especially Samson the silverback gorilla, who hid secrets behind his worried eyes. Lucy liked to ask him questions and claimed every tilt of his head contained a coded answer.

Rick worked nights and took care of Lucy when she was at the cheese market during the day, but on Mondays, she took off all day. They'd go to the zoo, or the park over in Brookfield or West Allis, and hike trails in the woods that reminded her of home. She recalled one Monday when Rick came to the zoo with them. He was having a good spell, occasions lasting a few weeks when he'd drink less and focus more on family. He was taking pictures of them on the merry-go-round as they passed by.

"Daddy!" Lucy waved at him, drinking in his attention like water. She patted the mane of the stallion. "That's my dad," she said to the hard plastic.

"Next time smile, Charlie," he yelled.

Later they'd sat in the backyard and built a campfire, and Rick played guitar and sang songs with Lucy.

"We should do this more often," Charlie said.

"We should," he said.

But they never really did. He soon got busy with work and stayed late partying with his coworkers after closing time and Charlie went back to taking Lucy to the zoo alone.

～

Charlie took a last sip of tepid coffee and watched the merry-go-round slow, then stop altogether. She walked back to the truck and stared into the cargo bed. It was clean. Dad always kept it clean. She thought of all the years she and Dad had sold cheese at the county fair out of the back of this truck. They'd sell Morgan Cheddar and Cheese Curds. They always sold out. "Cheese never goes out of style," Dad had said. It was fun. She felt part of something, on a mission to sell cheese. She wanted Lucy to experience the same kind of lifestyle, close to family and old friends, where they spent more time outside than inside and went to simple things like county fairs. She told herself she'd concentrate on building this new life and put the sticky quagmire of divorce on the back burner for now. Divorce felt a lot like a long, drawn-out death, and she could not deal with another loss right now, not while she was still moving through the hot pain of losing Dad and this hornet's nest of past memories stirred up by his passing.

As Charlie started up the engine, she shoved her dark feelings aside and steadied herself with a new resolve to stay in Falls River and get Morgan Cheese up and running again. Dad was right. People loved cheese, and she loved making and selling it. She needed money, and making cheese was her best bet. She certainly didn't want to teach high school science or work quality control at the canning factory, the few jobs her biochem degree might get her up here. Uncertainty creeped into her thoughts as she neared Falls River. Could she ever get back that kind of life? Or was it just a pipe dream?

Chapter 16

The loan officer wore a tan polyester suit coat with wide lapels and matching pants. He'd embraced 1970s expansive fashion trends with obvious enthusiasm—wide sideburns, wide tie, wide bell bottoms. He had it all. As Charlie and Jenny followed him to his office, Jenny raised her eyebrows and mouthed, "It's called a leisure suit."

Charlie whispered, "Don't make me laugh."

They sat in two chairs across from him, Jenny easing herself down slowly, one hand on the chair arm, the other clutching her large stomach. Charlie wondered if she was having twins. She was huge, but that didn't slow her down. To the contrary, with each week of pregnancy, she grew more outspoken on topics ranging from nuclear energy (she was opposed) to the dangers of microwaves (she was convinced they gave you cancer).

"What can I do for you girls?"

The name plaque on his desk said "Jerry Noth, Loan Officer." Never having requested a loan, Charlie wasn't sure how this went, so she jumped right in. "I'd like to get an extension on this loan, so I can get the factory up and running again." She pulled papers from an accordion file and handed them across the desk. Then her nerves took over, and she began talking, telling him about Dad dying, the cheese factory, and her plan to restart the business. She pointed out to him that Morgan Cheese had been in the black and her father had been making cheese up until this past year when he lost his milk supplier, then recently started having memory problems.

"So, as you know my father took out this loan for equipment."

"Yes, I handled the loan. Your dad is two months behind in payments, Mrs. Sobczak. I don't have to point that out to you. We've been patient. First because your father was well respected in this town and second because he passed. Sorry for your loss." He sat back and took a moment to adjust his belt.

His words were not encouraging. Despite feeling deflated, she forged ahead. "These are revenues from thirty years of sales." She reviewed the liabilities that had led them down the rabbit hole into the red: the equipment loan, Dad slowing down on production and sales, a poor economy, Dad's memory issues. What had Doc Cooper called it? Early signs of dementia possibly caused by cerebrovascular disease. She ended her litany of woes by saying, "I know my dad was behind in payments and I want to have a chance to catch up if you just give me an extension on the loan."

"It's really good cheese, Jerry," Jenny offered. "Can I call you Jerry? Do you think leisure suits are here to stay or just a passing fad?" She wasn't helping.

Jerry ignored her questions and put on reading glasses. He spent a moment reviewing the numbers Karen and Charlie had put together working at Dad's desk the past few days. He raised his eyebrows when he reviewed the copy of the Raines lawsuit she'd included with the accounting numbers.

"First of all," he said as he looked over his glasses, "your profit and loss statement indicates outstanding debt."

"Yes, but I have projected we can make up for it in about a year or two." Charlie leaned over the desk and pointed to numbers showing milk and other costs she had itemized. It had taken her long hours over the past several days to calculate the cost of milk, rennet, Larry's salary. Uncle Jack and Karen had said they'd work for free to help out, at least until they left for Key West for their get-out-of-winter trip.

"Your dad put up the land, the factory, and the house as collateral for the equipment loan," Jerry said, leaning back. "I'm afraid we're going to have to foreclose."

Charlie couldn't believe it. Could he do that? She felt a stab of pain in her forehead, a headache coming on.

"The land, the house, and the cheese factory are all encumbered with the debt. Your dad knew, if he went into default, he'd lose everything." He glanced at the papers. "You got six months to figure this out. After that, we'll take them."

Six months? Stunned, her thoughts raced. She could make cheese, though she needed more than six months to get things running. She felt tears forming and her head pounding, but she was determined not to cry.

Jerry seemed to lose interest. He tossed his glasses on the desk and placed his hands behind his head. "Even if I could give you an extension, you would need your husband to come in and sign with you. We don't even issue credit cards to women without a husband's signature."

"Okay, that's bullshit," Jenny said, flinging her arm up as if she were singing opera to the balcony.

"Yeah, that's not happening." Charlie kept her head down, trying not to start bawling. She stuffed the papers into her bag.

"Quite frankly, when I saw your name, Charlie, I thought you were a man."

"Clearly, she's not, and that shouldn't matter." Jenny stood up and placed her hands on her hips.

"It's our policy."

"You can take your policy and shove it." Jenny stared at him until he looked away. Charlie studied Jerry, who had turned red in splotches, with an inflamed area next to his nose lit up. He moved his neck around, then ran his hand down his tie.

"I suggest you get a private loan, a family member, someone willing to invest," he said.

"I suggest you rethink your wardrobe. This polyester is not working for you." Jenny pointed her finger in swirls at him and then turned toward the door. "Come on, Charlie, we'll take our business elsewhere."

Okay. Charlie thought. *Where?*

"Thank you," Charlie said. *For nothing.*

Chapter 17

On the ride back to Falls River, Jenny would not stop ranting. "Hell if he thinks that you won't get a loan just 'cause you're a woman."

"He said it's the law," Charlie said. "Or their policy. Whatever."

"We can't accept that."

"Or, maybe I need to rethink this, sell the land, sell the factory and the house, go back to Milwaukee." It was the last thing she wanted to do.

"Hang on." Jenny slammed her hand on the dashboard. "What are you saying?"

"Maybe I should just go back and work at the cheese market. At least I get a paycheck there. I haven't had a paycheck in a month. Lucy needs clothes for school. She needs to see the dentist, get her shots."

"Whoa, whoa, hold your horses, pull over, just pull over. I need to talk to you about this."

"All right." Charlie slowed down and turned onto a country road, then into a gravel driveway that led to an abandoned barn.

She turned to Jenny. "So?"

"You were quiet in that meeting." Jenny rolled her window down further and reached her arm out, searching for cool air.

"No, I wasn't. I showed him the numbers, and he told me it didn't matter because I'm a woman."

"Why do you want this?"

"What?"

"To make cheese, to move up here?"

"It's not obvious?"

"No, it's not. Not when you don't talk about it." Jenny pulled a rubber band off her wrist and tied her hair into a ponytail. Without wind blowing into the windows, it was getting stuffy.

"I thought you knew. I want to make cheese again. I want to get us away from Rick. I want to live somewhere where I can breathe. Go outside, walk in the woods with Lucy. Where I know people. Where I have a best friend." Charlie looked at Jenny, really looked at her, and saw how ginger freckles covered her arms and even her cheeks, how her eyelashes were reddish blonde like her hair. She was always so pretty, but now she glowed.

"There, that's what I was looking for."

"What? Me being pathetic?"

"That passion. You got it, Charlie. You always had it. You just need to use it. Speak up: this is your passion, for Pete's sake. Stop holding everything in."

Sometimes there's an emotional numbing after multiple or very traumatic loss. It's you trying to protect yourself. It's how you survived your sister's death and what happened to your mom. The VA counselor's words started to make sense. *An emotional numbing.* Charlie studied the barn in front of them. It was weathered, its gray boards sagging under the weight of neglect, but still, there was a raw beauty about it.

"Maybe I'm quiet because that's how I survive." It was clearer now than when the therapist had explained it. She was numbing herself to minimize the hurt.

Jenny turned to her. "Yes, you have been through a lot. Yes, Rick is not getting any better." She raised her arm up and slammed her hand on the dashboard again, causing the glove compartment door to fall open like a gaping wound. "But no, I don't feel sorry for him, and I don't think you need to take care of him anymore." She closed the glove compartment. "You take care of everyone—Ria, your mom, Rick. Take care of yourself a little. You want to make cheese? It's gonna be hard. But I think you can do it. Shoot, how many women run cheese factories on their own?"

"I don't know any."

"That's because women don't have the rights men do. We need to change that. Be able to get a loan on our own. We need more women lawyers, doctors." Now Jenny was talking to herself more than Charlie. "You know you can't find a woman OB-GYN? I've tried. I chose a midwife instead. The point is, think outside the box. Get out there, stick up for yourself, stop trying to please everyone."

Charlie sighed, started the car, turned it around, and headed back to the highway, thinking about what Jenny had said. How did this get so complicated? She just wanted to make cheese. She thought of how far she'd come; how she'd left Rick in Milwaukee; how she was close to perfecting the white cheddar recipe, though she still needed to find Dad's notes. From her years working as a cheesemonger, she knew what cheese sold well, and this cheese would sell. "I can fight for this. You think I can't."

"Oh, I know you can, that's what I'm saying." Jenny dug around the bag containing Charlie's 8-tracks. "You got any Bowie? Ha!" She pushed in the tape, and David Bowie's voice began one of their favorites, "Changes."

"Wait," Charlie said. "Did you say you are having a midwife deliver this baby?"

"Yup, at home."

"Oh, Lord." Charlie thought of Lucy's birth, and how she'd been terrified. The nurses at St. Joe's Hospital in Milwaukee were so kind. She'd never want to do that at home, but Jenny was stubborn and it was pointless arguing with her about it.

As the fields flew by and the wind from the open windows whipped their hair around, they sang off-key, falling back on high school habits, rolling around country roads taking the long way, the scenic route, up and down hills, past lakes and forests, paper mills and small towns. Navigating their lives together always made everything easier, more fun. When the song ended, Charlie looked straight ahead at the highway. "Why is everything so hard?"

"Tell me what's not," Jenny said.

She thought for a second. "Making cheese. Actually making cheese. Pouring milk into the vat, pressing the curds into forms, stacking them in the aging cellar. It's what I want to do, what I do best. I need to come up with Plan B. Let me think."

They rode in silence for a few miles.

"How did you start the food co-op?" Charlie asked. "I know you said Pete's family helped."

"His family gave us the money outright to buy the building, to pay for renovations, no strings attached," Jenny said. Pete's parents had money. His dad owned a big cabinet-making company. "If only you had someone like that."

"Or, if someone invested," Charlie said.

"I like how you're thinking."

Charlie snapped her fingers. "I got it. Let's meet with everyone—you, me, Walter, Larry, Uncle Jack, Karen. Maybe they know some people. There's got to be someone."

"Wait, I just thought of someone. Remember Walter's son, Jake?" Jenny asked. "He's pretty wealthy now, lives in Chicago."

"Of course, I remember him. I had such a crush on him, then turns out he's gay."

"Yeah. Everyone knew but you. So he stopped by the food co-op a few months ago. He was looking at some land up near Rosewood. Said he had some friends who started a dairy farm up there."

"It's worth a try," Charlie said. "I'm sure not getting a loan from officer Jerry."

"Talk to Walter about it. He wants to help. He's been pretty lonely after Ruth died, comes into the food co-op a lot. Always asks about you."

They slowed as they drove through Falls River. At the park, a few boys wearing Brewers caps were playing catch, a couple walked along the river path with their dog, and several older women got out of their car in front of Booths Landing. It was the lunch crowd.

"Let's get everyone together for a meeting," Charlie said. "It's worth a shot."

Chapter 18

Back home it was bedtime for Lucy, so Charlie snuggled next to her with Mom's old copy of *Winnie-the-Pooh*. Reading books together in bed had always been their safe spot, especially when Rick was drinking at home. Lucy smelled like strawberries from the bubble bath Karen had supervised before she left.

"Why is Eeyore sad?" Lucy asked, tilting her head back to look up at Charlie with her big, green eyes.

"Some people are just sad that way."

"Are you sad from Grandpa dying?" *Yes, and from Ria and Mom and leaving your dad.* She sighed out her sadness to keep it from taking over.

"Very sad. I miss him already."

"Me too. Uncle Jack said Grandpa is looking down on me through the stars. That's where he lives now, Mom. He said he might be in the wind. If he's in the wind, can I hug him?"

"Sure. That's how he's hugging you."

Lucy put her finger to her lips. "Shhh." She looked at something in front of her, something Charlie couldn't see.

"It's the wind," she said.

They listened to the wind blowing through the eaves. "A storm is coming," Charlie said.

"It's Grandpa."

Lucy fell asleep just as the rain began. At first tentative, it soon turned into a loud rumble on the porch floorboards. Charlie slipped out of the bed, turned off the light, and lay down on the couch in the living room. Thunder rumbled in the distance and lightning flashes lit up the room. The television encased in a colonial-style wood cabinet, a TV tray covered with stacks of Dad's books and papers, the recliner where he'd spend the evenings reading: all took on an eerie glow. She closed her eyes and fell asleep to the sound of rain falling.

A loud clap of thunder woke her just after 6 a.m. Her heart raced from the dream that had been interrupted, one she'd had off and on since Mom died: Water everywhere. Oozing over the riverbanks, it crept up the hill toward the house. Always the sense of terror as the water rose. The familiar feeling of being paralyzed, wanting to run but unable to move, unable to help Mom in time.

Relieved that she'd woken up and been spared the rest of the dream, she tiptoed into Lucy's room to check on her. She slept curled up in a fetal position, her blonde hair covering her face. She was so peaceful. Charlie went into the kitchen to make coffee. She pulled open the can on the counter and realized she had forgotten to replenish the coffee when she went shopping yesterday. Perhaps Dad kept some in the old cold storage they used as a pantry. She searched the shelves until she spotted a can on the top shelf tucked behind some jars of homemade tomato sauce, likely from Karen, who canned just about everything. After a few tries with her tiptoes digging into the dirt floor, she was finally able to grab the can just as it teetered on the edge of the shelf. Strangely, it was taped closed with duct tape. *Just like Dad.* He used duct tape for everything. Charlie opened the can and peered inside. A slightly nutty smell emitted from long-gone coffee. Several small black leather notebooks were tucked inside.

She reached in and felt the soft leather, worn from use, folded one open, and recognized Dad's careful handwriting. It filled the pages in swirls of notes about bacteria levels, milk quality, and time samples. She scanned old recipes from years ago. Dad had hundreds of recipes from decades of making cheese. Toward the back of the notebook was an entry: white cheddar. She held it close to her face, reading the notations with a surge of excitement. It looked like the white cheddar recipe they'd been working on. Holy crap, she'd found them! Dad's recipes. The new white cheddar. Thank God. Now she wouldn't have to guess at the recipe based only on her phone conversations with Dad and her own sketchy notes. Now she could replicate the recipe, follow it to a T, and sidestep months, even years, of trying to get it just right.

A cascade of questions gnawed at her. First, why would Dad hide the recipes? Was he, as she'd suspected, confused and maybe paranoid about something, or worried he'd lose them, so he stashed them in what he thought was a safe place? She couldn't help wondering if it had something to do with Casper. Had he threatened Dad? She had so many questions. A strong gust of wind rattled the branches of the trees outside the kitchen window, and, in the next instant, a huge branch fell to the ground in the yard, startling her with a loud thump. The wind died down. A sudden calmness settled on the trees outside. What was it Lucy had said? Grandpa was in the wind. Was he speaking to her now?

Steady; don't hurry it. Making cheese is taking it one step at a time.

One step at a time.

Chapter 19

"We got some good news and some bad news," Walter said.

"Let's get the bad news over with first." Charlie sipped her second coffee of the day and looked around the table at Uncle Jack, Larry, Karen, Jenny, and Walter.

"Casper Raines made an offer," Walter said. "He'll settle the debt you owe him if you sign over your wooded acres out back."

"No way." Charlie was angry but not surprised after that day in the woods when she'd run into Casper trespassing, cataloging their trees, and creeping around their property like a predator.

"They're paying good money for lumber in Europe," Walter said.

"He must be desperate." She looked out the window of the factory at the dense woods out back and thought of how Dad told her these woods were special. They were old woods with hundreds of trees that had survived the clearing of Wisconsin land by farmers in the late nineteenth century and the culling of whole forests for timber with cross saws in the early twentieth century. They'd nicknamed them Benny's Woods for the Scandinavian hermit who lived on the land in a cabin when Dad had purchased the property in 1947. Charlie didn't know for sure if he was really a hermit, but he looked like one. He had a long, gray beard and dressed formally in a gray suit with a white buttoned-up shirt, and carrying a walking stick. Picking his way through the woods, head down, his face would light up when he'd see her. *Little Charlotte*, he'd called her. Benny and Dad would talk about cheesemaking in Europe; the aging caves; the use of cloth, not wax; and the sharper flavors of European cheeses compared to Wisconsin cheeses.

When Benny's brother got sick, he'd gone back to Sweden to live with him. Apparently, he had a whole big family back there—nieces, nephews, cousins. Charlie missed him and thought of him often when she looked at the trees. The massive white pine, yellow birch, and thick maple trees they'd tap for syrup each fall were stunning. Dad taught Charlie how to identify each tree by the shape and color of its leaves. These woods were where Dad showed her how to find mouse bones coughed up from owls that lived in the tallest branches, how to track fox and coyote, and how to shoot deer in season. On her good days, Mom would take Ria and Charlie deep into the woods to collect the pine cones they'd use to make bottom-heavy dolls with old scraps of material for dresses, using raisins for eyes and yarn for hair.

"Dad would have never wanted to cut down these woods."

"Can Raines force it?" Jenny asked Walter.

"If we go to court, the judge could force Charlie to sell or turn the land over to Raines in order to settle the debt."

"He'll need to get in line behind Jerry Noth, Loan Officer," Charlie said, sighing. Was there any way out of this mess? "What's the good news?" she asked, unwilling to spend another moment contemplating losing the woods.

Walter cleared his throat, setting off a loud process that involved a once white, now gray handkerchief and thirty seconds of coughing that worried Charlie.

"I talked to Jake like you asked and told him how you want to get the factory going again and how you couldn't get a loan," Walter said when he'd stopped coughing. He placed his elbows on the table, folded his hands, and leaned in. Even though it was Sunday, he wore a suit and tie with his VFW pin on his lapel. "He's got those friends moved up to Rosewood from Chicago. They built a commune. Want to get away from the city, farm the land, raise cows, that sort of thing."

"They're communists," Larry said.

"They're hippies." Uncle Jack chuckled.

"They sound like farmers to me," Karen said.

"Whatever. Stop dithering; just tell the story." Larry lifted his Packers cap off his head, then replaced it a couple of times, a habit that became more vigorous when he was excited.

"They want to start a dairy farm," Walter said. "They've got really good pasture."

Start with good milk, Charlie heard Dad's voice advise.

"So, you're saying we buy milk from them?" She looked at Uncle Jack, who raised his eyebrows.

"It could work," he said. "They're good people."

"You know them?" she asked.

"I've been over there."

Jenny laughed. "Sure you have."

"Cripes' sake, Jack, that where you been getting your marijuana?" Larry lifted his hat and resettled it. A few tufts of gray hair flew up, then disappeared.

"Don't go getting all worked up about it," Uncle Jack said, accustomed to Larry's rants about the dangers of marijuana.

"Stuff's gonna kill ya," Larry said.

"We're all going to die of something," Uncle Jack reminded him.

"I'll give you that."

"What are you proposing?" Charlie asked Walter.

"Here's the deal: they're buying the cows next month, and need to sell the milk," Walter explained. "I suggested Larry here be their milker."

"They got some real up-to-date milking equipment," Larry said. "I'm starting next week, figure the rest of you can handle the cheesemaking."

"With you in charge of the milk, I know it will be good. How many cows are they buying?" Charlie asked.

"Fifty or so," Larry said.

Her mind was racing. She quickly calculated the numbers. It was more than enough.

"How would we pay them?" she asked. "We are not going to get a loan, that's for sure."

Jenny rolled her eyes. "Don't get me started."

"About how the banks discriminate against women," Charlie told them.

"I'll ask Jake to look into it. He's had more experience with that sort of thing," Walter said. "Meantime, he's interested in investing in the cheese factory. He bought some land up there that borders the commune, and he wants to spend more time up here. He's building a house."

"Tired of being a flatlander, eh?" Larry said.

"Should be nice to have your son around more," Karen said.

"I think he wants to keep a closer eye on me," Walter said. "Anywho, he's driving up tomorrow to talk particulars."

"Seriously? This is fantastic," Charlie said. "We should have started with the good news."

Walter smiled, taking a bite of a cookie. They'd always been there for her. Uncle Jack visited her in Milwaukee, each time leaving her with a couple hundred bucks in cash. Walter was calm and steady, and Larry was such a hard worker at the cheese factory. She was worried about losing him but knew he'd always wanted to be in charge of a milking operation.

She looked around the table. Jenny and Larry were helping themselves to some cookies on the plate Lucy was holding, arguing which one was best—Pawlowski's Kolaczki cookies or Karen's molasses. Walter was brushing cookie crumbs off his tie, laughing as Karen handed him a napkin. Uncle Jack sipped his beer.

"You guys think I can do this?" Her gaze fell on Jenny, who raised her eyebrows. *Speak up: this is your passion.*

"You'll do real good," Larry said.

"I'll help with any legal issues that come up," Walter said.

"Here's the numbers based on the new milk supplier." Karen slid some papers across the table. "I think if we start producing right away, we can have some batches ready by next spring."

Anxiety gripped Charlie, contracting her stomach. If she failed, she failed this group of people she loved so much. She knew having Dad's notes was not enough. Cheesemaking was as much art as science. Making cheese without Dad felt like jumping off a cliff, sailing through the wind without a parachute, or falling without a net.

"What the heck," she said. "Let's do it."

Chapter 20

That night Charlie sat on the porch, unable to sleep, too keyed up about the plan to work with the farm co-op and Jake. She'd told herself it just might work but knew she'd feel better after she met with the co-op owners tomorrow at what Larry had called the Commune but what Jake told her on the phone was really known as the Rosewood Farm Cooperative.

Cicadas were screaming a high-pitched tirade into the darkness, reminding her of Ria and how they'd hunt for cicadas and fireflies. When they'd catch one, they'd put it in a box with holes poked in the top and handfuls of grass and let it go after a few moments. Ria couldn't bear to keep them cooped up. Lucy was the same. Last night's rain had released the sweet smell of soil, and Charlie breathed it in, searching for something, anything, to settle her anxiety. In the yard, a single post light illuminated the day lilies, phlox, coneflowers, black-eyed Susans, and hydrangeas blooming in the space between where the grass ended and the forest began. Fireflies lit up, faded, and lit up again in a silent dance produced by a chemical reaction called bioluminescence—glows used in attracting mates and at the same time, discouraging predators. She sipped her beer and realized how good it felt just to sit and take in the summer night. Closing her eyes, she gently moved back and forth in the old rocking chair. A distant engine rumbling got closer, then bright headlights swept the front yard, settling on her for a disconcerting second before extinguishing and leaving her in darkness again. Who would be coming here at almost midnight?

A man stepped out of the truck. It was John. As he walked toward her, hands in his pockets, her own hands felt tingly and her face flushed. He gazed past her, and, as he got closer, she could see he looked troubled.

"Sorry, I couldn't make the meeting of the minds today." His mouth smiled but it didn't reach his eyes.

"What's wrong?"

"I was at a meeting to plan the new school district on the reservation. Tonight, we heard stories from students about some teachers at the high school over in Shawano doing things like kicking them out of class or suspending them more often than white students, not allowing them to wear beaded headbands."

"Can't they report that to the principal?"

"Some of them said it got worse when they did. That they were just seen as troublemakers." He sat down in the chair next to her, tipped his head back, and closed his eyes. "Kids shouldn't have to put up with being treated like this. They've been through so much. I worry about them."

"Did that happen to you in Madison?"

"Not really." He opened his eyes and grinned. "Grandma thought Madison schools would be better than up here and it wasn't too bad. I got a good education. Never got harassed or anything. But I was like a fish out of water and I sometimes felt kind of alone. The new schools on the reservation will teach our language, our culture."

"Grandma Stone would love it," Charlie said.

"You know, she went to the boarding school in Keshena," he said, "and she had some stories."

"I remember she told me she ran away, didn't like it."

"She could only see her parents like once a month, and she missed them."

"That must have been hard for her."

"Assimilation. She resisted, got in trouble with the nuns a lot. So she ran away."

She thought of Grandma Stone, imagined her planning her escape, then quietly leaving, making her way alone through the woods back home to her family. "What happened?"

"All I know is she had to go back. But she held onto her family, her culture." He rubbed his hands together. "You got a beer, by any chance?"

"You thirsty?"

"Now that you mention it," he said. "And I want to hear about your meeting."

"First things first," she said. "I'll be right back."

Two beers later, John laughed and shook his head.

"So let me get this straight: Larry is working at the cooperative, Jake's going to invest in the factory, and you're going up to Rosewood tomorrow to meet these people."

"That's pretty much our plan. What do you think?"

"It sounds solid," he said. "Jake's a good guy. I ran into him in Chicago once. We used to play marbles at recess back in sixth grade."

He held out his beer bottle. "To new beginnings." They clinked bottles and toasted the factory and the new Menominee Indian School District.

Charlie was pleased that John liked her plan. She loved talking to him, the way he listened and responded, unlike Rick, who always seemed so distracted. "You want to come up to Rosewood with me tomorrow?"

John shook his head. "I can't. I'm going to Chicago—there's a conference at the University of Chicago. Plus, I need to take care of something."

Was it about Kate? Suddenly he seemed a hundred miles away. Where did he go? She felt disappointed and embarrassed for asking. She didn't want to feel so vulnerable, not anymore. Not after all she'd gone through with Rick.

"Sounds serious," Charlie said. "I should go inside." She got up and walked past him with her head down. She didn't want him to see the hurt on her face.

"Wait."

She stopped. John reached out and took her hand.

"I don't." He hesitated. "I don't want to hurt you."

She'd always trusted him, but she suspected he wasn't telling her the truth. Screw it. She pulled her hand away. "Then don't." *Don't lie to me.*

"There is a conference, but I'm also going down there to talk to Kate." She watched his jaw clench. "I guess I owe her that much."

Charlie thought about chances. Second chances. Third chances. A hundred chances. No matter how many she gave Rick, it never worked. But who was she to tell John not to? Her feelings toward him were a conflicted bundle she barely understood. She had to admit, the thought of John with another woman made her incredibly sad. She was attracted to everything about him—his looks, his smile, talking to him, hearing how excited he was about the new school district.

"I guess so," Charlie said. She hated this new awkwardness that had crept into their relationship. "I really need to check on Lucy."

"Okay, see you soon." John sounded confused. He got up, walked down the porch steps, and headed toward his truck.

It was becoming clear to Charlie that John wasn't over Kate. She walked into the kitchen, stood at the sink, downed the last of her beer, and watched John's truck lights disappear.

Chapter 21

There were four homes on the land owned by the cooperative—a log cabin, two geodesic dome homes, and a flat-roofed modern home with a south-facing wall of glass windows. They were tucked into gently rolling hills traversed by a gravel road Charlie followed to the end, where a two-story stone building stood next to a red weathered barn. Jake had set up the meeting with Michael Roth, who Charlie assumed was the man walking toward her as she parked the car. He was tall, with sandy hair, a trim beard, and an easy smile. He didn't look like a hippie, or a communist. He looked like a young farmer.

"I'm Mike. You must be Charlie." He extended his hand to her. "I understand you need milk."

"I hear you have some." She shook his hand. It was calloused but warm. His green eyes reminded her of Rick's.

"I do."

"Jake's not here yet, but let's go in."

Mike led her into the stone building, where an old copper cheese vat sat in the corner at one end and an office was set up on the other end of a huge rectangular room. The floor and walls were stone. Oak beams ran the length of the ceiling, giving the room a rustic, Old World feel. The windows looked new and ran floor to ceiling, revealing fields on which several cows were grazing. The air was cool and smelled of herbs.

A woman walked into the room. She was as short as Mike was tall, with long brown hair and hazel eyes with flecks the color of cinnamon. She wore jean overalls tucked into black Wellington boots.

"You must be Charlie. I'm Christine." She held out her hand. Her grip was firm, her smile wide. "Please sit down."

They sat around an oak table on red vinyl chairs that looked like they belonged in a Wisconsin supper club.

"We're really excited about working with you," Mike said. "Jake tells us you have quite a talent for cheesemaking."

"He's very kind," Charlie said.

"I'm looking forward to learning," Christine said, "if you don't mind teaching me."

"I'd love to."

"I know something about growing corn," Christine explained, "and a lot about milking cows, but never did learn how to make cheese."

"It was Christine's dream to get the cows," Mike said.

"I missed having them around," Christine said. "Growing up, we had over two hundred."

"We both grew up on dairy farms, me in Wisconsin, Christine in Minnesota," Mike said. "We quit our jobs last year and moved here."

They all turned when the door opened to reveal Jake standing there, arms flung wide open.

"I'm here!" He came over and hugged all of them. "Sorry I'm late, the traffic in Chicago was horrible. Charlie, so sorry about your dad. He was a good guy. My dad's going to miss him."

Jake had dark hair like his father, thinning already, but he had maintained his good looks, with a square jaw, dimpled smile, and crinkles at the corners of his eyes.

"Come sit." Christine pulled over a chair. "Let me get everyone some coffee before we start talking business."

Christine disappeared into what looked like a kitchen from what Charlie could see—wood counters and an old, porcelain farm sink.

"So, how do you guys know each other?" Charlie asked the men.

"Mike managed the apartment building I lived in." Jake turned to Mike and raised his eyebrows. "Until you checked out of city life." He turned back to Charlie. "They went all *Green Acres* on me."

"About four years ago, Jake helped us find this land and the Chicago investors who built the homes," Mike said. "People who want to have a place in the country but can't be here all the time. After a lot of driving back and forth to oversee the building projects, we were finally able to move up here last year."

Christine walked in with a tray of coffee cups and a small pitcher of cream. "We'd been looking for land to start a farm. This made sense," she said, distributing the coffee. Charlie took a sip. It was suitably strong for sipping in a stone country farmhouse.

"So, you guys are both from Falls River?" Christine asked.

Charlie nodded. "Jake was two grades ahead of me."

"Rub it in."

"We'd hang out once in a while," Charlie said. "Our dads were good friends."

"After I told Dad I was gay, it was his friends who helped him come around."

Charlie remembered that Walter didn't quite know how to handle his son's revelation. "Of all people, Larry helped your dad through it."

"Karl and Larry got Dad to call me in Chicago." Jake put his hand up to his ear, holding an imaginary phone. "You're my son. I love you. I don't want you to go through this alone anymore. I'm right here with you." Jake paused. "It meant a lot to me."

"We met Walter. He is a gem," Christine said.

While on a tour of the property, Mike and Christine explained how they just finished setting up the dairy operation, showed them their state-of-the-art milking house, and walked them through the cow barn. Back at the office, Mike pulled out some paperwork from a legal file folder, and they began the process of working out the details of the agreement. Jake would become Charlie's partner, and his investment money would be used to pay for the milk. They'd share profits and he would work with Karen on marketing the cheese.

He'd agreed to take over the equipment loan from the bank. Charlie could pay him back over several years, a big relief. When they had first discussed the partnership, Charlie had told Jake she was a little worried about losing control of the cheesemaking end of the business. He'd assured she would have complete control. He explained how he'd been looking for investment opportunities up north and that he planned to build a home at the co-op. Morgan Cheese, he said, was the perfect investment for him. Wisconsin cheese was big in Chicago and Morgan Cheese would do well there.

From outside, bleating sounds interrupted them, and they all turned toward the noise. Several sheep congregated at the window.

"They're East Friesian," Michael explained. "Good for milk production."

"Hadley!" Christine called. Soon a boy about the same age as Lucy poked his head into the room from the direction of the kitchen. He had light-brown curly hair and a smattering of freckles across his round cheeks.

"Hello." His smile was toothless on top.

"This is our son." Christine introduced everyone to Hadley.

"Where's Tato?" Christine asked.

"Right here." A black-and-white collie showed his head around the corner of the door.

"Send him outside, please. He needs to earn his keep," Christine told Hadley.

In seconds, the dog appeared outside and began yapping at the sheep, which caused them to turn around and move out to the fields. There was something mesmerizing about the way they moved together, Charlie thought while watching them.

The phone rang. Charlie was surprised when Mike handed it to her.

"It's Walter."

"Charlie, we have a court date," Walter said without preamble. "It's next week."

"So, the judge wouldn't postpone?" A sense of dread crept over her. Suddenly the room didn't seem so quaint. The stone walls just looked cold. The air felt damp.

"I'll stop by tomorrow, and we can talk more," Walter said. "We'll figure this out."

Charlie passed the phone to Jake, who filled Walter in on the details of the deal they'd made. Charlie gathered her things and mouthed to Jake that she needed to get on the road. Mike and Christine walked her out to her car.

"We know this lawsuit is stressful," Mike said. "From what you shared, we believe you've got a good case to ask for more time."

"Let us know what we can do to help," Christine said.

Charlie tried to hide the anxiety she felt. She didn't want them to see how terrified she was. "I appreciate your understanding about the lawsuit." She and Jake had kept the lawsuit out of the deal—she wasn't going to ask him to pay off a debt of questionable validity from so long ago, and as a limited partner, he was not liable for past business debts. The money she owed Raines would be separate. If she could convince the judge for more time to pay off the debt, she could get the factory going. It was a big if. She felt like a juggler balancing on a high wire.

As Charlie drove back to Falls River, she ruminated about the lawsuit, her anxiety increasing with each mile. If she lost in court, she could lose everything. She began having second thoughts about the agreement she'd just signed with Jake. Buyer's remorse. What was she thinking? It was all so overwhelming. None of it mattered if she lost the lawsuit. She knew if that happened, she'd have to sell the factory, the house, and the land. All would be liquidated and sold at auction. She'd seen plenty of farm auctions over the years to know it was a real possibility. To calm her nerves, she slid in an 8-track tape and opened the window wider. She slowed to twenty-five through the small unincorporated town of Truly. She passed Fisherman's Diner, quaint houses on main street, and two churches. On the outskirts of town, there were trim, one-story homes with picket fences and clusters of hydrangea bushes. There was a white farmhouse with a clothesline in the side yard, and sheets and pillowcases flapping in the wind. Joni Mitchell's voice sang "River"—a song that matched her melancholy mood.

~

She was helping Mom hang wet clothes on the line. Charlie must have been about eight years old. The line ran from a hook on the corner of the house to a hook Dad had drilled into the giant maple tree in the middle of the backyard. From their yard, corn fields spilled down the valley to the Fox River. Across the river, cows casually grazed on the soft grass or stood still in placid contemplation, occasionally flicking their tails at horseflies.

"Is this how you washed clothes in England?" Charlie asked, eager to get Mom talking. It was rare she came outside these days.

Mom clipped the cuffs of Dad's work pants to the line with wooden clothespins she kept in the pocket of her apron, then placed her hands on her waist and stared at the dark clouds in the west. Storms always came in from the west, from Minnesota, Iowa, and Missouri. Some days they brought rain; some days they just threatened it.

"Sure. Mum had me pin up the wet clothes on a line just like this one. Of course, we washed them by hand. No one had machines then, not in my neighborhood."

Her neighborhood had been near Piccadilly, London, where her parents owned a small cheese market and the apartment above it, large enough for her and Edward, her younger brother, to share a bedroom. Piccadilly Circus. Outside the cheesemongers' windows, Charlie imagined streets filled with clowns, bright-colored tents, Ferris wheels, and carnies hawking games where kids could win huge stuffed animals like the ones at the Outagamie County Fair.

"How did you do the wash if you didn't have a washing machine?" Charlie asked as she flipped a towel over the line.

"We used a dolly tub," Mom said. "And a dolly peg to turn the clothes 'round until your back was sore and your arms felt like they'd fall off from churning the blessed thing."

"'Round and 'round," Ria said. She took one of Mom's stockings and twirled it around, spinning it like a wooden spoon in a mixing bowl.

Mom was quick with her anger. "Victoria, stop it." She grabbed Ria's arm, pried open her fingers, and wrenched the stocking from her. Ria's look of surprise was instant. When her tears started, Charlie rushed over to pick her up.

"What's all the fuss about?" Dad asked, walking up to them from the direction of the cheese factory. He headed over to Mom, put his arm around her, and whispered something in a soothing voice. They all rode her mood cycles—happy one minute, the next, angry or despondent—which were happening more and more frequently. Dad was in his work clothes: white pants, a white cotton button-down shirt, white apron, and rubber boots. He was tall, with thinning blond hair and blue eyes, a striking contrast to Mom with her hazel eyes and dark-brown hair, which she wore in victory rolls, the sides turned and pinned, old-fashioned even for Falls River. Sometimes her hair was unkempt, smashed on one side from sleep, and the hair around her face floated around her face unpinned. She had pale, flawless skin and high cheekbones.

"Mom was telling us about doing laundry in England," Charlie said.

"She was the prettiest girl in London," Dad said. "And we went to the dance halls and all the men were jealous of me. Come on, Ev, let's show them."

Mom surprised Charlie by agreeing, and they danced a few steps of the Lindy Hop, slower than she'd seen them dance this one before. They both looked unusually happy.

When, after a few moments, her parents stopped dancing, Charlie said, "Tell us about how you met again, Dad." She desperately wanted to hold on to this feeling of being a family.

"Daddy!" Ria echoed.

"All right, off we go." Dad kissed Mom on the cheek, then lifted Ria from Charlie's arms and carried her to the back step, where she settled in close, arm around his knee. Mom continued hanging the wash, her flowered skirt nipping and dancing around her legs from the gusts of wind that blew off the river. Charlie picked up a wet sheet, smoothed it over the line, and pinned it in three places.

"I was out walking." Dad dug into his pocket, pulled out his pipe, squinted at Ria's red-rimmed eyes, and smiled. "It was a Sunday afternoon in Piccadilly Circus. You could smell the sea. I remember thinking if I could just find some cheese, it would cheer me up. I missed Wisconsin." He lit his pipe and took a few puffs.

"Just then I looked up and saw the sign, Morgan's Cheese Shop." Dad spread his hands wide above his head like he could see the words written in the space above him. "I went in the shop and saw your mom behind the counter. Funny, I forgot all about that cheese."

Charlie breathed in whiffs of the sweet, familiar tobacco smell that drifted over the yard. She knew what came next.

"Your mom said, 'Can I help you?' And I said, 'Yes, if you'll marry me, I'll be the happiest man in London.'"

"Stop exaggerating, Karl." Mom's voice sounded tired. She pinned a pair of socks on the line. "You didn't ask me to marry you right then."

"Maybe not, but I sure wanted to."

"No, you left after two months, and I stayed in London." Mom's voice was quiet. Charlie knew Dad had been part of the Allied invasion of Normandy. And Mom had endured the London bombings that had killed her brother.

Mom pinned up a last pillowcase, picked up her baskets, and looked at the clouds.

"Charlotte, you need to watch Victoria, and mind you, if it rains, take in these clothes." She walked away from them, not at a fast pace but not slow either. The screen door creaked when she pulled it open and smacked loud and sharp against the wood frame after she disappeared into the house, and Charlie's sense of foreboding increased.

On days Mom left her in charge of Ria, they'd spend time with Dad in the cheese factory and soon her worries would diminish as they helped him stack cheese in the cooler or salt the curds. Occasionally, she and Ria roller-skated around on the smooth floor of the factory.

∼

Now, Charlie pulled into the driveway, parked the truck, went into the garage, and found the roller skates she'd used in high school. In the factory, she turned on the radio, laced up her skates, and wheeled around to the sounds of David Sanborn playing sax to David Bowie singing "Young Americans." She relaxed as she navigated around the equipment, pausing to inspect the vats and cheese presses. Being back in the factory buoyed her confidence and she allowed herself to feel excitement—she'd made a deal to get milk! It was a big hurdle. To top it off, she'd really enjoyed talking business today and had taken an instant liking to Michael and Christine. Most importantly, she felt she could trust them. Her plan was going to work, she told herself. It had to.

Chapter 22

The night before court, Charlie's anxiety was back. Even hours spent in the aging cellar taking inventory with Lucy hadn't calmed her. She put Lucy to bed, then sat on the porch, rocking and watching fireflies spark and ebb, reminding her that these summer days were fleeting and would end soon. Her mind sifted through what could go wrong in court tomorrow. First, being a woman put her at a disadvantage, something made very clear at the bank. She hoped the judge wasn't one of those people who believed a woman couldn't run a business. Second, she'd worked the numbers, but was the plan sound? In her favor was bringing on Michael and Christine; though new to running their own dairy farm, they both had grown up in the business of milking cows. They knew what they were doing. Plus, they had Larry, one of the best milk guys around. Her ultimate hope was to buy time. If she couldn't get more time to pay off the debt to Raines Dairy, she'd lose the cheese factory for good.

Third and lastly. Casper. Sure, he wanted revenge because Dad had reported him for selling bad milk, but there was something else: Something Charlie figured he harbored against her. Something that happened when they were in high school. An incident she had kept to herself, indeed had spent years trying to forget, ignore, and file away as insignificant.

She stilled the rocking chair and was back in high school, walking home on a hot September day during freshman year.

～

The day had been uneventful. Algebra and English were boring, but not science. The young biology teacher, Miss Gilbert, said they were going to design their own projects, and Charlie had already decided she was going to develop a new cheese, one that was sharp, maybe even a white cheddar. After class, she took the path through the woods because it was shorter than walking home on the county road. She was already missing John, who had moved to Madison the week before, and, in her head, she was telling him about the science project she planned. There was no breeze and the woods were heavy with humidity, so Charlie was sweating even though she wore shorts and a tank top. As she neared the turn on the path that ran along the river and straight to their property, she felt uneasy, a weird prickling on the tops of her shoulders, a sense someone was behind her. A twig breaking confirmed the feeling. She stopped, turned around, and peered down the path.

Ferns covered the forest floor like an emerald carpet. The trees were still and silent with a canopy of lush leaves and branches so dense she couldn't see the sky. No one was back there. She continued walking, but after a few steps, she heard the sounds again. They seemed closer. She gripped the strap of her book bag carelessly slung over her right shoulder and walked faster. Now she could definitely hear footsteps. She hoped it was one of the young kids who lived up the river past their place. Still walking, she turned and looked. She could see a figure with a white stained T-shirt and stringy blond hair emerging from the woods. Casper Raines was looking straight at her and laughing. She had a weird thought. He wasn't bad looking when he smiled. He had unusually straight, white teeth. But his laugh was creepy. In an instant, she felt a rush of adrenaline, and she took off running. But the path was riddled with tree roots, and, after a few yards, she tripped and crashed to the ground. Casper was standing above her when she pushed herself up into a kneeling position. He was chuckling. "Well, if it ain't cootie girl from crazyville." He'd called her this once before, in grade school, at recess, when she'd come back to school after her mom died.

Charlie caught her breath and checked her knees. They were bleeding. "Leave me alone."

"Why should I?" Raines bent down, grabbed her arms, and pinned her onto the ground, using the full weight of his body. Her head snapped back and hit hard on a tree root. Momentarily dazed, she smelled the stink of his sour breath as he sucked on her neck. She felt his dirty fingers slip between her legs, pull away her shorts, and creep up inside her underwear. He moaned and whispered, "Nobody here to help you. See how it feels."

Fierce hate shocked her into action. She used her free arm to push his chin up, and in one quick motion, she wrenched away from him, jabbing her elbow into his gut. He grunted but then started laughing. Charlie looked up and was relieved when she saw two young boys emerge through the woods. Casper saw them too, and she used his distraction to haul herself up from the path and grab her book bag.

Head and heart pounding, she sprinted the rest of the way home.

~

Charlie had avoided Casper Raines the rest of high school, or at least for the time he was there. He dropped out after three years. She'd heard he went out west and was glad she didn't have to run into him in town. He was creepy. She did not want to see him tomorrow. How could she ignore him? Maybe if she focused on Walter. Kind Walter. Unlike Casper, who was a bully. What had Lucy said about bullies? Her teacher had told her to tell them to stop, to walk away from them, to be strong. That was it. Charlie hung onto the phrase. Be strong.

Chapter 23

The Outagamie courthouse bathroom in Appleton reeked of body odor and the misery of all the people who'd come here before her. Charlie slid the lock on the stall door in place before she vomited her breakfast of coffee and dry toast into the toilet. At the sink, she wiped her mouth with a paper towel, looking into the mirror at her reflection. Dark circles beneath her eyes told the story of last night's bad memories and worries about having to speak in court. Unable to sleep, she'd finally slipped into bed next to Lucy, listening to her soft breathing.

Shoot, was she going to throw up again? Cramping in her stomach sent her back to the toilet. Would she be able to testify like this? She knew Walter wanted her to. She knew Casper Raines would be sitting at the table next to his lawyer, his fake smile the same as when he'd taunted her in grade school and done worse on the river path back in high school. Charlie steeled her stomach to be strong, took three deep breaths, reminded herself how fear was her worst enemy, unlocked the stall door, washed her hands, and walked out of the bathroom to the courtroom down the hall.

Walter motioned her over to the defendant's table in front of the judge's bench. He nodded to her. She could see he was sweating, his skin pale. When she turned around, she saw Uncle Jack, John, Jenny, and Larry sitting in a row of seats beneath a giant mural depicting fields of corn, cows, and a red barn with a lone figure riding an old red tractor in the foreground. Jenny waved, Larry lifted his cap off his head and tipped it toward her, and John lifted his chin. Great. Now, she was even more nervous. Everyone could watch her freak out.

Walter was first to talk after the judge settled himself and called the court to order. "Judge Flynn, we are asking for a stay on the enforcement of the judgment so as to acquire funds to pay what is owed. They are asking for payments from twenty years ago. Surely another year won't matter."

"How does she intend to do that?" the judge asked.

"Your honor, she has a plan," Walter started to explain.

Judge Flynn interrupted, "I'd like to hear it from Mrs. Sobczak."

Oh boy. Her hands felt sweaty and her heart raced and there was a weird buzzing in her ears. Was she having a heart attack? Walter and the judge were looking at her. She wished she was somewhere else—in the factory, listening to music, making cheese. Be strong. What the heck. All she wanted to do was make cheese. That was all she was asking for.

Charlie pushed back her chair and walked up to the witness stand, conscious of Casper watching her. She forced her hand to be steady when the young clerk swore her in.

"Mrs. Sobczak, can you tell us your plan to pay the estate's debt?" Judge Flynn asked. His eyes appeared expressionless behind rimless glasses.

Shoot. She searched her brain for the words she'd practiced, for the numbers she'd gone over again and again. But nothing came to her. She blanked, then remembered Jenny's words: *Speak up: this is your passion.* After a long pause, what came out of her mouth was unrehearsed.

"Your honor, my father started Morgan Cheese after serving in World War II. He named it after my mom's family, who ran a cheese market in London. Dad came from a family of dairy farmers in Sheboygan. He and his brother, Jack Mayer, built up the business. Morgan Cheese was sold in four states." She paused to take a deep breath. "Sure, it was a small operation, but it was a source of pride for Dad, our family, and kind of a meeting place for the people in town. I believe my father got behind in payments for about one year in 1956, after my mom died. Casper's father never asked for the money from this time, and the unpaid bills stayed on the books. As far as I can tell, my dad and Casper's father had a gentlemen's agreement. They helped each other out. They were friends." She stopped, looked at the judge, and then back at Walter. Stay strong. Better yet, fight back. "I believe Casper is acting out of revenge because my father had reported him to the milk council."

Casper's lawyer, Gerald Grubb, cut her off.

"Judge, that accusation is false, and, even if it was true, it has nothing to do with this case. The fact is, Karl Mayer owed the dairy money. Casper's father was willing to carry the debt year after year. Casper is just trying to collect on what the family is owed."

"Damn right," Casper spat out.

Judge Flynn pounded his gavel. "Keep your comments to yourself, Mr. Raines, or I will fine you. Go ahead, Mrs. Sobczak. As I said before, I need to hear your plan to get the factory up and running, or we will move toward liquidation."

"Your honor, I have a cheese factory with up-to-date equipment. I have plenty of rennet and the recipes I've inherited from my father. I have located a source for milk to replace Raines Dairy and have an investor who is coming in as a partner, providing start-up money."

Walter gave the judge the spreadsheet they'd developed, and he studied it for a few moments.

The anxiety she felt about these numbers bubbled up. The plan, pretty damn ambitious, did not give them any wiggle room.

"Mr. Grubb, do you have any questions?" Judge Flynn asked.

Charlie forced down a feeling of panic as Raines's attorney stood and walked over to where she sat. Up close, she could see his black suit was expensive, his white shirt heavily starched. His gray hair was cut close to his scalp.

"What are your qualifications to run a successful cheese factory, Mrs. Sobczak? Wasn't your job a cashier at a grocery store?" Grubb asked.

Charlie bristled. Without thinking twice this time, she defended herself. "Making cheese is in my blood, Mr. Grubb. I worked alongside my father and Uncle Jack for twelve years, until I went to college. During college summers, I worked at the vats. After college, I set up my own kitchen cheese-making operation to develop new recipes with my father." She thought of making cheese in her kitchen like immigrant farm women at the turn of the century. "For the past seven years, I worked at the Milwaukee Cheese Market. I helped with buying. I sold cheese from all over the world. I'm a cheesemonger, Mr. Grubb. I've applied for my license from the state of Wisconsin to make cheese, and I've got a degree in biochemistry."

"Surely, you don't think making cheese with your father qualifies you, a woman, to run a business?"

What right did he have? An attorney from Appleton? Dad never trusted people coming in from the outside telling them what to do.

"Yes, it does qualify me. And if I don't, what's the alternative? The town loses an important business? People in this state know the value of my dad's product. It's his legacy, and I intend to carry on that legacy. I can produce a product that will benefit not just the community but the state of Wisconsin. As for being a woman, for Pete's sake, back in the old days making cheese *was* woman's work." She looked past Grubb and noticed Jenny vigorously nodding her head. Charlie kept going.

"On the farm, it was women who made cheese for their families in their kitchens before factories started popping up. I, for one, think it's time more women got into the business of running cheese factories." A cheer went up in the back galley. Jenny. Charlie felt her face flush. She looked over at Walter. Were those tears he was wiping from his eyes? She couldn't tell for sure. His head was down, and he fumbled for his handkerchief before blowing his nose with a loud honk. From the back of the courtroom, she heard someone slowly clapping. It was Uncle Jack. Relief washed over her and another feeling, joy, came at being supported by this group of friends and family, who had all joined in with Uncle Jack clapping, and pretty soon the judge was pounding his gavel again.

"Thank you for the history lesson, Mrs. Sobczak, but I want Mr. Grubb to finish his questioning."

"Just one more." Grubb fumbled with a file on his desk and pulled out some papers. "Mrs. Sobczak, can you tell me what these are?"

She studied the papers, several invoices made out to Morgan Cheese from 1956. She had copies of the same invoices.

"They're invoices from Raines Dairy to Morgan Cheese."

"And does it say paid or outstanding?"

"Outstanding."

"Thank you. That is all for this witness. Now, I would like to call Casper Raines."

Casper sat in the witness chair and glared at Charlie as if they were having a staring contest. He was the first to look away after his lawyer asked him a question.

"Mr. Raines, tell us the status of your account with Morgan Cheese."

"We provided milk in good faith—for over twenty years. When Dad went into the nursing home, I needed to clean up the books. I'm just asking for what is owed us. It's only fair. If she can't pay, she should sell the land to pay the debt. She thinks she's some kind of women's libber. She ain't gonna be able to keep it going. And pardon me for pointing this out, but her mom killed herself in the river. And you know what they say"—he looked straight at Charlie and sneered—"crazy runs in families."

There was yelling coming from behind Charlie. Larry. The judge was pounding his gavel.

Charlie gripped the table, shaken to the core at his mentioning Mom.

"Your honor, I object," Walter finally managed to blurt out. Gamely, he struggled to stand for a few long seconds until Charlie finally got up, discreetly put her arm under his, and helped him up.

"I do too," Judge Flynn said. "You have gone too far, Mr. Raines. But that's not why I've decided to let Charlotte Sobczak here have one year to begin repaying her debt to Raines Dairy." He turned to Charlie. "Mrs. Sobczak, I am making this decision based on your obvious passion for reviving your father's business. I am giving you a one-year redemption period. After that, your land and factory could be liquidated to pay off the debt. We'll have a status update in a few months. This court is adjourned."

~

Afterward everyone stood under the giant maple in front of the courthouse and congratulated Charlie.

"You should feel good about this," Jenny said.

John approached her, smiling. "That was so cool," he said. "Call me, I need to talk to you." She wondered if it was about Kate, then pushed the thought aside. She'd had a good day in court and didn't want to spoil it with more worries. Before she could answer him, Jenny stepped closer and John moved away.

Her friend beamed. "I saw your passion. Way to go."

"Thanks for coming, everyone," she told them. "It really helped." She nodded to Walter. "I couldn't have done it without you."

"Now let's make some cheese," Jake said. He was driving back to Chicago but handed her a bottle of champagne before he left. "I knew you'd do it."

After everyone was gone, she got into her truck and paused before starting it. This felt good. But there was one more thing. She needed to make a stop on the way home.

Chapter 24

The cemetery was outside of town, on the edge of a soy field next to the church. The only trees were in the center of the graveyard, giant maples with gnarled roots that didn't allow for grass to grow beneath. It was the first time she'd been there since Dad's funeral. Overwhelmed with emotion, she knelt in front of her family's graves. Ria's headstone, the oldest, had an image of an angel Mom had insisted on having carved into the stone. It was one of those angels that looked like a fat baby with wings. A cherub. It scared Charlie when she first saw it. Her nine-year-old self couldn't quite process it. Was it supposed to be Ria? Or just keeping her company? She supposed Ria would have liked it, would have thought it was cute. Dad's headstone hadn't been installed yet. Mom's was simple: *Evelyn Morgan Mayer, 1926–1956*, it read, *Beloved Wife and Mother*.

"Thought you might have come here." Uncle Jack walked over and stood next to the tree that towered over the three graves. "You were good in there." He placed his hand on the tree.

"Thanks. It wasn't easy, especially hearing what Casper said about Mom." A butterfly flitted around Mom's headstone and settled there. A monarch. "Do you think she actually tried to kill herself? I've always wondered." She'd never said this out loud. She held her breath and stared at the butterfly.

"Well, you know the coroner said it was an accident," he said. "She'd taken those barbiturates. Probably took a few more than she should have. Either way, she wasn't in her right mind."

"I told the therapist about Mom. She said some people have a harder time recovering from grief, especially if they were already depressed."

"No parent should have to bury a child."

"Dad tried to hide it, but I'm starting to understand he was more affected by losing them than I'd thought. After Mom died, he didn't bring in any money for almost a year."

"He blamed himself for what happened to your mom. Had a rough time. You're right; he tried to hide it from you. Said you deserved a happy childhood." Uncle Jack stooped down and ran his hand over the new sod on Dad's grave. "He made some cheese, but his heart wasn't in it. Threw out most of what he made. Stopped selling but kept making it, testing recipes. Then he had that bout with phage, lost some batches to the attack virus, and got discouraged. He came over to my house a lot when you were in school. Sat with me while I made cabinets. That's when the debts piled up. He finally pulled himself together, started making cheese again. Put all his energy into raising you and building up the business again."

"What was their connection? Why didn't Old Man Raines call in his debt?"

"They were in the same unit during the war. They always looked out for each other," Uncle Jack said. "I avoided Raines. He was not a nice guy. Whenever he'd come over to meet with your dad, I'd leave."

"Do you think he'd talk to me? I want to hear from him why he didn't call in his debt."

"You can try. He's not going to hurt you. I know that much. I heard he's in a wheelchair. He's got early-onset dementia, probably caused by alcohol. Sleeps most of the time."

~

The nursing home was housed in a nondescript, one-story white brick building in Appleton. Worried about running into Casper, Charlie tucked her hair into a Brewers cap and put on sunglasses. Undercover, she hoped she could turn and walk the other way if she saw him. It didn't take long to find Old Man Raines. He was sitting in the hallway at the nurse's station, head flopped forward. She asked the nurse if it was okay to talk to him, explaining her dad was an old friend. The nurse nodded and smiled her encouragement. Charlie pulled up a metal chair, sat eye level with him, and placed her hand on his shoulder. "Mr. Raines."

He surprised her by lifting up his head and looking straight at her. "Who are you?"

"I'm Karl Mayer's daughter, Charlie." She took off her cap. Growing up, she'd often been around when Old Man Raines had made his monthly visits to the factory. She would listen to them talk until her dad told her to go outside and play. She was sure the old man would recognize her if his dementia hadn't diminished his memory of those earlier times.

"Karl. We met during the war, you know." Old Man Raines winced and closed his eyes as if remembering was exhausting, reminding her of how Dad never talked about his experiences, how Rick never talked about Vietnam.

After a few seconds, Charlie tried again.

"Mr. Raines?" Was this going to be futile? Perhaps she should just leave him be.

"Mr. Raines."

This time he looked up, squinting at her, trying to focus.

"Who are you?"

"I'm Karl's daughter."

"How is he?"

"Dad died, Mr. Raines. That's why I'm here."

"Died?"

"Yes."

"You know . . . Karl helped me start the dairy."

"He helped you?" she prompted, hoping he'd continue talking.

"Logging was done. The good forests were gone."

"How did he help you?"

"He knew cows. Who did you say you were?"

"I'm Karl's daughter, Charlotte." She noticed his eyes and skin had a yellowing she associated with the very sick.

She pushed on. "He owed you money, but you didn't ask for it. Why?"

He closed his eyes, tipping his head forward and down. Then he yanked it up, startling her. "Karl told me not to hit my son." Old Man Raines licked his lower lip, and Charlie saw his tongue looked swollen. "How's he gonna learn?"

He was talking about Casper, how he'd abused him. They'd seen it more than once. The second time was worse than the first.

~

After that day raccoon hunting with Larry, when they'd witnessed Old Man Raines backhand Casper, she and John had taken it upon themselves to spy on Casper and Old Man Raines. They'd hike along the river to the abandoned sawmill and sit on the forest floor watching the goings-on at the yard, hidden by the brush. Some days, no one was out, and they left disappointed. Other days, they saw Old Man Raines barking orders at dairy workers, but one day they saw Old Man Raines beat up Casper until his head was bloody and they thought he was dead.

It was early summer, several months after Mom died, and John and Charlie had spent nearly every day together. They wandered the woods, hiked up to the falls, walked the river trail over to the old mill, and waited for Old Man Raines to make an appearance. On that particular June day, they were just about to leave their spy headquarters, hunkered down behind a fallen log, when they heard it. "Git over here, boy."

It was him.

From behind the beat-up trailer, Casper approached his dad with a scared look on his face.

Old Man Raines pointed a fat finger at Casper. "You think you can just up and take my keys, boy?"

"You're drunk," Casper yelled at him. "You can't drive around like that."

"I'll decide when I can drive." Quicker than Charlie thought possible given his state of drunkenness, the father pushed Casper to the ground. She heard a crack as his boot hit Casper's skull. Casper went limp. Fear spread through her body, and she clutched John's arm.

"Is he dead?" she whispered. She'd never liked Casper, but this was different. Nobody should be kicked in the head like that. Her stomach tightened. She felt sick.

"We've got to get help," John said as the color drained from his face. "Let's go." He grabbed her hand and pulled her up. She took a last look at Casper, at the blood pooling on the ground near his head, saw Old Man Raines standing over him shouting, "Get up, boy," and saw how his command was useless to Casper's still body.

They ran straight to the factory, where Dad was sitting at his desk, working on his notes.

"Call the police. Casper's dead. His dad killed him." Charlie panted, out of breath.

"It's true," John said.

"Where are they?" Dad stood up.

"They're at the old mill."

"You wait here." They asked to go with him, but Dad refused. "Just wait here," he said again, and drove off in his truck.

~

Old Man Raines slumped in a wheelchair, spittle on his chin. His hands, puffed up and discolored with purple and red splotches, lay on the plastic tray attached to his wheelchair.

"Why would you hurt your son?" Charlie asked.

The old man looked at her with watery eyes sunk deep into his skull. He blinked a few times. Charlie could tell he was fading, so she nudged his arm to try to wake him. It was useless. He was asleep, heaving wheezy, uneven breaths. For such a violent, unhappy man, he looked pathetic now. His mouth hung open and a string of saliva dropped onto his geezer bib. Dad never called the police that day, and, when he came home, all he said was that Old Man Raines had been drunk, that he'd never meant to hurt Casper.

She turned around and walked away. What he'd said, she already knew. Once he'd decided to quit logging, Dad had helped him set up the dairy farm. He didn't tell her why he'd carried Dad's debt all those years. They'd helped each other out for reasons left on the battlefield in Europe, stories her father couldn't or wouldn't tell.

~

Charlie drove over to Booths Landing, asked Jim Booth to use the phone, and called John. He was at his place in De Pere and agreed to meet her at the restaurant. She called Karen and asked her if she didn't mind staying with Lucy for another couple hours. Karen congratulated her on her success in court and reassured her not to hurry home; she and Lucy were busy making chocolate chip cookies. Charlie needed a drink. After ordering a beer, she sat down at a table in the corner facing the river. Aside from the grinding current, the river was quiet with no boats in sight. She didn't recognize the two old farmers sitting at the bar. She settled into anonymity. Soon the dinner crowd would be arriving. No doubt she'd see people she knew.

John walked into the restaurant thirty minutes later, calling over to Jim behind the bar. "Hey, Jim, can I have a beer?" He looked at Charlie's empty bottle. "Make that two."

"What's up?" John sat across from Charlie, smiling at her in a way she found utterly sexy. She hadn't spoken to him alone since he'd gotten back from Chicago, where he'd presumably met with Kate. Had they decided to get back together? The thought made her profoundly sad.

"I went to see Old Man Raines this afternoon." Charlie studied John's reaction. She knew he'd be interested.

"No shit?" John looked up at Jim, who placed two beers on the table. "Thanks."

"Enjoy," Jim said. "Good to see both of you."

"What happened?" John asked her as Jim walked away. "Did he talk to you?"

"It was so weird. He told me Dad helped him start the dairy, which I knew. But then he talked about how he beat up Casper. Claimed Dad told him not to hit him." Charlie took a long swig of beer, watching John's reaction.

"I'm sure he did." John looked at the river. She wanted to touch him, to reach out and hold his hand. But she didn't.

"I'm not saying Casper isn't an asshole," Charlie said. "But he was just a kid. Dad should have called the police. We told him to."

"I know how much you respected your dad. Like anyone, he made mistakes he probably regretted."

Charlie thought about what Dad had said in the hospital. *I should have helped that boy.* It finally dawned on her. "He told me something in the hospital. I wasn't sure what he meant at the time. He said something like 'I should have helped that boy.' Shoot." Why hadn't she seen it before? "He must have been talking about Casper."

John winced like he was imagining Casper beat up, blood pooling near his head. "He regretted it."

"Yeah, I guess he did." She peeled the label off her beer bottle, watching it break away until the bottle was bare. "Old Man Raines was such a mean drunk. Looks like he's paying for it now. He didn't look good."

Charlie paused. She wanted to talk to him about what Casper said in court. "Mom died when she was only thirty. I knew she wasn't well, but I wouldn't have called her crazy." She felt exposed, the hurt was so raw. They had never talked about this.

"Maybe it wasn't about what was wrong with her but about what happened to her," John said, and his eyes narrowed as if he was looking at something in front of him she couldn't see. "I saw it on the reservation, after termination, the lack of jobs, health care." He sat back, rubbing his eyes. "People really suffered. Still are suffering."

"It's heartbreaking." She knew from Karen about the high levels of poverty experienced by the Menominee after the tribe's status, terminated by the government in the 1950s, became effective in 1961. They'd won back federal recognition just a couple of years ago.

"The point is, people are suffering and sometimes we don't know how much." He took a swig of beer. "One thing I do know: don't listen to what Casper says. He was out of line. Don't let him get to you."

"It's just . . ." She paused, searching to name what she felt. "Sometimes I miss my family so much. Then, other times I feel so much joy, like when I'm with Lucy, or making cheese, or sitting on the porch just watching the fireflies." *Or when I'm with you*, she wanted to say but held it back. "I want to be happy." *I don't want to be like my mother.*

John spoke slowly, drawing out his words like a poem. "Happiness can be hard to hold on to. But you know how if you wait long enough, you'll see another firefly light up, and then another." He ran his hand up her arm, calming her. "The light always comes back." They hadn't touched each other in so long. It felt right.

"It does, doesn't it?" She thought about the passage of time. After a week, a day, or an instant, the sadness faded, her mood lifted, and she felt better. In that way, she wasn't like her mother.

"Lucy says watching the fireflies dance is her favorite sport," Charlie said.

"Here's to watching fireflies dance," John said as he raised his bottle. Charlie did the same, and they clinked their bottles together. She took a swig of beer and laughed.

After a few seconds, she inhaled and said what she'd been wanting to ask since he sat down. "Are you leaving?"

He seemed surprised. "Why do you ask that?"

"You went down to Chicago."

"It's over with Kate, if that's what you mean," John said.

"Oh." She exhaled with relief.

"So, after what happened in court today, I assume you're staying too?" John leaned forward, hands flat on the table, waiting for an answer.

She smiled. "I'm working on it."

He sat back, picked up his beer, and took a sip. "You did good."

"You didn't see me throwing up in that dingy bathroom before it started."

"But you went in," John said. "Kicked ass."

"I am kind of a badass." She laughed. Again. It felt good.

"Damn right." He set his empty bottle on the table. "Still, you should be careful. Casper has something against you."

"Yeah, he does," Charlie said. Visiting Old Man Raines hadn't given her more insight about why Casper was so vengeful against her, but she had a greater appreciation of how he'd gotten that way.

"Just be careful."

Chapter 25

Ten days later, Charlie walked over to the cheese factory at 4 a.m. under a full moon, visible in the spaces between the pine boughs above the cheese factory. She sat at Dad's desk and studied his notes on the white cheddar. Recorded in his precise handwriting was the condition of the milk, the weather, the culture and rennet he'd used, acidity levels, the amount of time before he'd called a clean break, how much salt he'd added, how long he'd left the cheese in the presses, the temperature of the cooling unit, and humidity levels. *Be gentle; let the milk do its own work.* Charlie's nerves calmed down a notch after reviewing Dad's careful notes.

Uncle Jack opened the door. "Milk's here."

He sounded so calm. She was excited and thrilled to finally be making cheese. It was their first milk delivery. Yikes.

"How's it look?" She followed him out to the truck. The sunlight was moving in, slow and tentative.

"Looks good. Check it yourself."

They hoisted the milk cans onto rolling platforms. "We've got to invest in a better system," Charlie said. "This is going to kill my back." Big arms and bad backs was an old adage about the physical characteristics of cheesemakers. Lifting milk cans, coupled with hours spent bending over the vats, could leave cheesemakers with bad backs and strained muscles.

Inside, they poured the milk into the vats. Making cheese six days a week meant they would slowly build up their inventory of six-month, one-year, and two-year aged cheddar. With the help of Jake, Charlie and Karen had worked hard to find customers ready to purchase the white cheddar. She was thrilled to watch the list of customers grow each week, thanks to Dad's reputation of integrity and quality product. Karen had even added some Key West restaurants and stores. Charlie figured if all went well, she'd be able to make enough money for her and Lucy to live on and to pay off the debt to Casper. She glanced into the woods, half-expecting to see him lurking out there. She was anxious to pay him off and never have to see him again.

She turned on the radio, tuned into the student-run university station; fired up the propane ring under the vats to pasteurize the milk; then washed her hands for the third time that morning. Next, she added starter culture and waited for the mixture to attain the right acidity level, checking periodically with a pH meter. It was the starter culture she'd worked on in college. This pleased her, knowing her biochem degree did not go to waste. She waited. Expectant. Excited. Making cheese was a process of muscle-straining activity punctuated by periods of waiting. She danced a few steps to Aretha Franklin's "Respect," swaying back and forth to settle her nerves as she waited for the pH level to reach an acceptable range. She added rennet and waited for the mixture to turn more solid than liquid, patting its surface softly with the back of her fingers. Almost ready. Give it ten.

The door slammed and Lucy ran in.

"Mom, I gotta get on the bus."

She wasn't wearing the outfit they'd agreed on the night before, the new one, pink jeans and purple top. Instead, she was wearing her overall jeans, a red shirt, and her Wellington boots.

Charlie decided to let Lucy be Lucy. "You look groovy."

"That's cheesy." Lucy rolled her eyes, and Charlie saw the future teenager in her.

"I know. I'm the queen of cheese!"

"The queen of cheddar," Lucy corrected, flinging her arms overhead in a flourish. Her clear green eyes and the hair that fell across her forehead just like Charlie's own overwhelmed her with emotion. This was it. This was happiness. She recalled her conversation with John at Booth's Landing—about how the light always returns. Remember this, she told herself, wanting to fix this feeling firmly into her brain.

Karen walked in. "She's all ready. How does it feel to be back at the vat?"

"It feels wonderful."

Charlie bent down and reached for Lucy's hands. "Have fun today," she whispered. "Sorry I can't wait for the bus with you." Her heart tugged in Lucy's direction, but she couldn't leave the vats at this critical moment.

"It's okay, Mom," Lucy whispered as she wrapped her arms around Charlie. She smelled like cereal, toothpaste, and Prell shampoo. *Don't ever change, Lucy. Always embrace life like you're doing right now.*

Charlie watched Lucy walk out of the factory holding Karen's hand, her book bag hanging from one small shoulder. It was the first day of school, and she showed no fear. Last year, in kindergarten, Lucy had been anxious about leaving Charlie on the first day of school, crying and clinging to her each morning for a week until she settled in. She was grateful Lucy was going to attend school in Falls River for first grade. Thankfully, it hadn't been hard getting Rick to agree to Lucy starting school here. He had seemed distracted when she told him on the phone that she'd enrolled Lucy at Falls River Elementary, saying, "Do what you want, you always do." Even though they both knew this wasn't true, she hadn't responded to his accusation. She didn't want to provoke an argument. She was just happy he hadn't objected to her plan.

Charlie returned to her vigil at the vats. *Listen to the whey. It will tell you what it needs*, her Dad had always said. After two more minutes of watching, she patted the spongy mix, allowed it to run off her fingers, and called it.

"Ready," she told Uncle Jack. "A clean break."

"Copy that," he said. In the vat, the milk was rapidly involved in the process of separating the curd from the whey. As the mixture heated, they cut the curd to release the excess whey, until the curds knitted together into large sheets, which they cut into long loaves. Next, they began piling the loaves on top of each other, the weight of the large slabs forcing the whey to expel itself. It was the age-old rhythm of cheddaring—stacking and flipping the loaves. Uncle Jack continued the process while Charlie checked acidity levels and wrote the numbers in Dad's notebook.

"We're ready to mill," she said. They fed the slabs into what amounted to a kind of wood chipper for cheese, used to grind up the loaves into small pieces.

"This mill is amazing," she said. "That old one took two times longer."

"Your dad liked it too."

Bruce Springsteen's new song, "Thunder Road," came on the radio, providing a sweet mix of piano, harmonica, and melancholy lyrics as they salted the curds. Salting, an important part of the process, slowed bacterial growth and added flavor.

The curds were now ready to be packed into molds. "Let's do this," Uncle Jack said.

They scooped the salted curds by hand into the forms, then pressed the cheese with the new stainless-steel press Dad had purchased. After an hour or so, they had almost all the cheese loaded into the forms and placed into the presses.

"How you doing?" Uncle Jack asked.

"I feel good. Like I never left."

"Like riding a bike." He patted her shoulder, and they worked in silence until the last of the cheese was in place in the forms and the sun drifted lower in the western sky.

"Can I ask you a question?" Charlie had been waiting to ask Uncle Jack about Casper.

"Sure. Let's sit for a minute. I'm worn out."

They pulled up chairs at Dad's desk, and Charlie told him about what Old Man Raines had said about Casper. She filled him in on how Old Man Raines had abused his son. Uncle Jack didn't seem surprised.

"I heard about that from your dad."

"So why did it keep happening?"

"Some of these old guys, they do what they want. I've seen too much of it."

"On calls?"

"Yeah, they only started requiring us—medical people, doctors, including us EMTs—to report abuse in the mid-sixties."

"Before then, what happened?"

"Sometimes neighbors or family tried to stop it. Sometimes the sheriff got involved if it was really bad."

"Well, Dad went over there, that time."

"I'm guessing he told Old Man Raines to lay off his son."

"John thinks I should be careful."

"Charlie, you got all of us here." Uncle Jack paused, looking at her with an intense expression she'd never seen before. "You call me anytime."

"I will." She was somber now, thinking about the time she saw Casper lurking in the woods out back.

"Let's finish up," Uncle Jack said.

"You bet."

As they checked the forms in the presses, Charlie thought about how Uncle Jack and Karen would leave for Key West soon. She was nervous about losing them for the few weeks they spent living on a houseboat, fishing, sailing, and scuba diving, but she knew they deserved a break from the snow and freezing cold. Problem was, she wasn't sure who she'd get to replace Uncle Jack. Or Karen, for that matter. She'd relied on her to help with the business side of things and, most important, caring for Lucy.

The molds were ready, so they lifted each block of cheese out of its mold and placed it on pine boards, where it would dry for a few days before the waxing process could start.

By the time they'd cleaned up the factory, it was three o'clock. Lucy would be coming home soon. Suddenly Charlie's whole body ached. She was tired. *But it's a good tired*, Dad always said about cheesemaking. After she hung up her apron, she surveyed the factory, satisfied. This was it: what she'd planned for, dreamed about; why she'd worked so hard in college on the new starter culture; why she'd learned everything she could about European cheeses working at the market. Getting to this point had been a long, circuitous journey that hadn't been easy, especially in college at UW–Madison, where she'd been one of a small number of women enrolled as a biochemistry major. She eased herself onto the rocking chair on the front porch and thought about those days: How she'd had to work hard to prove herself. How she'd spent hundreds of long hours in the lab, most often alone, but sometimes with Wyatt.

Chapter 26

"Are you going to the protest?" Wyatt asked. Chomping on an apple, he planted himself on a stool next to Charlie at the lab bench where she'd spread out her notes. They'd met when they were freshmen in the chemistry lab at UW–Madison three years ago. Like her, he was a biochemistry major and had grown up in rural Wisconsin.

"Nah, I've got to get this research project finished." She was doing experiments on starter cultures, bacteria added to milk during the first stages of cheesemaking to metabolize lactose and produce lactic acid to form the curd.

"Come on," Wyatt urged. "You can take some time off. I don't want to go alone."

"When has that ever stopped you?" Wyatt was all about the protests. In fact, he lived for them. If there was a protest, he would be there, drawn like a moth to a flame. He turned up the radio. "For What It's Worth" was playing. Appropriate.

"It's not stopping me," he said. "I heard Bill Peterson is involved in setting up the interviews." The look he gave her was wary.

"He's not my teacher anymore. Thank God." She shrugged. "What a pain." Last year, Peterson had tried to get her to go out with him, had insisted until she'd agreed to meet him for a drink at a bar on State Street one night after class. It was a big mistake. He'd attempted to kiss her, but she said she wasn't interested. She hadn't thought too much about the incident until he seemed angry with her in class—ignored her when she raised her hand to answer a question or unfairly criticized her work. She transferred out of his chemistry lab, annoyed she'd lost the opportunity to work on important cancer research being conducted by the professor Peterson TA'd for—the reason she'd taken the class in the first place.

"He's showing them around," Wyatt said. "He's like a napalm ambassador." Dow Chemical produced and sold the napalm used by the U.S. government in Vietnam. Recruiters were on campus to interview prospective graduates to work at the company. When Charlie was given the opportunity to interview, she'd turned it down, unable to see herself working for a large company involved in producing chemicals used in war.

"That stuff is really scary." She measured some milk and poured it into a beaker. She knew about the effects of napalm on the human skin. A mix of naphthenic and palmitic acids and gasoline, it earned the name liquid fire because it melted flesh, causing deep wounds and extreme pain. She'd seen disturbing photographs of children being burned with napalm gas, and it turned her stomach. "I'm just gonna stay here," she said. "I heard university administration said students participating in the protests could be kicked out of school. I can't risk it." Dad was working so hard, helping her pay tuition. She didn't want to earn a double claim to fame—first person in her family to go to college, first person to be kicked out.

"I'll be over at the Commerce Building if you change your mind," Wyatt said before he tossed his apple core in the wastebasket, got up, and walked toward the door.

"Be careful." She went back to her lab work. It was her bailiwick. She was developing a better culture to stave off attack viruses called phage that could ruin an entire batch of cheese. She poured a starter culture into the beaker. The next phase of the experiment would be testing the culture in the small cheese plant located in Bascom Hall. One of the teachers in the Department of Dairy Industries was allowing her to use their cheese-making equipment tomorrow. She also planned to test the starter culture with Dad at Morgan Cheese. He was helping her with the project, sharing his experience and knowledge about phage-resistant starters, having had several batches ruined by the attack virus back in what he called the great phage disaster of 1956.

Two hours later, she'd finished up her work at the lab and headed back to her apartment, looking forward to making popcorn and watching *The Smothers Brothers Comedy Hour*. On the way, she decided to walk by the Commerce Building and see what was happening. There was an ever-increasing number of protests these days—mostly antiwar, but she'd seen others for civil rights of Black people, Native Americans, and women. It was eye-opening after growing up in the relatively isolated cocoon of affirmation from her family and Dad's friends in Falls River, though she was deeply familiar with the fight for restoration of Menominee tribal rights and lands from conversations with John and Karen.

When it came to women's rights, Charlie gave her dad credit. He'd never placed limits on her because she was a girl. He'd always encouraged her to follow her dreams, even when her high school counselor had questioned her plan to study biochemistry in college. She'd wanted to be a research scientist after reading about Alice Evans in biology class during her junior year of high school. Evans had discovered that bacteria in unpasteurized cow milk caused undulant fever in humans, a dreaded disease at the time. She'd also worked in the Washington, DC, lab where other scientists were developing treatment for influenza during the flu epidemic of 1918 and still others were working on treatment for polio sufferers. Charlie had imagined herself following in the footsteps of scientists like Evans and Marie Curie.

She'd been so excited after her biology teacher suggested she apply to UW–Madison, but her counselor had tried to steer her toward being a teacher. She'd ignored the counselor and, buoyed by her biology teacher's encouragement, went ahead and applied. She was thrilled when she got accepted and was offered a scholarship to the same school Alice Evans had attended back in the early part of the century.

Aside from the experience with the counselor, it was at UW–Madison that Charlie had experienced weird, subtle slights like not getting called on in class. Or, when she did get called on, she was often interrupted by her male classmates. She'd had male classmates attempt to tell her what she already knew on various topics in class. Sometimes she'd just let them drone on when she'd had absolutely no problem understanding the material. She'd considered these mild irritations because there were so many professors who encouraged her and generously shared their wisdom with her. She soaked it all in.

As she neared the Commerce Building where the Dow interviews were being held, she saw a huge crowd was gathered. Right away she could tell that something wasn't right.

There were angry cries of "Down with Dow" from protesters. Two students walked past her, holding their heads, blood covering their fingers. Sickened, she scanned the crowd, looking for Wyatt. He was tall and should be easy to spot, she hoped. Anxiety flooded her body with adrenaline. She didn't want to be arrested or get hurt. She moved closer to the crowd, smelled the humanity, and felt the heat. Feeling claustrophobic, she looked up and noticed the clouds overhead.

"What's going on?" she asked a student holding a sign that read "Up against the wall Mother Dow." He wore a peacoat and looked like one of the fraternity members who lived on Langdon Street.

"The students were in the hallway. It was a peaceful sit-in. Then about twenty minutes ago, the cops went in, trapped them, started hitting them with billy clubs."

She couldn't believe it. "That's nuts."

"Be careful." He stuffed his hands into his pockets and ducked into the crowd.

Where was Wyatt? It would be just like him to be in the middle of it all. He was brilliant at science, reliably kindhearted, passionate about civil rights, but she worried about him. She knew he was gay and had suffered harassment over the years for it. She walked around the perimeter of the group so she could get closer to the front.

Sure enough, he was up in front. Relieved, she inched her way toward him. He was near a group of protesters who'd stationed themselves on top of a cement pillar. One of the guys wore a sheepskin coat, and others wore suits and ties. One was older and looked like he might be a professor.

"Charlie!" Wyatt yelled. He jumped off the pillar and grabbed her upper arm when she approached him. "They're beating people up."

"I heard. You okay?" She never saw him look so upset.

His voice was rushed, fueled by adrenaline. "I'm fine. We were in the hallway at Commerce, sitting on the floor for a couple hours. It was calm until the police came. They just started beating people. I was able to get out 'cause I was near the door."

～

It was ironic that just before graduation from college, she'd been offered jobs with a couple of the large chemical companies. She turned them down. She was not interested in working for chemical companies, teaching, or even working in a research lab on campus. She'd lost the fire to be a research scientist. It was during that fateful senior year of the protests, when she'd focused on starter cultures in cheese, that she'd admitted to herself she was more interested in studying cheese bacteria than anything else. Yet she wasn't quite ready to move back to Falls River, and when her dad mentioned his friend needed a cheesemonger at a cheese market in Milwaukee, she applied. It seemed just what she needed after the intensity of her coursework in Madison, and she was intrigued by the opportunity to sell cheese from all over the world. She packed up and moved to Milwaukee and found working in the cheese market was fun, especially after Wyatt joined her.

~

Charlie walked from the front porch to the road and waited for Lucy's bus to arrive. As she spotted the yellow cab coming toward her on Cricket Road, she thought about how everything she'd done the past twenty-five years had culminated in today's cheesemaking—from apprenticing with Dad, to studying bacteria at college, to cheese mongering in Milwaukee, to putting together a business plan for Morgan Cheese. It was learning, dissecting, selling, and creating: her favorite part. She'd accomplished a lot today. She was all in. This business would be her income for years to come, or so she hoped.

The bus stopped, doors opened, and Lucy appeared at the top step. As she grabbed the handrail to steady her balance, she turned and looked at the bus driver. "Thanks for the ride."

"You bet." He was an older man, about Dad's age. "I knew your grandpa."

"You did?" Lucy began to climb down the stairs and Charlie smiled when she noticed she still wore her Wellies. "I did too!"

Chapter 27

Two weeks later, driving up to Legend Lake, Charlie was ready for a break from making cheese. It was the first day off she'd taken since reviving the factory. She could feel late summer's gentle nudge toward autumn, her favorite time of year. Leaves were starting to change on the maple and birch trees and she and Lucy wore sweatshirts against the early morning chill. Legend Lake, located on the south end of the Menominee Reservation, was less than an hour away from home. Charlie had been up to the reservation a few times with John back in grade school. She admired the wild beauty of the land and the clean waters of the rivers running through it. The reservation was more than 235,000 acres, much of it dense forest with the largest single tract of virgin trees in Wisconsin.

"How many horses does John have?" Lucy asked her umpteenth question.

"Just one, honey."

"What's her name?"

"Honey."

Lucy giggled. "You just called me honey. I'm not a horse."

"You're not?"

"Honey is John's horse." Lucy had her usual mess going on. There were coloring pages, picture books, crayons, and a bag of pretzels on the floor at her feet.

"Actually, Honey belongs to John's friend. He's just taking care of her," Charlie said.

Forty minutes from home, they turned off the highway and drove down a narrow, paved road. Soon, they found the road to Legend Lake, and, as John had instructed, they pulled into the second driveway. The moment they parked, Lucy sprang out of the car and ran over to John, who was feeding a carrot to a honey-colored mare. As Charlie joined them, she could hear John talking to Lucy.

"Would you like to feed her?" He handed her the carrot.

"She's eating it," Lucy whispered as Honey took a gentle bite. "That's a girl."

John turned and smiled at Charlie. "You made it."

"The directions were perfect." He wore a plaid shirt and jeans, and his hair was pulled back with a rubber band. Smoke drifted up from a fire next to the corral. The air smelled sweet, like burning pine.

"So how does it feel to be making cheese again at the factory?"

Charlie thought for a moment. "Pretty darn good. But I've got to admit, it's nice to take a break today." She smoothed back her hair, which was falling into her eyes. "How long are you staying here?" She knew he spent most of his time at his house in De Pere, close to the school where he worked.

"Just a few weeks." John nodded to the far end of the field and pointed to a small one-story structure with wide windows. "The house back in the woods there was built by my friend Joe. He's out east now and I'm just staying here until he comes back."

Charlie scanned the lake and the surrounding shore, dense with trees. Here and there were homes, but they were few and far between.

"It's gorgeous," she said. "Especially with the colors changing."

"I like it," John answered.

"I like it too," Lucy said.

"Want to ride her?" John asked.

She clapped her hands together. "Can I, Mom?"

They both looked at Charlie while she hesitated.

"You can sit behind Lucy. I'll lead her," John said. "A slow walk, Charlie. We can take the trail through the woods."

"A very slow walk." She told herself this was John; she could trust him. She was so used to not trusting from the past few years with Rick, who couldn't be relied on, much less trusted.

John saddled up the horse and helped Charlie get settled before lifting Lucy up to sit in front of her. Lucy turned around. "Don't worry, Mom. Honey's a good horse." She spoke as if she'd known the mare for years.

John led them on a trail through the woods. The gentle rocking rhythm of the horse felt good. They were quiet for a while, taking in the beauty of the forest, with the wind rustling the leaves the only occasional sound.

"Holy cow, these trees are big," Lucy said. "What's your favorite, John?"

"Umm, I suppose I like pine trees—they're so tall and magnificent, green all year round—and I like pine cones, but I also like maples because you can tap them for syrup."

"I like syrup on my pancakes."

"She does like her syrup," Charlie said.

"So how do you *get* the syrup from the tree?" Charlie could almost see wheels turning in a thought bubble above Lucy's head.

"Well, let's see, I used to do it with my grandma." He stopped, stood next to Lucy, and patted the horse. "We'd go out late winter and tap the trees. It's like putting a straw in the tree so the sap runs out. Then, you collect it in a big jug for like a week. After that is the fun part: you boil it on a fire outside and it turns into syrup."

"My grandpa taught me how to make cheese," Lucy told him. "Maybe I could teach you."

"That would be nice," he said. "And I can teach you how to make syrup."

Lucy turned her head. "Can we, Mom?"

"Of course," Charlie said. It struck her how relaxed she was, content to listen to their conversation.

Later, John took them out in his boat and told them the history of Legend Lake, how the lake was really nine separate lakes now made into one.

"The Menominee have fished these lakes for thousands of years."

"How many?" Lucy asked.

"Ten thousand," John answered. "We are the ancient ones."

"What does ancient mean?"

"It means old."

"You're not old. How old are you, fifty?"

"I'm almost thirty, like your mom. Once you're fifty, you're almost a grandparent."

"I believe I can feel Grandpa in the wind," Lucy said. "Do you believe angels are in the wind?"

"'Course I do." John looked up at a formation of geese flying south.

"Why do they fly in a line like that?" she asked, pointing to the perfect V formation the geese created.

"To save energy. It's easier to fly when they're behind each other in a line," John said.

"Where are they going?"

"South, to where there's food," he said. "They know winter is coming."

"I love snow," Lucy told him. "Mom's gonna teach me how to skate this year. I want to play hockey."

"I am going to teach you how to skate," Charlie told her. "But playing hockey is a maybe." The thought of Lucy playing such a violent sport scared her.

"You promised."

"We'll see."

"That means yes," Lucy told John conspiratorially.

"It means we'll see," Charlie reminded her.

Lucy's mouth fell open as she looked up at the geese and studied them for a long time. As they approached a boat with two men in it, John waved, slowed to idle, then cut the engine.

"Hey, Jeff." John nodded at the driver of the boat, who was wearing an army jacket. His son, Daniel, was a teenaged version of him. John introduced them, explaining that Jeff's family had been their neighbors when he lived on the reservation with Grandma Stone, before she and John moved to Falls River.

"You catch anything?" John asked.

Jeff reeled in his line and tossed it out again. "They're not biting. Caught a nice northern yesterday though." John chatted with Jeff for a while about fishing and Lucy started asking Daniel questions.

"How old are you?"

"I'm eighteen," he said.

"That's pretty old. I turned six August twentieth and I'm in first grade. We didn't have a birthday party this year because Mom was so busy but she made me cupcakes and we went for hot dogs at Booths Landing with Uncle Jack and Karen. You ever go there?" Lucy finally paused to let Daniel talk.

Charlie watched the lake turn gray from the sun setting behind the trees and took in its quiet beauty. She could feel the air cooling and dampness coming off the lake, so she grabbed a blanket from the bag she'd packed and wrapped it around her and Lucy.

It wasn't long before John told his friend he needed to leave, then turned to face them. "Let's go fire up the grill, make some dinner."

"Sounds good," Charlie said.

"See you guys soon," John told Jeff and Daniel. He gunned the motor and silently pointed to the sky overhead, where more Canada geese flew in V formation.

"Winter's coming!" Lucy cried, following their flight with her small hand cupped in front of her right eye.

For the rest of the way back to the house, Lucy sat on Charlie's lap, cuddled under the blanket. The ride was exhilarating, and Charlie was happy to forget about her financial worries. Being out on the water was always a calming force, and she had missed it. Lucy insisted they sing "Row, Row, Row Your Boat" in rounds, and the sounds of their voices rose above the noise of the motor, lifted, and were dispersed by the wind.

After a dinner of grilled hamburgers and chips, Lucy was tired, so Charlie set her up on the couch with the blanket and turned on *Toby Tyler*, playing on *The Wonderful World of Disney*.

John washed and Charlie dried the dishes in the adjoining kitchen.

"What are you teaching about now?"

"Current events. I'm teaching about the Menominee termination and successful fight to restore tribal status."

"It's good you came back here. We need you."

John stopped washing the bowl he'd been scrubbing. He became very still.

"Are you saying *you* need me?" He said it to the soapy water in the sink, so quietly she almost didn't hear.

"I . . . never mind." How could she ask John for anything? True, they had a history, but they were in their thirties now, no longer young kids playing in the woods together, or college kids watching the Northern Lights from the back of his truck.

"Say it." He turned and looked at her. "Don't go all quiet on me. Just say it."

She didn't want to risk getting hurt again. She hadn't even gotten a divorce yet. She had a six-year-old daughter.

"Charlie, you're doing it again. Talk to me."

"Doing what again?"

"Closing me off from what's in your head." He placed his hands on her head and lifted them up like he was flinging confetti.

Screw it, she thought. Just say it. "How can we do this? I'm still married."

"Are you?"

"No. You're right. My marriage started ending years ago. But seriously, I have a daughter."

"Who's a gift." John smiled at her. "I'm willing to wait. Until you work things out. I'll help you. I want to. Don't you know that?"

"I didn't know. A lot of time you don't talk about stuff either."

"So, are you going to say it?"

He looked so earnest. What the heck. "I need you." Embarrassed, she started talking weirdly fast. "We should spend more time together. Do stuff like today. Maybe go bowling, fishing, dancing, whatever."

"You said you need me." John laughed. "Ha, I knew it."

"Now it's your turn," Charlie said.

He didn't hesitate. "I need you too. I need you around, to go fishing, bowling, hiking together, to do nothing with me, talk to me, to dance with me." He stopped short, distracted by the song on the boombox. "Here, we can start right now."

John went over to the table and turned up the song playing on the radio. It was "Blackbird" by the Beatles.

"Dance?"

She reached her hand out and he took it, placed his other hand on her back, and pulled her close. They swayed together to the music as she wrapped her arm around his neck. She was sure he could feel her heart pounding.

"My heart's beating so fast," she told him.

"Mine too." Suddenly, he took her face in his hand and kissed her—his lips warm and soft. She kissed him back hard, searching with her tongue to find his. He ran his lips down her neck, and she got goosebumps. Charlie slipped her hands beneath his shirt and felt his warm, muscled back. She breathed. It felt so good. It felt as though the world had stopped, reduced to this perfect moment; as if everything that came before today needed to happen in order for them to be together in this kitchen, on this cool, late summer night with Lucy sleeping in the next room and the moon shining on the lake outside.

"I can't believe you're here, Charlie. It's been way too long."

"I'm not going anywhere."

"So then, it's what, fishing next?"

"If you don't mind a six-year-old who talks a lot."

"I don't mind at all. Hey, do you want to drive down to Madison with me next week? I have a meeting, and I was thinking you could do a little research about the Raines family. I know your dad and Old Man Raines were army buddies, but maybe there was more. The library there has a good collection of old state newspapers you could check out. I did research there for history classes in high school all the time."

"Good idea. I agree, I think there's got to be more to it," Charlie said. She could take one day off, make it up on the weekend. "I just have to be back by three."

He pressed his hips against hers, and she leaned into him as close as she could get.

Chapter 28

Holding hands, Charlie and John walked around the State Capitol, and Charlie became nostalgic about college. This place had changed her. Its atmosphere was everything she wanted to be (strong-minded, independent) and everything she feared (drug infused, spinning out of control, with packed bars spilling onto State Street on weekends). She'd stayed away from the parties. She had bad memories of how the drugs her mom took in her last days made her so disoriented. Doing drugs scared her and she couldn't understand how students were so carefree about it. Just the thought of doing drugs gave her low-level feelings of dread. The one time she tried weed, her anxiety skyrocketed. Then toward the end of senior year, she'd relaxed a little. Maybe it was knowing she was sure to graduate—with high honors, no less. She'd started going to a few parties and football games. She drank beer and played pool and foosball at the bars on State Street. On Saturdays, like today, she'd go to the farmers market and browse the stalls set up along the sidewalk around the State Capitol building.

It was sunny and warm, and the market was crowded with students and families buying pumpkins, apples, cider, maple syrup, honey, bakery items, and cheese. She bought a pound of cheddar from Hook's Cheese and some apples from Door County. Along State Street, the mile-long pedestrian mall between the State Capitol and the university, artists offered chalk portraits to tourists, and crafters sold handmade jewelry, scarves, and hats in anticipation of winter. On one corner, protesters carried signs demanding justice for women who developed cancers from menopause estrogen therapy. Further down State Street, toward the university, Vietnam veterans sat on picnic tables smoking cigarettes, while a guy in dirty jeans played guitar and sang a James Taylor tune. Little had changed.

At a coffee shop, John sat across from her, and she felt such a combination of attraction and comfort, she reached across the table and covered his hand with hers.

"Was this your hangout?" he asked, nodding to the room filled with students studying large tomes, the smell of coffee heavy in the air. He turned his hand over and held on to her smaller one.

"One of them," she said. "What about you?"

"There was this diner in the neighborhood near the University of Chicago. It was always packed and I'd go there and have big breakfasts, strong coffee. It kind of reminded me of Booths Landing." He poured cream into his coffee and took a sip.

"Ha. All the way to Chicago and you were back in Falls River."

"I liked going to high school here in Madison. I liked Chicago for college, especially being around my mom. Did I tell you? She and Nick, her husband, helped me out with school. What my grants didn't cover. But yeah, you're right, I did miss Wisconsin."

"I know the feeling," she said.

"And I get to renovate the old house in De Pere, teach in Wisconsin, help out with the new school district on the reservation. He checked his watch. "Speaking of, we should go in about twenty minutes."

"What is the meeting about today?"

"There's a hearing at the State Appeal Board set for February. Today we're meeting with the lawyers to prepare for it. I'm a small part of this; the women and men who have led this effort are the ones doing the heavy lifting."

Later, they stopped in front of the Wisconsin Historical Society library near the student union, and John cupped the side of her head with his hand, kissed her, and told her he'd see her at the union after his meeting.

At the library, she sat in front of the microfiche machine, studying articles from state newspapers: the *Appleton Post-Crescent*, *Shawano Leader*, and *Green Bay Press Gazette*. She wasn't sure just what she was looking for but was intent on finding information to explain what Casper had against her family.

First, she searched for articles from 1945, figuring that, because Dad had met Old Man Raines during the war, there might be some mention of them in a story about returning soldiers. She found nothing. She searched

1950s articles and read stories describing the polio epidemic. Mostly children were affected, and, according to a UW–Madison scientist, leaky septic systems were the reason for the spread of the disease. Bad water. Grandma Stone knew this. *Take care of the earth; listen to what she tells you.* John and Charlie would nod, and Charlie would study Grandma Stone's kind eyes. She seemed to understand everything about this life that, for Charlie, was such a puzzle.

She found an article about Dwayne Raines purchasing the property that was to become the sawmill and later the dairy. She figured Dwayne must have been Old Man Raines's father, Casper's grandfather. More articles included descriptions of the lumber business in Wisconsin, how men used horse-drawn sleighs to pull felled logs from the forests and send them down rivers. Log jams on the rivers were a frequent story. It was interesting history but nothing of substance, and Charlie was ready to give up after two hours of searching. What did she think she'd find anyway?

She walked over to the large library windows with a view of the water fountain and stretched her neck, moving it from side to side. Her eyes were drawn to the fountain and a couple standing in front of it. The woman was gesturing with her hands. The man had his hands in his pockets. Charlie squinted to see better. It was John. Now he was nodding his head. John reached his arm out and touched the woman's shoulder. Charlie realized the woman was crying when she wiped her eyes with the palm of her hand. They stood there talking for a minute more, then turned and walked toward the union. Was it Kate? It had to be. Why was she crying? A familiar feeling engulfed her. Betrayal. She'd felt it so many times with Rick. Then another familiar feeling—disappointment bordering on profound sadness. How could she have trusted John? Better yet, why? She desperately wanted independence, to be free of Rick, and now she'd landed on the same runway—with John, no less. It was awful to feel this way about her old friend.

Charlie forced herself back to the desk and her seat in front of the microfiche reader, but her heart wasn't in it. Why bother? She should be working at the factory making cheese rather than taking time out for this wild goose chase. She should be at the co-op in Rosewood with Lucy, Hadley, and Christine, making ice cream. Instead, she was sitting here, feeling like crap, the way she'd felt so many times with Rick. She absently scanned an article in the *Appleton Post-Crescent* about Old Man Raines, whose first name was really Roland, selling a piece of land on Cricket Road. Wait. She peered at the black-and-white photo. That's her road. She recognized her driveway. Weird. The article described how Dwayne Raines, Roland's father, had bought the land in 1905. Dwayne Raines. It sounded like the bad guy in an old western. She looked closer at a grainy photograph of a forest. Cricket Road. She saw her house next to the woods. The article went on to describe how Old Man Raines had sold the land next to her house to Karl Mayer. Sold Benny's woods? How was that possible? She had assumed Benny owned that land. It must have been owned by the Raines family. The time of the sale was just after Benny left for Sweden. She made a copy of the photo and stuffed it into her pocket.

An hour later, Charlie walked over to the union, bought a beer, and scanned the tables on the terrace, searching for John, half-expecting to see him with the woman from the fountain. She still felt deeply hurt but pushed the feeling aside, knowing she had no claim on him. She was married, after all. Weaving through the brightly colored metal tables and chairs, she spotted John sitting alone at a table near the lake.

"Hey." His smile seemed strained. Or was she just imagining it?

Here it comes—he's going to tell her he's getting back with Kate, if that was Kate. She didn't know for sure it was her. Or, he's going to tell her he had a new girlfriend. Or, she's pregnant, whoever she was, and he's going to be a father. Yes. Maybe that's why the woman was crying.

"I want to hear about what you found out, but first I have to tell you what happened." He ran his hand through his hair, which was uncharacteristically messy.

"Say it." Charlie sat down and took a swig of beer.

"Wait, say what?" He looked confused. Was he now going to make up some story? Rick used to tell some whoppers. Or, come to think of it, sometimes he'd just be honest and figure she didn't get it. He would just admit it, whatever he'd done. Now she was angry.

"You're getting back with Kate, I'm guessing." Charlie winced, waited, worried. Her anger made her think she needed to leave now. *I can't do this anymore. It's too hard. Tell me and I'll go home. I'll take the bus.* On the bus, she could regroup. There should be a bus going back to Appleton at least. She could call Larry and ask him to pick her up at the bus station there.

"Getting back?" John shook his head. "No."

That one word. No. Charlie pushed out the air her lungs had been holding since she'd asked the question.

"I saw you talking to someone at the fountain," Charlie explained. "I figured it was Kate."

"It was. She was at the meeting. She still wants to get back together. I told her no. Again. It was that simple. She cried. She's upset." He seemed slightly shaken-up about it. "I feel bad, but I'm not going to pretend I'm in love with her."

"Whew, I really thought you were going to say you're getting back with her."

"Why would I do that?" He seemed genuinely surprised. "I want to be with you, Charlie."

Whoa. Hold on. Her anxiety intensified. They were together? Sure, they'd decided to spend more time together after they had danced in the kitchen up at Legend Lake. And even though Charlie was relieved by his sentiment that he wanted to be with her, she was wary and hesitant all of a sudden. Her rapid heartbeat and churning stomach told her she needed to rethink this relationship. Put the brakes on. Seriously, after wanting to be on her own, without Rick, why was she jumping into another relationship? Was she ready to anguish over John now? What was it about relationships these days? Were they always this tricky? Was it because she wanted it all? Maybe—and she hated to give him any credit whatsoever—Casper was right. She *was* a women's libber. She wanted to run a business *and* have a family. She didn't want to feel trapped, cleaning, cooking, and doing laundry. It was Charlie's least favorite part of growing up when laundry and kitchen work fell to her after Mom died. She'd always preferred working in the factory or peering into her microscope over doing housework.

"That's nice" was all she managed to say. She studied a sailboat out on the lake. Who sails in September? Rich people. That was one of the things she'd noticed about Madison: so many people had money to burn, something she'd never known. Was she crazy? John just said he wants to be with her and she's thinking about rich people and sailboats, about not belonging. Maybe it was because she was the child of an immigrant. Being an outsider lived inside her. *Stay in the lab; stick with what you understand: bacteria, cheese.* Her rising panic helped her focus. She had to tell him. "I'm just not good at trusting, you know."

"So we'll take it slow." He looked worried. She could tell by the way he squinted. She never wanted to hurt him, but in his gaze, she felt herself bogged down into mendacity. She couldn't trust. Not yet. Memories flickered, triggered by what she'd felt when John and Kate stood together at the fountain: The hurt. The boredom she rode like waves, the ever-present desire to leave, the anger and resentment so strong she'd wanted to scream. The dream to get away. To start her own business. Just tell him.

"I can't," she said. "I'm not ready."

Chapter 29

As autumn unveiled its colors, they settled into a production schedule at the factory, making cheese six days a week. It was grueling, but Charlie loved every minute of it. Uncle Jack brought the milk around five, and they'd immediately start making a new batch of cheese that would take until late afternoon to finish. Lucy helped on Saturdays, after she'd finished her "homework." Since school started, she was obsessed with homework, which she assiduously assigned to herself. She practiced writing words in a notebook she'd carry around the factory and in which she also kept careful track of how much cheese they made. "Mrs. Lindeman said we need to do real-life math," she'd announced. Charlie suspected Lucy's first-grade teacher was referring to simple tasks like counting apples at the grocery store but kept her mouth shut, just happy Lucy was happy. Watching her studiously bent over her notebook reminded Charlie of herself as a kid with her own notebook, following Dad around. With all of Lucy's activities and six days of cheese production each week, September flew by before Charlie realized she hadn't seen Walter or Larry in three weeks. John called once. Just checking on her, he'd said. And in a move that made her want to reach into the telephone line and hug him, he said he'd found someone to help her out at the cheese factory: Daniel, the teenager they'd met on the boat ride on Legend Lake. She thanked him profusely before the conversation dissolved into an awkward silence, but not as awkward as the drive home from Madison the day he'd told her he wanted to be with her and she told him she wasn't ready. When he dropped her off, all he said was "Tell me when you're ready."

The first Sunday in October, Walter and Larry came for dinner. Karen was cooking for them and said she had a big announcement, something about marketing the cheese.

"Holy smokes, Charlie, look at all this cheese," Larry said when she showed him the aging cellar. "This is a beautiful sight." It was. Seeing the floor-to-ceiling shelves of cheese covered in wax placed roughly two inches apart gave her the feeling she'd accomplished something worthwhile. Rather than just selling cheese at the market, she was finally making cheese again.

"Looks like you'll be running out of room soon," Walter commented.

"Sure does." The problem had been nagging at her, but she'd been so busy, she'd not yet figured out what to do about it. "Maybe we could build out over there." She gestured toward the door. "But that's going to be expensive."

"I got an idea," Larry said. "What if we made rolling shelves that could fit between the shelves already here?"

"You could put wheels on them," Walter said.

"That's what I just said," Larry said.

"You said rolling shelves," Walter pointed out.

"Well, what'd ya think I meant?"

"It could work," Charlie said.

"Ask Jack to build them. He can make anything," Walter said. He leaned heavily on his cane. Today he was walking slower than ever and wheezing with each breath.

"How about we go get some dinner," Charlie suggested.

Karen had cooked wild rice with roast beef and gravy. The rich smell of beef coupled with the earthy sweet scent of the rice reminded Charlie of when Dad was alive and Karen would occasionally come over and make dinner for everyone. These family dinners included Uncle Jack and often Larry and Walter and Walter's wife, Ruth, before she died. Jake joined them a couple of times.

"Lucy set the table for us," Karen said.

"There are five plates, five knives, five forks, five glasses," Lucy said. "Let's see, that makes twenty." She turned to Walter. "I'm learning counting by fives."

"You just keep doing what you're doing, little lady. That's good counting," he said.

Lucy beamed.

"So, what's the news?" Charlie asked Karen.

"I've heard from my sources that this is a perfect time to sell cheese like our white cheddar." Her sources, Charlie knew, were her friends from an investment club consisting of Sheila, a retired librarian who'd become a reasonably successful artist; Hannah, who owned Pawlowski's Polish bakery; Sara, who ran the beauty salon; and Tilda, the mayor's wife. They'd made a good deal of money from their investments over the years, and they even went to New York City for a field trip to the stock exchange one year. They saw *Jesus Christ Superstar* on Broadway, toured Ellis Island, and had drinks at the Rainbow Room at the top of Rockefeller Center.

"There's a whole back-to-nature movement out there. People are looking for the real deal—fresh veggies, farm-made cheese, homemade bread," Karen explained.

"It's the hippies," Larry offered. "They're all about living off the land. Heck, that's how I grew up. No indoor plumbing. No electricity. We called it being poor."

Karen leaned forward with her elbows on the table. "I contacted all the stores Karl sold to in the past and got orders. They can't wait to get Morgan Cheese back on the shelves. I called some new stores that opened in Appleton, Stevens Point, Madison, and Oshkosh. They want to taste the product first, but I think they'll buy from us. And, here's the big news, I got you and Jake a meeting with the regional manager of the biggest grocery chain in Wisconsin!"

"Wow, you're amazing," Charlie said. It was happening. Things were coming together.

"I have those new contracts for you, Charlie," Walter said. "You can start writing up orders whenever you're ready."

Charlie felt a surge of excitement. She quickly ticked off her to-do list: health department inspections were up to date, which was a big accomplishment; the updated logo design was almost completed; and the first batch of cheese would be ready in about four months.

"I believe we are about ready to sell some cheese," Charlie said, looking around the table at everyone minus Uncle Jack, who was training new volunteers at the fire department. "And, by the way, I think we have the best team in the business." They clinked glasses, laughing when Lucy hopped up on Charlie's lap, threw her arms around her, and gave her a hug.

"I'm part of the team, right?" Lucy asked everyone.

"You bet," Walter said.

"You can't leave this team," Larry added.

"To Karl." Walter raised his glass. "Prost!" They all clinked glasses again.

Walter set his glass down on the table, grabbed his hanky, and began to cough into it. What started as a quiet cough turned into violent spasms. Soon his entire body shook as he gasped for breath.

Lucy watched him, mouth open, anxiety obvious in her wide eyes.

Charlie put her hand lightly on his back and felt spasms rock his body. His shirt was wet with sweat.

Larry jumped up and stood next to Charlie. "We should call Jack."

Karen scooped up Lucy. "Let's go in the living room."

Walter's lips were turning blue as he struggled to breathe. It had happened so fast. One minute they were toasting, and the next Walter was—what? Having a heart attack? He slumped forward onto the table.

"I'll do it." Charlie grabbed the receiver on the wall and dialed the emergency number. Uncle Jack answered.

"Walter's collapsed, and can't get his breath. Please come quick."

The ambulance came within ten minutes, with Uncle Jack supervising. "Didn't think I'd see you tonight" was all he said. With calm efficiency, the paramedics took Walter's vitals, put him on oxygen, then lifted him onto a gurney and wheeled him out to the ambulance. There was little Charlie could do but follow behind. She felt helpless, the same way she'd felt watching Ria and Mom get worse. She should have known Walter was sick. He'd seemed tired when they'd gone down to the aging cellar. She shouldn't have let him walk so far.

As her noisy Volkswagen chugged along the empty highway, she felt herself submerging into the familiar void of melancholy where the air was thick with dread. She looked up at the moonless sky and wondered if Walter would make it.

Chapter 30

It wasn't a heart attack. Walter had pneumonia. His lung collapsed, and he was lucky they got him to the hospital as fast as they did. Charlie stayed at the hospital until midnight. The next morning, Lucy had a lot of questions.

"What happened to Uncle Walter?"

"He had a collapsed lung. That's why he was having trouble breathing."

"Can they fix it?"

"They did." Charlie didn't tell her the details of how the doctor had inserted a needle into Walter's chest, allowing air flow. "He's okay, but he needs some time to recover since he's older."

"He's not that old, fifty maybe." When would she figure out that everyone older than a teenager was not fifty?

"He never seemed that old to me," Charlie agreed. On second thought, it was in the last few months she'd noticed he'd aged. The coughing spells had increased. He was out of breath easily. His face was often drained of color.

"I have something for him." Lucy went to the porch and retrieved a rock she had found at the river's edge. She'd collected them in fives, lined them up according to size, and painted them. This one had a red heart with pink polka dots. With a sharpie, she'd written *I love you* inside the heart, then signed her name.

The rock sat on the dashboard as Karen and Charlie drove back to the hospital to see Walter that afternoon while Lucy was at school and Uncle Jack finished up some work at the factory.

They talked about Walter's late wife, Ruth; and about Jake, who was already at the hospital; and then Karen told her about the first time she met Walter. "It was after my first husband, Bill, died. Bill worked at the mill on the reservation up in Neopit. He was a manager. People always came to him for advice." She rolled down the window, taking a deep breath of the crisp morning air. The Volkswagen chugged along. Charlie still liked to drive it. The truck felt sturdier, but the Volkswagen had a better sound system and was cozy. She popped in the Joni Mitchell tape.

"We had a good life," Karen continued. "We'd picnic at the river on weekends, go canoeing. Then with termination came so many changes. People started being let go at the mill. Bill lost his job too. He decided to look for work out west. The plan was I'd join him out there when he found a job."

"What happened?" Charlie knew there had been an accident but had never heard the details.

Karen looked out the window at the lush green pines that lined the highway for miles, mixed with the birch trees, their stark white trunks ethereal, medieval almost.

"A semi ran him off the road in the dark, in a snowstorm out near Denver." She folded her hands in her lap.

"I'm so sorry," Charlie said, on the verge of tears, imagining Karen, a young widow alone.

"Back in the sixties, I was looking for work. I wanted to leave the reservation for a while. There were no jobs. Especially for women."

It struck Charlie how they'd faced similar challenges with having to start over, with being a woman in business. She saw how fortunate she was to have Karen as a mentor and friend.

"So how did you meet Dad?"

"Well, first I met Walter and Ruth. It was at the farmers market in Appleton. I was selling baskets, and they bought three of them. After that, Walter convinced Karl to sell the baskets at the cheese store. I set up a display of baskets on a table at the store, and started cleaning and organizing the coolers. Your dad offered me a part-time job."

"Of course he did; your baskets are amazing. And you helped him with accounting and marketing. He always said you were brilliant at business."

"Thank you for saying that," Karen said.

"That must have been rough, having to start over like that."

"It was terrifying," Karen said. "But sometimes the universe doesn't give a choice. Change is hard, but its path can lead us to beautiful, unexpected gifts. Like how I met you." She reached over and gripped Charlie's forearm, then as quickly let it go.

It was a rare show of emotion from Karen, who was so generous but always kept her feelings well hidden. She felt a rush of affection toward her. "So you met all of us through Walter—Dad, Uncle Jack, me. We wouldn't know each other if not for Walter."

"I wouldn't have married Jack," Karen said.

"I'm so glad you did." Charlie thought of how she'd come home from college for their wedding, how they got married at St. James Catholic church and afterward in the church hall, they all danced to Elvis singing "Can't Help Falling in Love."

"I was lucky to find him," Karen said. "And what about you? Have you seen John lately?"

What was she getting at? "I haven't seen him too much lately." She was vague since she didn't want to tell Karen they'd had a rift after she'd told John she wasn't ready to date. "He's busy teaching, helping plan the new school district."

"He seems happier, now that you're here."

"Does he?"

"You know what I'm talking about," she said. "You two were meant to be together."

"Were we?" Charlie asked. This was good, right? But then the thought crept in. What did Karen see?

"Stop answering my questions with questions. Don't overthink it. I know how you analyze everything to death."

"You're right," Charlie admitted. "Man, I'm gonna miss you when you're in Florida. Lucy will want to call you every day."

"That sounds like a good plan," Karen said. "If you need someone to watch Lucy after school, I heard of a woman who watches kids in her home."

"Give me her number. I'll call her."

"Her name's Susan. She's from my friend Barb's church and you know Barb; she's a holy roller."

"It's worth a try." With John's help, she'd found Daniel to take over for Uncle Jack at the factory, but she was hoping to find someone to watch Lucy two nights after school so she could get more work done during the week. Now that Karen was leaving, she'd need to take over all the accounting.

They rode the next few miles listening to a Buffy Sainte-Marie song on the radio. When they arrived at the hospital, Charlie found a parking spot, then reached over to embrace Karen in an awkward hug, with the stick shift digging into her side. "Thank you." *For helping me navigate this difficult time, for taking care of Lucy, for saying I make John happy.* "For everything."

Walter was sleeping when they arrived at his room, so they sat with him in silence. There were signs Jake had been there—newspapers, books, a pillow and blanket on the chair next to the bed. He'd driven up from Chicago and stayed the night with his father but must have slipped out for a moment. When Karen went to find him, Charlie stayed, thinking about how worried she'd been that Walter wasn't going to make it after he'd collapsed at dinner. It was Walter who'd helped her when she was afraid after Mom died, when she was so scared her Dad would be next.

~

It was snowing and close to Christmas. They were playing cards at the kitchen table. Uncle Jack shuffled the deck, elbows slightly raised. He'd shuffle, tap the deck two times, divide it in half, shuffle again, and repeat three times. Always three times. Then he dealt the cards, shooting them with precision across the table to land in front of Walter, Larry, and Dad.

"You sure you shuffled these?" Larry asked, examining his cards. He didn't have much of a poker face. Dad said you could read his face like a *Dick and Jane*.

"You saw him do it," Walter pointed out. "Just play the hand you're dealt."

Charlie could hear Larry mumble something about the correct way to shuffle cards even though she wasn't standing in her usual spot next to Dad, so she could easily peek at his hand. She was decorating the Christmas tree in the adjoining living room.

It was a small spruce Dad and Charlie had cut down and dragged in from the woods that morning as a light snow fell and the river watched, stoically still.

Charlie hauled out a dusty box of ornaments from the living room closet and began unwrapping them just as Mom had done each year. There were antique angels with glass faces sent from Mom's family in England after her parents died. There were whimsical Santas; red, green, and silver orbs; a delicate chandelier; a toy train; a tiny pair of ice skates; a bright-orange carrot; and a delicate pickle from Germany. She placed them on the sturdy branches, then dug into the bottom of the box and pulled out an ornament wrapped in canvas, secured with a piece of twine tied in a neat bow. Her hands began to tremble as she carefully unwrapped the ornament. It was a delicate wood fairy with purple wings and a red flower hat: Ria's favorite ornament. She'd insisted on hanging it front and center. All by myself, she'd said. Charlie remembered the game they created—at night Charlie moved the fairy to a different branch and each morning Ria would search for it, find it, and exclaim, "You're a sassy one."

"Why are you crying, Charlie?" Walter sat down on the couch in front of the tree.

"Why did they have to leave?" Charlie asked.

"It was just their time." Walter placed his hand on her shoulder.

"I'm scared." Her hand closed over the ornament as if she could channel Ria through it, as if she could wish her back.

Walter followed her gaze. Dad was laughing at something Uncle Jack had said.

"Honey, your dad is strong," Walter assured her. "He's going to live a long time. And he needs you."

Charlie looked into Walter's kind, brown eyes. Puppy dog, his wife, Ruth, called them because of how they drooped down at the corners. Her tears spilled onto her sweater.

"Come on, I want to tell you a story." Walter patted the couch next to him and they sat and looked outside. It was snowing harder—the wind was whipping the flakes into frantic swirls, and sideways, so the driveway was covered in drifts. Walter handed her a white cotton handkerchief from his pocket.

"Have you heard about Franklin Roosevelt?"

"He was president during the Depression and the war." Charlie stared out at the white flakes against the tall pines and stark black branches of the leafless oaks and maples.

"He got polio in his twenties, but that didn't stop him from becoming one of the best presidents of the United States," Walter explained.

"Dad said Lincoln was the best."

"Both were great," Walter agreed, then cleared his throat. "Here's the story—it was March 1933, Roosevelt's inauguration. As you said, the country was in the middle of the Depression with millions homeless, lots of people out of work. It was bad."

"Dad said his parents almost lost their farm."

"Being a little older than your dad, I was lucky to be in school," Walter said. "But I took the bus to Washington, DC, to hear FDR's speech. I finagled my way up to the front, so I could see him getting out of the car. He leaned on another man's arm. It may have been his son. In his other hand was his cane. He had braces on his legs, and walking took some effort. I saw it myself. The strain on his face. He was sweating. Everybody knew he'd had polio, but people didn't know he'd spent most of his time in a wheelchair. He was paralyzed from the waist down."

"He couldn't walk?" Charlie asked.

"Not without some help. He made it to the podium and gripped it hard with his hands, leaning on it. Later, I realized he must have been holding himself up. I listened to what he said, and I will never forget it."

Walter sat up straight and adjusted his tie. "This great Nation will endure as it has endured, will revive and will prosper. So, first of all, let me assert my firm belief that the only thing we have to fear is fear itself— nameless, unreasoning, unjustified terror which paralyzes needed efforts to convert retreat into advance." He stopped.

"Remember, Charlie." Walter looked at her with a kind smile. "The only thing you have to fear is fear itself."

~

Now she understood the truth of those words—how, because of her fear of losing him, she'd lived her father's death a hundred times. She was doing the same thing with Walter. He was a dear man, a little rough around the edges, but he was so kind. She was relieved he looked better; his color was good.

Karen and Jake came into the room. "Look who I found," Karen said. Jake looked so much like his dad, Charlie startled. Maybe it was because he was tired. She stood up and hugged him.

"Thanks for taking care of Dad," he whispered. "I just talked to the doctor. I think he's gonna make it." He wiped a tear from his cheek.

"Hey, he took good care of us all those years," Charlie said, grinning, relieved to hear his news. "I was just thinking about how your dad told me this story, about how he'd seen FDR give a speech and how he always told me I had nothing to fear but fear itself."

"Oh, yeah, he told me that too." Jake crossed his arms and looked down at his father. "Pretty amazing that he saw FDR so close. They say he didn't want people to see him struggle like that."

"Maybe we need to see more of that," Karen said. "How we all struggle. So we know we are not alone."

Charlie nodded, dug in her purse for the painted rock Lucy sent along for Walter, and placed it on the table next to the bed so he could see it when he woke up.

Chapter 31

Susan's home was on Main Street, not far from Booth's Landing. It was an old Victorian, with a wide, wraparound porch, fluted columns, and a second-story corner turret. Close up, Charlie saw the paint was peeling and the porch floorboards were uneven and needed repair. She knocked after she realized the doorbell didn't work. Finally, after what seemed a long time, Susan opened the door. She was a large woman with thinning hair, wearing jeans and a sweatshirt that said "Follow me. I walk with Christ."

Above the folds of her chin was a face that once was pretty. Now, the corners of her lips drooped and puffs of skin under her eyes were a pale shade of pink. Charlie wondered how she kept up with young kids; she didn't look healthy.

"I'm sorry, you probably had to wait on the porch. My hearing is not too good these days."

Charlie followed her into the house and sat down on the red plaid couch that didn't fit in with the room's ornate chandelier, carved fireplace, and tall ceilings.

"So, you need someone to watch your daughter a couple days after school?" Susan asked.

"Yes. Lucy, she's six, in first grade. She's very well behaved, talkative." The room smelled of cat litter.

"Well, I have lots of experience, have three of my own. They're all grown now. My husband worked at the mill in Green Bay. He passed four years ago."

"I'm sorry."

"Thank you. And I want you to know, I understand what you're going through, dear." She pulled a clump of tissue from her sleeve and wiped her nose. "So young to be a widow."

Does she think I'm a widow? Charlie wondered. "I'm sorry if I gave you the wrong impression. I'm not a widow. My husband is alive."

"Oh, that's good, dear. I thought you were alone."

"Well, I am, I will be." Charlie searched for what to tell her. She wondered why it even mattered to the woman. Warning bells rang in her head. She'd been down this road before. There was the time she'd tried to rent an apartment near Milwaukee and was turned down for being a woman alone. She decided to be honest. If this woman was anything like those apartment owners, she didn't want Lucy anywhere near her.

"My husband and I are split up; he's in Milwaukee."

"Oh dear." She looked up at the ceiling and sighed. Her eyes darted around the room. She pursed her lips. "How old did you say your daughter was?"

"She's six." Charlie sensed this meeting was just about over.

"Oh Lord, I should have told you earlier. I only take children above eight years old. It's my policy."

~

After a hurried exit from Susan's house, Charlie walked over to the food co-op where she'd planned to meet Jenny for lunch. The smell of lavender was strong as she opened the door. At the front of the store, Jenny was arranging bars of lavender soap on a nicked-up, pine board table. Bunches of lavender in jam jars were placed in the center of the display.

"How was your meeting with the babysitter?" Jenny adjusted her jean overalls and tightened the red bandana she used as a headband.

"Horrible, strange. Let's just say, it's not going to work out. I would never send Lucy there. It was gross."

"Sit. I'll get the sandwiches," Jenny said.

"I should help you."

"I'm pregnant. I'm not an invalid."

Charlie dropped herself into a soft club chair covered in a flowered chintz fabric. Bluegrass music was playing from a stereo near the cash register. Her muscles relaxed. It felt so good to sit. She should come here more often, she thought. The smells were comforting.

Jenny set a tray on the side table and sat down in a matching chair. She'd made ham-and-cheese sandwiches on homemade Italian-style bread, served with iced tea and chocolate chip cookies.

"So, what happened?" Jenny asked.

No one else was in the store so Charlie felt free to vent her frustration. "Everything seemed fine until I told her I was basically a single mom, then she said she didn't take kids under eight years old. I was surprised and confused, but it was just so blatant. Tell me I'm not imagining this." She took a bite of her sandwich, savoring the sweetness of the ham. Why did everything up here taste so much better than in the city?

"You're not. She's discriminating against you."

"Except for the school counselor telling me not to go into science, I never ran into this kind of stuff growing up here," Charlie said.

"That's because your dad basically treated you like a son," Jenny told her.

"True," she said. "So when I run into this kind of thing, it's so weird. It happened before. Did I tell you that?"

"Maybe. I can't remember." Jenny took a bite of her sandwich. "Tell me again."

"A couple years ago, during a bad patch with Rick, I decided to try to move out, so I applied to a few apartment buildings. I found an apartment I could afford, west of the city, in the suburbs. It was really nice and had a backyard for Lucy to play in. I was excited. But after the landlords got my application information and found out it was just me and Lucy, they turned me down. They seemed like a nice couple. I was so disappointed. I ended up not moving."

"What's the big deal, renting to a single mom?" Jenny asked.

"I guess they were worried I wouldn't be able to pay rent. I don't know." Charlie shifted through the theories she'd considered. "Or is it some kind of prejudice? Some religious belief against divorce?"

"Maybe they thought you'd have wild sex with a different man every night. Whatever. It's just wrong, not renting to single moms." Jenny finished her sandwich and took a bite of a cookie. "It's like what happened at the bank. I looked into what Jerry Noth did to you that day, denying you a loan because you're a woman."

"By 'looked into,' you mean you talked to Jake?"

"Yes, and he said it's illegal now not to loan to someone because of gender under the Equal Credit Opportunity Act that was passed in 1974. You could sue that bank, probably sue that Susan lady too."

"Forget it. I don't want anything to do with her," Charlie said. "And Jake took over the equipment loan, so I don't need the bank."

They sat in silence for a moment, eating their lunch, listening to John Hartford sing "Gentle on My Mind" as a woman came into the store. She looked like a student.

"It's kind of lame when you think of it," Charlie said. "Susan made this excuse that Lucy's too young. Like oops, I just forgot, she's too young."

"She could have just been honest," Jenny said. "She could have just admitted that she's a narrow-minded phony. Try that cookie. One of the owners made them."

"Chocolate chips and oatmeal. My favorite." Charlie bit into one.

She paused, savoring the combination of chocolate and crunchy oatmeal. "I'm still left with the problem of how I'm going to get the accounting done."

"Why not just let Lucy hang out with you?" Jenny asked.

"I guess I don't have much choice. I'll set up a desk for her. She can do her homework at the factory." She took another bite of the cookie. "I did it."

"And look how you turned out," Jenny said, "obsessed with bacteria and making cheese."

"And your point is," Charlie said.

"That's my point."

Chapter 32

A few days later, Charlie and Jenny prepared to drive to Milwaukee to pick up winter clothes and whatever else they could fit in the truck. Charlie was tired of wearing the same two sweaters she'd brought to Falls River, and Lucy needed her winter gear. They planned to stay the night because Charlie and Jake were meeting with the regional manager of the largest grocery chain in Wisconsin about selling Morgan Cheese.

The first time Charlie and Jenny had taken a road trip was when they drove down to Florida the summer after senior year in high school. They drove straight through the night to Ft. Lauderdale beaches, donned new bikinis, and slathered their skin with baby oil and their hair with Sun In and lemon juice. Listening to Peter, Paul, and Mary and Beach Boys tunes, they drank beer and smoked weed with long-haired guys from Ohio. In a bar near the beach, live women swam around in tanks alongside neon-colored plastic seahorses. They were a long way from the corn fields of central Wisconsin.

Jenny tossed her suitcase in the cab of Dad's truck. The large bed would have ample room for their winter clothes, Lucy's toys, their books, bedding, and kitchen stuff.

"No Lucy?"

"No way. Rick was bad last night when I talked to him," Charlie told her. "Something's up with him."

Charlie had considered taking Lucy, but, in the end, left her with Uncle Jack and Karen. It was a weekday, and she shouldn't miss school, she told herself. Rick could come up north to see her soon. But really, she didn't want Lucy to see him in such a bad state. Last night when she'd talked to him, he sounded so out of it: slurring his words, making little sense, repeating over and over how he was going to change.

Jenny hauled herself gingerly into the cab, wearing a Bob Marley shirt under a pair of Pete's jean overalls, which she called her uniform. She wore her hair in a side braid and large hoop earrings.

"You look so cute pregnant," Charlie told her.

"You really think so?" Jenny asked. "I don't feel cute."

The drive seemed quick, though they stopped three times—twice at cheese markets along the way, and once to get gas at a truck stop near Oshkosh. In Milwaukee, they headed straight to the east side near Lake Michigan to pick up Wyatt at his apartment. Having nearly completed his master's degree in journalism at Marquette, he worked as a freelance journalist covering medical and science news. Working at the cheese market part-time helped pay rent. He hopped into the truck, looking like a different person, his hair shorter now and his beard cut close.

"No more long hair?" Charlie asked. "So, you're going for what now? Handsome, gay, investigative reporter?"

"Yes, as a matter of fact."

"You nailed it," Charlie assured him.

"You look good, kid," Jenny said.

Wyatt turned to Jenny. "And you look, er, large."

"Really?" Jenny asked. "And you're a writer? You can't come up with a better adjective?"

Their easy banter reminded Charlie of the fun times after college when she and Wyatt lived together. When they weren't working, they traveled together around Wisconsin, camping occasionally with Jenny and Pete. They took what they called their grand circle tour of Wisconsin cheesemakers. They visited Roth Cheese in Monroe, Carr Valley Cheese near Madison, Widmer's Cheese Cellars in Theresa, Sartori in Plymouth, Decatur Dairy in Brodhead, and Hook's Cheese Company in Barneveld; then drove up to Falls River, where Wyatt and Larry would discuss cows and milking processes for hours on end.

Now Wyatt and Jenny were talking about his freelance work, and his latest story about Howard Temin, a former professor of his at UW–Madison who had recently been awarded the Nobel Prize in physiology or medicine.

"So you talked to him?" Jenny asked.

"I did. He was really cool. He remembered me."

They drove from the east side to the duplex in Pigsville, reminiscing about going to college in Madison. Charlie felt bittersweet nostalgia for those days working in the lab, attending classes, and walking the lake path in winter when the lake was frozen or in fall when the leaves were a rage of yellow, orange, and red.

After passing through downtown Milwaukee, it was only a few minutes until she pulled into her old neighborhood. Known as Pigsville because a large pig farm had dominated the neighborhood in the last century, it was located on the northern rim of a low-lying swath of river valley between the city and the western suburbs. Though the stink of pigs was long gone, the inhabitants of the neighborhood could often smell the pungent odor from the Red Star Yeast Company when the wind blew from the southeast. Some people hated the smell. Not Charlie. She knew it was simply olfactory evidence of the production of an ingredient essential to bread making—saccharomyces cerevisiae, a sugar-eating fungus that causes bread to rise.

As she pulled the car into the driveway, she felt sad to see the front yard looked unkempt with long grass, leaves everywhere, and weeds in the garden where she had planted hydrangeas. Upstairs, the duplex was empty. No Rick. Her relief was instantaneous. But then, where was he? He'd promised to be home to help Wyatt with the heavy stuff.

The place was a mess. Dirty dishes, fast-food wrappers, pizza boxes, empty beer cans, and full ashtrays filled the space.

"I'll open the windows," Wyatt said as Jenny, claiming she needed to move her legs after sitting so long, slowly surveyed the chaos in each room.

It took them a half hour to get the garbage out. Charlie made coffee, and they sat in front of the fireplace to plan their next moves.

"Before we get started," Wyatt said, "I want to know how you're doing."

Charlie breathed in deep and sighed out the air. "Better. The cheese-making is going well. I love being up north again. Lucy adores it."

"We love having her. Sorry, Wyatt." Jenny took a sip of water, claiming coffee wasn't good for the baby.

"I'm happy for you, running your own factory," he said. "It's what you should be doing. I felt bad I couldn't make the funeral. I had that hiking trip to Montana planned for so long, I couldn't cancel."

"It's okay," Charlie said. "I told you, don't worry." It seemed ages ago: the funeral, the court case.

"Did you bring some cheese?" Wyatt asked. "Come on, I know you did."

"Of course." Charlie stood up, rummaged in her purse, and pulled out a half-pound wedge she'd cut that morning from the batch that Dad had made. "Remember that cheese from Somerset we were selling right when I left? It's kind of like that. It's got a more European feel. Stronger than the usual Morgan blends." She handed him the wedge.

Wyatt got out a Swiss army knife from his pocket and cut off a slice. He smelled it, then broke the piece in two.

"Nice break, not too rubbery, or crumbly." Wyatt took a bite and closed his eyes. "It's good. Very old worldly, strong, a little salt on the back end."

"Thanks. You know how hard we worked on this. Lots of bad batches and do-overs."

"You're a perfectionist," Wyatt said. "That's why this is so good. Let me know when you're ready to sell. I'll pick up the order myself."

"Give me a few months." Charlie allowed herself to feel excitement at the prospect of selling the white cheddar at the cheese market. She imagined stacked rows of it in the cooler, with their signature label—Morgan Cheese—written in block lettering above a simple black cow.

"So what did you do with the batches that didn't turn out?" Jenny asked.

"We tossed them," Charlie told her. "Sometimes it's best to cut your losses."

"Like what you're doing here now," Jenny said. "Right?"

"I'm trying," Charlie said, suddenly weighed down by the feeling she'd failed at something bigger than making a bad batch.

"Cut your losses." Jenny nodded her head, encouraging her.

"Right," Charlie said, "let's get this over with."

Wyatt stood up and rubbed his hands together. "Where should I start?"

They divided up the work. Charlie and Wyatt packed the living room and bedrooms while Jenny boxed up the kitchen, leaving a good amount of what was there for Rick. It took all day, but they cleared everything out of Lucy's room and had loaded up most of what Charlie was going to take. She'd leave the furniture for Rick to deal with—there was nothing expensive. All was either picked up from yard sales or Goodwill, except the living room couch they'd bought new. She remembered how excited they were to be getting a couch that wasn't soiled with someone else's stains.

On their last trip down to the truck, Langston opened his front door and stepped onto the porch from his place downstairs. He had a trim-cut beard and a short Afro. He folded his muscular arms and gave her an easy smile.

"Hey, Charlie, sorry I didn't say hi sooner. I've been sleeping. Still working nights. Anyway, I just got a call from the bar. Rick's over there, and he's apparently really drunk. I'm going to get him."

Charlie felt a wave of dread spread through her body. She turned to Wyatt. "Can you finish up? I'll go with Langston."

Wyatt didn't hesitate. "Call me if you need help."

~

Langston and Charlie walked into the Batting Cage, a bar frequented by neighbors, Brewers Fans, Miller Brewery employees, and Vietnam veterans. Rick slouched at the bar. When they approached, he lifted up his head.

"Hah, Charlie, you're here," he said in a slow drawl.

"We've been packing up the house." She didn't ask why he hadn't helped. She didn't want to sound accusatory and set him off.

"They've been packing up the house, everyone," Rick shouted. People looked at him, then went back to talking with each other. A couple of guys watched Rick with wary side glances.

"Let's get you home," Langston said, placing his hand on Rick's arm.

"I don't have a home," Rick said. "Didn't you hear? No more Lucy. Charlie's leaving me." He shouted the last part.

"Keep your voice down, man," Langston said. "Let's go."

"Fuck off." Rick was on his feet now, swaying slightly, fists clenched.

"You don't want to do this," Langston told him.

Charlie stepped over to Rick. "Come on. Let's go back to the house."

Rick acted fast. He swatted at the bar stool. It tipped and toppled over, hitting Charlie in the foot.

Langston moved in. He grabbed Rick by the shoulders and led him toward the door, all the time talking in a low voice. "Remember that time in Frankfurt? We were on leave. You got up and sang in the bar and the whole crowd sang along, what was it?"

"Some damn song." Charlie followed close enough to hear his remark.

"It was a Bob Dylan song," Langston said. "'You Ain't Goin' Nowhere,' that was it." Langton started singing. He had a nice voice.

"Not the best choice of songs for this particular moment." Rick laughed a little too loud and long.

"Sorry, man," Langston said. "I had to get you out of there."

They were outside now, standing in front of Langston's car, a yellow Fiat. Rick leaned up against the car and put his hands over his face. "I got nothing, man. I fucked it up."

"You don't see all you've got," Charlie said softly.

"And I drink because I don't want to see." He stared at the asphalt near his feet. "It's a vicious, fucking cycle."

"Would you let me take you to the VA now?" Langston knew who Rick needed to see. He'd been getting therapy at the VA for two years now. "It can help you. It helped me."

"It's too late," Rick said.

"It's never too late," Langston told him. "Guys are coming in after years of suffering. And now there's guys just like us who run the groups. Who have been there. Who know."

"Is it too late, Charlie?" Rick asked. He seemed to shift from being dead set against treatment, to at least considering it. Charlie found the slight change in his demeanor encouraging. He was referring to more than treatment, though. He was asking about them—if it was too late for their marriage to be saved. "No, you heard what Langston said. Just go. Give it a chance," she urged him, ignoring his implied reference to their relationship.

"Let's go," Langston said. "Come on."

"Okay." Rick gave in. It wasn't a resounding commitment. But it was a start.

They drove to the VA in Langston's car, not talking. Langston pulled up to the emergency room entrance. Charlie couldn't go in. She needed to get back to the duplex. She'd drive the car home, and Langston would walk back. Langston and Rick walked up to the hospital entrance. They passed two long-haired veterans wearing army jackets. One asked Rick for a cigarette.

"Sure, buddy." He pulled out a pack.

"You go to Vietnam?" the guy asked.

"Yeah," Rick said, and turned around to look at Charlie with a weary expression. "Yeah, I did."

Chapter 33

Charlie and Jenny stayed at the Pfister Hotel that night. The downtown hotel was unabashedly opulent with a four-story lobby, wrought-iron balusters, crystal chandeliers, and marbled columns.

While Jenny checked them in, Charlie studied the mural on the ceiling, immersed in an earlier time when lavish details represented the wealth and power of a new city. Many of Milwaukee's buildings were constructed by Germans who'd come here like her father's family, fed up with living under a monarchy and searching for a more democratic society. They were artisans, carpenters, stonemasons, and bricklayers who knew how to craft buildings that would become the city hall, mansions, and hotels like this one.

"You sure you can afford this?" she whispered to Jenny, who was handing the clerk cash. Though she'd never stayed here, the hotel wasn't far from the cheese market and she liked to wander around the lobby on her work breaks.

"It's my in-laws' treat." Jenny gave her a key looped on a green plastic fob. "They suggested it. Plus, I can go to Gimbels when you're at the meeting. I need baby clothes."

"You're saying you won't make our big sales meeting tomorrow?" Charlie was nervous about her meeting with the regional manager of the biggest grocery store chain in Wisconsin.

"As much as I like getting up at seven a.m. on a Saturday morning, I have to pass," Jenny said. "Besides, you've got Jake for moral support. And do I need to remind you how many years you worked as a cheesemonger? You should be able to sell cheese to a cow, for shit's sake."

"I could sell cheese to a cow," she agreed.

It was an extravagant comfort, to stay here after the day she'd had, and she was content to order room service that evening and forget about her upcoming meeting. They talked about high school and old friends and processed what had happened with Rick. When Jenny brought up John, Charlie didn't say much, unsure where their relationship stood. She hadn't spoken to him in several weeks. It was just after ten o'clock when they both fell asleep in the plush bedding.

In the morning, Charlie arrived early at the grocery store in a suburb west of downtown and saw Jake was waiting for her in the parking lot. She removed the cheese samples from the cooler in the back seat and they walked into the store together. It was huge compared to the stores up north, emblematic of the large chain stores that had popped up in cities in the last few years. With many of the specialty shops closing, this was where people bought their cheese now. Granted, they sold some of the processed cheese popular these days, what Dad had called glorified cardboard, but she was sure they'd be willing to sell Morgan Cheese after tasting it. Or so she hoped. She was nervous but calmed herself by knowing she had a good product, and as a former cheesemonger, she knew how to sell it.

"Do I look like a monger in training?" Jake asked. There to provide moral support and learn how to sell cheese, he was dressed in a tweed vest over a white shirt with jeans.

"You look like an English guy ready for his afternoon tea," she said. "Kidding. You look great."

"You English, always about the tea," he said. "Didn't cheddar get started in England?"

"Indeed it did," she joked in her best English accent. "Well done then."

The regional manager, Tom O'Hearn, was round everywhere—his bald head, his large belly, and his big blue eyes. Even his hands were puffed round from fat.

"Thanks for coming in on a Saturday, our busiest day. Let's go to my office, it's quieter," he said after shaking Jake's hand and nodding to Charlie. They walked through the bustling aisles, weaving between women pushing full carts. They passed the bakery and delicatessen counters with customers waiting for their number to be called. As they passed the cheese section, Tom pointed to the rows of yellow boxes. "We have a large selection of American cheese. It sells well." He turned to Jake. "Don't you just love a good grilled cheese?"

"Sure. Morgan Cheese is great for that too, melts nicely." Jake turned to Charlie and shrugged his shoulders into a question mark as they followed Tom into his office. She managed a tight-lipped grin. Her stomach muscles contracted, and she struggled to stay calm. She was representing herself, a businesswoman, no longer the daughter of the owner, but the owner. She wasn't going to screw this up. As they sat around a white-topped, Formica table, Charlie quickly set up a cutting board and sliced off some cheese from a wedge of the white cheddar.

"I've been here five years; before that, I was the manager at Big Boy." Tom turned to Jake and chuckled. "Ever bring the little lady to the big boy?"

"I, er, we're not married." Jake raised his eyebrows at Charlie when Tom looked at the cheese she had placed on a cutting board.

"Not married, eh?" He winked at Jake. "Still haven't gotten around to asking the question?"

Charlie had a swift impulse to laugh and bit her cheek to stop herself. Did he really say that? She decided to ignore his comments. "I've been to Big Boy, love their burgers."

"So, what do you have here?" Tom asked. He directed his question at Jake, ignoring her again. He reminded her of that loan officer Jerry. Same ilk.

Jake remained silent, his mouth open, his arms crossed over his chest. He was studying Tom like a specimen and she could tell he was pissed because he was biting his lower lip. She hoped he didn't do a Jenny and start yelling at the guy. She placed her hand on his arm. "I can answer that, Jake." She turned to Tom. "I've got a Morgan cheddar; it's a white cheddar in the English style." She offered Tom a slice of cheese.

"White." He took a piece off the cutting board. "Don't know if my customers will go for that. Kind of weird."

This guy did not know cheese. No problem. The trick was to educate him without sounding condescending. She had a lot of experience doing this with customers at the cheese market, winning them over with a history lesson and samples. She loved talking about cheese, so it wasn't hard.

"The whiter color here is natural; the orange color you see with a lot of Wisconsin cheddars is from annatto, a food coloring added to get that yellowish-orangish look. We've found lots of customers quickly get used to the white cheese, and even start to prefer it."

Jake took a slice and both men bit into their cheese—in unison. Charlie breathed in the smell of the fresh cheese, listening to the quiet ticking of the clock on the wall behind her. A lot was riding on this sale: her company, being able to stay in Falls River, her sanity.

He was taking his time, savoring the taste. That was good. She respected that. How could she connect with him? Dad. Tell him about Dad. Her dad was interesting, a self-made man. "My dad and I developed this cheddar; it took us a couple of years to get just right. We were going for an English version of a Wisconsin cheddar because my mom was from there and she told us about white cheddar, the kind they made before the war. She sold cheese at a store in London from extended family's farms in Somerset, where cheddar originated." Was she saying too much?

Jake spoke first.

"It's really good. What do you think, Tom?"

"Can't argue with you, Jake. It's damn good. I like it." He reached for another slice. "I've been to London myself, back when I was in the service. Great town."

He said this while looking at Charlie. Yes! She'd made some progress. She got him to address her.

"My parents met in London when my dad was there, before the Normandy invasion," she told him, slicing more cheese from the wedge.

"D-Day." Tom nodded with a look of respect. "You say you make this cheese with your dad?"

"I did. He died recently, so now it's . . . just me." She smiled at Jake. "And Jake, my business partner, along with my uncle and aunt. Our dairy is in Rosewood; their milker is my dad's friend Larry."

"Larry and my dad were friends with her dad," Jake told him.

"Sorry for your loss, Charlie," Tom said. "Now if you don't object, I'd like to order some of this white cheddar."

Yes! She had sold to the biggest chain in Wisconsin. We did it, Dad, she said to him. We did it together.

~

Later, they met Jenny and Wyatt for brunch at the Pfister Hotel's Rouge Restaurant. After the waiter poured them coffee, Charlie took in the room—red-and-gold-patterned carpet, red chairs, red velvet curtains, gold-framed pictures. "This room is amazing."

"My parents always took us here the week after Christmas," Jenny said. "We'd drive down, have brunch, then see *The Nutcracker* or *A Christmas Carol*."

"I remember that." Charlie took a sip of coffee. It was strong, hot, perfect.

"Tell us about the meeting," Jenny said.

"I'm dying to hear about it," Wyatt said.

"It was strange. The guy barely looked at Charlie, kept asking me questions," Jake said. "I didn't know what to say so I just went along with it."

"He didn't look at me much at first," Charlie agreed. "It was weird."

"Especially because I didn't know what I was talking about," Jake said. "We got the order though."

"He did like the cheese," Charlie said. She was relieved. She knew Tom's type from the way some male students had treated her in college classes and so she'd just dealt with it. "I told him about how my mom was a cheesemonger in London and how my parents met there. He'd been there. The London connection seemed to help."

"This Tom guy isn't used to a woman running a business," Jenny said. "Welcome to the 1970s, people. Get real. Women have the right to vote now and everything." She took a sip of orange juice from a crystal fluted glass.

"I just think about Alice Evans," Charlie said.

"Alice who?" Jenny asked.

"Alice Evans."

"Who's that?" Jake said.

"The scientist," Wyatt explained. "She worked at UW–Madison, also in DC at the National Institutes of Health, before it was called the NIH."

"Alice Evans was a scientist back in the early part of this century." Charlie turned to Jenny. "She started working before women got the right to vote and worked into her eighties. She died in September. Maybe that's why I'm thinking about her."

"I assume she discovered something," Jenny said.

"She discovered bacteria in unpasteurized milk that caused people to get sick," Charlie said.

"Undulant fever," Wyatt said, looking at Jake. "Called undulant because the fever came and went like waves."

"I like that analogy," Jake said, sipping his mimosa, handsome in his crisp white shirt.

Jenny and Charlie shared a look. Would the two men like each other? They'd talked about matchmaking Jake and Wyatt for years. Now they'd finally met. The women raised their eyebrows at each other. Jake saw this and kind of rolled his eyes. But his lips turned into a half smile and his eyes were twinkling, actually twinkling.

Wyatt just looked embarrassed. "She pissed off a lot of people—it cost money to pasteurize milk, to update barn equipment."

"The men scientists doubted her. She was a woman, and she didn't have a PhD," Charlie said. "They figured someone else would have already discovered it, if it was true."

"People try to diminish women all the time," Jenny said. "Not much has changed."

"But she persisted," Charlie said. "That's my point. She just kept going. She knew she was right. Finally, her findings were replicated, and she was vindicated. She helped the industry move to pasteurizing milk. It improved the safety and wholesomeness of milk, which greatly benefited the dairy industry."

"She got it herself," Wyatt said.

"Got what?" Jake asked.

"Undulant fever, from working with it," Charlie explained. "She was sick a lot after that. But she kept working, lecturing into her eighties, encouraging women to go into science."

"She downplays this a lot," Wyatt said, "but Charlie here was a star in the biochem department in college. She got recruited by a couple of big chemical companies."

"Yeah, but by that time I decided the lab wasn't for me. I didn't have the patience for it," Charlie said. "Plus, all I was doing my senior year was researching cheese bacteria. To me, it was a lot more interesting than anything else."

"Lucky for us," Jake said, then turned to Charlie. "I've had this question I've been meaning to ask you. What are we calling this cheese? Is it white cheddar or English cheddar?"

"I think I'd like to call it what Dad and I talked about. Name it in honor of Mom—Evelyn's Cheddar."

"To Evelyn's Cheddar, then." Jake lifted his glass.

Jenny wiped a tear from the corner of her eye and lifted her orange juice. "And to her daughter."

"Aww, thanks, guys," Charlie said. They clinked glasses and she took a sip of champagne, looked around the table at her friends, and felt content.

She thought about going back up north. They would leave soon. She was ready to get back to Falls River and anxious to see Lucy. She wondered what John was doing today. Her natural urge was to call him and tell him about the sale and what happened with Rick. She'd been trying to push him out of her mind on this trip, but she had to admit she missed him.

Chapter 34

One week overdue, Jenny claimed she was going crazy at home not being able to do any work on the farm. She said watching Charlie work was better than sitting on the couch watching daytime soap operas, which she claimed were both highly addictive and mildly nauseating. Three days into it, Pete brought in a television so Jenny could watch her soaps and the cheesemaking simultaneously.

Charlie hadn't heard from Rick in the five days they'd been back and figured no news was good news.

"How do you like dairy farming?" Jenny asked Christine, who was there to learn about the cheesemaking process.

"I'm loving it. Mike and Larry are doing most of the milking. I've been busy with the accounting, making contacts with cheese factories as we build the herd, but I want to learn about what these guys do here."

"We'll put you to work." Charlie was stacking and flipping loaves of cheddar to release the whey. She showed Christine how to manage the loaves. "Yeah, like that."

"You guys need anything, don't ask me. I'm living large. Literally living large." Jenny circled her arms around her huge belly. She was sitting at Dad's desk with her feet up on another chair and had the TV positioned in front of her on the desk.

"Go ahead and have that baby already," Charlie said.

"I'm ready. I pee every three minutes. Speaking of." She pushed herself up using the arm rests and walked to the bathroom in the back of the factory.

The front door slammed. "Hey, Christine, welcome to the land of big arms and bad backs." Uncle Jack pulled on his apron, tied it, and joined them.

"I'm good so far. Don't forget, I grew up milking cows and hauling milk barrels," Christine reminded him. "I hear you and Karen are leaving soon."

"Tomorrow actually. We're heading to Key West in the morning," Uncle Jack said. "I hate to leave Charlie on her own here."

"John is sending over his friend Jeff's son, Daniel, to help out. Says he's a good worker, needs a job." Charlie struggled to shake off the sadness she felt about Uncle Jack and Karen leaving. She struggled to be strong so they wouldn't feel guilty, even though she felt on the verge of a panic attack each time she thought of being here without them. "Lucy is sure going to miss you guys."

"We'll be back in a couple of months." Uncle Jack looked worried.

Charlie tried to lighten the mood. "Daniel's young. He'll be able to haul the milk around for me no problem. No offense, Uncle Jack." She was joking, but there was truth to it. Karen had told Charlie about Uncle Jack's back acting up at night, pain he addressed with a combination of aspirin and weed.

"None taken."

A shout came from the back of the factory. "Charlie!" They stopped and looked at each other for a second. Then it dawned on Charlie: it was Jenny. She ran toward the bathroom. When she got there, Jenny was leaning over the sink, her backside facing Charlie, a puddle of water at her feet.

"My water just broke. I'm starting to have contractions."

"No."

"Hell yes."

"Holy shit," Charlie said. "What do we do?"

"You're the one who's had a baby. What do you think we do?"

"Call the hospital."

"Wrong. I'm having the baby at home. I told you a million times. Call the midwife. Here's the number." She dug around in her bra, pulled out a small piece of paper, and handed it to Charlie.

Christine pushed into the bathroom, eyes wide when she saw Jenny, the water on the floor, and Charlie's anxious face.

"Is this supposed to happen this fast?" Jenny asked. "I feel like the baby is coming already."

"Let's get you a chair." Christine took Jenny by the shoulders, guided her a few steps out of the bathroom, led her down the hallway, then helped her onto a chair.

Charlie followed them, ran over to the phone, and dialed the number for the midwife, Naomi, who answered on the second ring. Charlie explained what was happening. "Where should we take her? She wants to go home but she said it feels like the baby is coming now." Her mind raced. Home birth? Were they back in the nineteenth century now?

"Just stay there. I'll be over in twenty minutes," Naomi said as Uncle Jack motioned to Charlie.

"I'm getting my bag from the truck," he called, seeming utterly calm but moving fast.

Charlie dialed Pete's number. "Pete," she said before he got a chance to say hello, "it's time. Jenny's in labor. Come quick!"

Charlie ran into the storage room and grabbed clean towels, then ran back and set them next to Jenny.

"What are those for?" Jenny asked.

"I don't know, they always get clean towels in the movies so I got clean towels," Charlie told her.

"Good thinking, Dr. Kildare," Jenny joked.

"Clean towels are good," Christine said. "Having a baby is messy."

"You guys going to boil some water now?" Jenny asked, grimacing from another contraction.

"Let's time these," Uncle Jack said, back now with his bag of medical supplies. He took her pulse, then checked her blood pressure. "You're good."

"Those contractions are buggers," Jenny said, calm now between contractions. After a few moments, she tensed. "Oh man." It was another one.

Charlie helped her through it. "Just breathe. Come on."

"Okay, okay, okay." Jenny mirrored Charlie's breaths. They held hands. Jenny's grip was strong. When the contraction passed, she asked, "How far apart are they?"

"That's about seven minutes apart," Christine said.

"Let's get you over to the house," Uncle Jack said. "You'll be more comfortable there."

~

After a slow walk to the house between contractions, Jenny sat down on Charlie's bed and rode out another one. They were four minutes apart now. Charlie checked her watch. Where was Naomi? It was twenty minutes since they'd spoken on the phone. Christine was waiting outside for Naomi, near the road, to make sure she found the house.

"It hurts so bad," Jenny panted. "Oh my God. Is this normal?"

Her voice was high pitched, strained with pain. Charlie handed her a glass of water after the pain passed.

"It's very normal, just a little fast for a first." Uncle Jack took Jenny's pulse again, looking up as Christine and Naomi entered the bedroom.

"Thank goodness," Charlie said. Naomi was slight, under five feet tall, with long black hair, beaded earrings, and various necklaces made of turquoise. She busied herself with checking Jenny's vitals and conferred with Uncle Jack.

Pete finally arrived. "Holy cow, it's happening." He was flustered and nervous, but his presence seemed to calm Jenny. He sat next to her, two ginger heads, though Pete's hair was a darker red than Jenny's, which had blonde tones. Pete tugged on his beard. "You okay, babe?"

"Hurts like hell." Jenny's face was wet with sweat.

"You sure you don't want to go to the hospital?" he asked.

"We're good," Jenny said. "Right?" She looked at Naomi.

"So far so good. Let me check for dilation," Naomi said.

They left Pete alone with Jenny and Naomi and waited in the kitchen. Charlie made coffee; Christine put together some sandwiches. Uncle Jack called Karen and brought her up to speed on what was happening.

Naomi came out into the kitchen. "She's at five centimeters. It shouldn't be too long. Charlie, can you boil some water? Get some clean towels?"

"Ha, I get to boil water," Charlie said. "And we need clean towels; lucky I brought some over from the factory." She said this loud so Jenny could hear her.

"I heard that," Jenny called from the bedroom upstairs.

After two hours of contractions, Naomi declared it was time. Jenny was fully dilated and ready. Naomi was all business and Charlie understood why Jenny had such faith in her as she readied for the birth. "Jack," Naomi ordered, "you're going to help me. This baby's coming out!"

Jenny screamed. "Hell yes. Get this baby out of me!" She screamed again.

"Just breathe," Pete told her.

"Stop telling me what to do."

"I'm going to ask you to push now," Naomi said. "Take a deep breath, ready, okay now, push."

Jenny bore down. "Holy crap!"

"You're good," Naomi told her after almost an hour of this. "The baby's coming. One more push."

"You got it." Christine encouraged Jenny with her eyes.

"She's here!" Charlie said as the baby slipped into Naomi's hands.

"She's a she?" Jenny asked, looking tired but smiling.

"She sure is," Charlie said as Naomi examined the baby, then handed her to Jenny.

"Oh my gosh, she's beautiful." Tears streamed down Jenny's face. "Look, Pete."

He stared at his daughter in awe as Jenny placed her in his arms. "She sure is."

"Well done," Naomi said, and expertly helped Jenny deliver the afterbirth.

"What are you going to name her?" Naomi asked. Charlie and Christine cleaned up using the towels Charlie had brought over.

"We both agreed on the name. No arguments there," Pete said.

"We did argue about the boy's name. I wanted Peter and Pete wanted Joseph. But for a girl . . ." Jenny looked down at the infant snuggled into Pete's arms, with her perfectly round head, wisps of ginger hair like her parents, and pink cheeks. "It was easy."

Jenny looked at Charlie. "We're calling her Charlotte. After her godmother."

Chapter 35

The next morning at the cheese factory, there was no sign of the holy commotion that had taken place the day before except for Lucy's crayon pictures of the baby taped up on the wall next to the cheese presses. Relying on Charlie's descriptions of the baby, the drawings resembled Lucille Ball with a mop of red curly hair, pink face, and big eyes. Lucy left for school with the promise of visiting baby Charlotte the following week.

Uncle Jack and Karen were on their way to Florida and Daniel had shown up as planned. He was taller than she remembered, with a soft step, and a quiet way about him. Today, he wore his long hair in a ponytail that hung midway down his back. He called Charlie ma'am and was a quick learner. She didn't have to tell him twice how to pile loaves of cheddar or how to work the cheese presses. And he didn't talk much, which was fine with her. After making their first batch together, they sat in the office, and she asked him about school.

"How many classes do you need to graduate?"

"Just one." Daniel stared at his hands, now puffy from cleaning. "I'm only going part-time now. It's a special credit recovery program at night. I should have graduated last year."

"So you only need one class. That's all?"

"It's math. I'm pretty bad at it."

"I know this guy, Walter, who's good at math. He could tutor you." Charlie knew Walter would be willing to help Daniel pass his math class. Thankfully, he'd recovered from the collapsed lung. He just moved slower now when he walked and talked more about retiring from his law practice.

"Sure." Daniel shrugged.

"How did you like school?" Charlie thought about what John said about Menominee students being bullied over at the public high school.

"It wasn't my favorite place," he said. "I liked cooking class. Science was okay."

"Then you'll love making cheese," Charlie told him. "When I was a kid, my dad gave me an old microscope, and I'd smear everything on slides. Study them. Everything from cow dung, to human saliva, blood, and snot."

"That's cool." He smiled for the first time that day. "Sounds like a kid."

She told Daniel about how she'd examined cheese at all ages and stages under that old microscope and learned how bacteria moved like river water. It flowed in and out of porous chambers, eventually transforming into cheese with varying tastes and textures depending on whether the cow had been fed grass or grain, the amount and type of rennet, how much salt was added, bacteria levels, and time. She shared with him how her life had been unpredictable, but cheesemaking became her safety net. She loved how each step built upon the last, how she could control the texture and flavor of the cheese by merely changing one ingredient or by deciding how long the cheese remained in the aging cellar.

Daniel listened to her with an intensity that reminded her of John.

"I can tell you'll be good at this," she said. "You're patient, something you need in this business." Waiting months, even years, was necessary when it came to making cheese. She paused, giving him an opportunity to say something. He looked at her expectantly. "You're a good listener. Thank you so much for your help today." He seemed to really care about making cheese, which was essential for this work. "Can you come back tomorrow?"

"I'll be here." Daniel stood up, pulled his shirt down, and turned toward the door. "See ya, Mrs. Sobczak."

"Call me Charlie," she told him. "Please."

After he left, she sat and stared at the factory: the bleached-clean, stainless-steel vats; the presses lined up like soldiers waiting for orders; clean towels stacked on the shelves. She allowed herself a moment of pride. And excitement. She was making cheese! The telephone rang. She let it ring a couple of times while she savored the moment, then reached for the receiver.

"Morgan Cheese," she said, shutting her notebook, eager to go meet Lucy in a few moments when she got off the school bus.

"Charlie? It's me." She recognized Rick's voice at once even though the line was crackling from a poor connection. "I want to see Lucy."

Immediately, dread spread through her from the pit of her stomach to the tips of her fingers. She hadn't talked to him in the three weeks since she and Langston had dropped him off at the VA, which had turned out to be a bust. Langston had called and told her Rick had left treatment after three days, claiming he didn't need it.

"Lucy hates to miss school. She's really busy," Charlie said.

"I want to see her," he repeated. "She won't need to miss school."

She struggled to think of another excuse, anything to put him off. If Lucy went with him, she wouldn't be safe. If he took her, he may not give her back. What if he just disappeared with her? Horrific scenarios played out in her head, making her crazy with worry.

"We need to talk anyway," he said.

"Yeah, we do. About why you left treatment. Why didn't you just give it a chance?"

"It was bullshit. Talk therapy, but don't talk about the war. It was fucked up."

"Langston said it was good."

"He's in a different program," Rick said. "Forget it. I don't want to talk about it. I'm coming up on November tenth. I'll take Lucy for a couple days, have her back Wednesday."

"I don't think that's a good idea." Charlie searched for more to say, terrified at the thought of sending Lucy alone with him. She clung to the telephone receiver as memories from the awful time he'd had a seizure gripped her. He'd been drinking all day. She'd gone out for ten minutes to the corner store to get some milk, came back, and he was on the floor in the kitchen, shaking violently, his skin chalk white as Lucy stood next to him screaming, *Daddy, wake up.*

"Please, Charlie." He sounded exhausted but sober.

"All right, but just for a couple hours." She relented; how could she not? He was Lucy's father. They needed to maintain some type of relationship.

Charlie hung up. She stared at the drawing of Charlotte on the wall. *How do we protect these kids from bad things happening?*

Chapter 36

"When's Dad gonna get here?" Lucy asked.

"He said around lunch." A jumbled pile of painting supplies was assembled on the kitchen table—five tubes of paint, two palettes, several brushes, and cups of spilled water. Painting with Lucy was an exercise in chaos.

"It's past lunch." Lucy dabbed her brush into a cup of yellow tempera paint, then swirled it onto her paper, creating a large sun in the center.

"I'm sure he'll be here soon." Charlie tried to hide the anxiety that gnawed at her gut. It was three o'clock. Would Rick show up? Would he be sober? She prayed he wasn't drinking this early in the day.

"Why is Dad always late?" Lucy asked.

"He's just . . ." She struggled to find words, so sick and tired of lying for him. "Busy." What else was there to say without criticizing?

"Will you come hiking with us?" Lucy asked. The plan was for Rick to take Lucy hiking, then out to dinner. Charlie was hoping to get some work done.

"Do you want me to?"

"What if Dad falls down again?" Lucy dabbed her brush into the white paint and began making clouds beneath the sun.

"What do you mean?"

"Like when he fell down and couldn't talk." Lucy swirled the clouds into the sun, turning the entire page into a dull puddle. "What if that happens?"

Charlie went on painting, trying to hide her alarm. Lucy had never talked about Rick's seizure from alcohol poisoning.

"Honey." Charlie set down her brush. "Are you afraid Dad's going to fall down?"

Lucy's eyes welled up with tears. "Yes." She plopped her brush on the table and climbed onto Charlie's lap.

"I don't want to be in the woods by myself." She buried her head into Charlie's shoulder. "I'm scared." She trembled.

"Don't be scared, sweetie." Was Lucy more traumatized by Rick's behavior and drinking than Charlie had imagined? She had told herself her daughter was young and didn't understand. But she was an observer. She watched and saw everything. Like Charlie, she took it all in and didn't talk about it until the fear and foreboding overwhelmed her like a river dam in a flood.

"You won't get lost," Charlie told her. "I'll come with you."

"Good, Mommy." Her body relaxed. She stared at the picture Charlie had painted, a carnival scene, with a Ferris wheel and a carny hawking a dart game with stuffed animal prizes in unlikely colors—green lions, pink elephants, blue giraffes, purple hippos. The guy had a cigarette hanging from his lips. He was leaning over the counter, trying to catch the attention of a little blonde-haired girl. In the background, a clown leered at her with a devilish grin. She ignored them, more interested in the cheese curds raining down from the sky, intent on catching one in her small, outstretched hands.

"You always paint her." Lucy wiped her tears away with the back of her hand. "Ria."

Charlie studied the girl in the picture. Was she still mourning Ria? Was she one of those people who couldn't live in the present because they were mired in tragedies from the past?

"I guess I do." You don't get over it, she mused. You moved forward but loss pulsed within you—at once dulled and intensified over time. Loved ones walked with you as life played itself out.

They both jumped when they heard the banging on the front door.

"Dad!" Lucy hopped off Charlie's lap and ran to meet him. She opened the door and hurled herself at Rick. "You're here!" She wrapped her arms around his neck just as she had done to Charlie moments earlier.

"I missed you, pumpkin." He grinned at her. "You're practically grown up." Rick lifted her from beneath her arms and twirled her around. Lucy squealed and laughed until he stopped and hiked her up onto his shoulder. "Good, I can still lift you."

"Charlie." He tipped the rim of his baseball cap, which Lucy promptly snatched and placed backward on her head.

Hoisting Lucy off his shoulder, he carefully lowered her to the floor in front of him. "You ready to go for a hike?"

"I'll get my boots." Lucy turned around and ran to her room in the back of the house.

"And your winter coat," Charlie called to her. "It's cold out."

"You're late," she said when Lucy was out of earshot.

"Sorry, the truck needed some work." Rick shook his head in disbelief. "Hear that? And you said I never apologize."

"I did say that." Trouble is, he often couldn't remember what he'd done to warrant an apology. After a night of drinking, he'd forget. At first, she kept it from him—the verbal insults, his stumbling around, his ranting about everyone and everything, the times he cried. Then, after the therapist said she needed to be honest with him, she began telling him. But he'd just get defensive.

When he stepped further into the front hallway, the odor of cigarettes came with him. He wore an army jacket over a tight chambray shirt, jeans, and hiking boots. There were dark circles beneath his eyes that, even so, were still striking, an unusual shade of light green. He was focused on Charlie, and she felt herself momentarily sucked into his orbit. She looked away, not wanting to feel this familiar attraction toward him. The front door was open, and, as she went to close it, she noticed his truck in the driveway, packed full of stuff.

"You moving?" Would he want to take Lucy? Charlie slammed the front door a little too hard. There was no way she'd let him.

"Yeah, I'm heading to New York. A guy I know needs a cook."

"The big city, huh?"

"I need a change." Rick looked around the living room, then out the window at the cheese factory.

"Change is good." Her words felt hollow.

"Is this good for you? An old cheese factory, this run-down farmhouse. Is this what you really want?"

Charlie felt hurt by his criticism. It was salt on an old wound—reigniting her own fears of failure. Just get through tonight and he'll be gone, she told herself. Don't be drawn in. Then the thought hit her again. What if he wants to take Lucy? Would he do it out of spite? *Breathe.* She forced herself to calm down and look at him. She knew he was waiting for an answer. *Your daughter is afraid to be alone with you.*

"You made your choice. This is mine," she whispered, familiar feelings flooding her cell memories with soul-crushing self-doubt.

He stepped closer to her and placed his hand on her waist. She felt uncomfortable. This was her husband, but they'd been apart for months.

"You sure?"

She stared at his mouth. The day he'd passed out, saliva oozed from its corner to the wood floor, where it formed a tiny pool. Lucy kept screaming, *Daddy, wake up.*

Charlie thought he was dead.

"I'm sure." She pulled away from him and his hand fell to his side just as Lucy's voice interrupted them. "Mom's coming hiking with us."

"Is she now?" Rick asked her.

She nodded. "Lucy asked me to come with."

Together they looked at Lucy clomping across the hallway in her Wellies. She stopped, laughed, and clapped her hands together. "Let's go."

Chapter 37

Ankle-high tree roots zigzagged across the narrow trails through the woods along the river. Canada geese congregated on the riverbank, and a mallard couple swam in domestic tranquility. Years ago, during a period of obsession involving birds, in particular geese and ducks, Charlie had learned that mallard couples stay together for the winter and spring months—the green-headed males diligently protecting the paradoxically drab females. After mating, she learned, the male mallard leaves the female to raise their offspring on her own.

"Come on, Mom," Lucy called from the trail a few yards ahead. As Charlie approached, she heard Rick talking.

"See the roots; they go down twelve inches deep and grow out farther than those branches up top." Lucy tipped her head back and stared up at the giant maple's leafless branches rising to join the tree canopy. Rick, Lucy, and Charlie always had this in common, a love for the woods. They'd taken Lucy hiking from the moment she could walk, instructing her about how to tell a maple from an oak, how to identify the various types of Wisconsin pines, why a tree rotted out and fell over on its own. What was happening here? Was Rick making up for lost time? Trying to insert himself back into their lives? His earlier question niggled at her, making her feel uneasy. *Is this what you really want?* Why did she sound so tentative when she answered?

Was it the promise of a good moment, like this one? Glimpses of the man she met in front of the cheese cooler years ago?

"Hey, tree, I'm gonna climb you." Lucy wrapped her arms around the tree nowhere near the next available branch. Rick turned to Charlie and smiled. It was a smile they'd shared before, the day Lucy was born.

"She's so beautiful," he'd said. He smiled that smile, took Lucy in his arms, and held her to his chest. At that moment she saw how their life could be, felt hope he could overcome his addictions.

"Let me take Lucy to dinner," Rick said when they started walking again. "You look tired. I can get her home to you by seven." He pushed his hair back from his face, and, for the first time, she saw a few gray hairs.

"I don't know." They arrived at the parking lot. Daniel's truck was there. Strange. He climbed out of the cab, still wearing his white apron. He'd been cleaning the factory. His presence here told her there must be a problem. He waved and walked over to them.

"We lost power in the cheese factory," he said. "I figured you'd want to know."

"Shoot, did you call anyone?"

"Called Larry, and he said to come get you."

Her mind ticked off what could go wrong. The cheese in the aging cellar should be okay for a few hours, but it was supposed to snow and get cold tonight. She turned to Rick.

"I need to get back to the factory."

"I'll take Lucy to dinner and bring her back," he said.

Should she trust him? The voice inside her head shouted no.

"We'll be fine," he said. Charlie studied Lucy, who walked along the edge of the parking lot, singing to herself, picking up brown leaves, and stuffing them into her coat pockets. The sun, weakened from the earth's rotation into winter, seemed far away, an indifferent steel orb peeking through the trees. Charlie zipped up her coat against the rapidly dropping temperature and strong wind.

"Okay," she said reluctantly, hoping Lucy would agree. Besides the electricity problem, there was so much work to catch up on at the factory. Rick was engaged and attentive with Lucy. She could use a few hours alone.

"Lucy." Charlie stooped down to face Lucy's eye level. "I need to go back to the factory. The power went out, and I have to get someone to fix it."

Lucy looked over at Rick. "Is Dad going home? I thought we were going to Booths Landing."

"You can go there with Dad." Charlie searched for any signs of fear in her expression and detected none. The hike and the prospect of having her beloved hot dog and ice cream dinner seemed to have overshadowed her earlier worries.

"Daddy will bring you home right after." Charlie hugged her and could feel the crunch of leaves in her coat pockets.

"Okay, Mom," she said, yawning.

"Seven o'clock," Charlie reminded Rick as she nodded and plunged her hands into her pockets.

"I'll see you then," he assured her.

She spent the next hour waiting for the electrician to drive over from Stevens Point, taking inventory by flashlight in the aging cellar. They'd need to start moving some of the cheese out of here. Soon, the four-month aged cheddar would be ready. Though Daniel was good, losing Uncle Jack and Karen had set them back at least two weeks.

Red, the electrician, walked into the factory. "I was wonderin' when you were gonna call. I told your dad to fix that fuse box the last time I came."

"Why didn't he?" she asked.

He scratched on his chin with one hand and hiked up his pants with the other. "He was a little confused last time I saw him. Seemed off. Said he'd call me but never did. It was about a month before he died."

"What's wrong with the fuse box?"

"The wiring's old. There's too much load on the one line."

"Just do whatever you can," she said after Red explained that the electrical system was straight out of the 1950s.

"I'll need to come back to update the wiring," he said.

~

By the time she'd finished inventory, it was almost seven o'clock. Red had gotten the electricity running in the house, set up Dad's old generator for the factory, and would be back next week to finish the job she was sure she could not afford. Anxiety crept around her like a predator as she sat at the kitchen table with a peanut butter sandwich and apples from the co-op. These were familiar feelings she'd had nearly every day living with Rick: Financial uncertainty. Fear of the unknown, of bad things happening. A dark highway of disaster at every turn. Where was he? It had only been three hours, but he was now ten minutes late. She felt panic rising, bottle-necking inside her chest and throat, spreading dizziness she fought off by drinking a large glass of water and pacing around the kitchen.

She'd described this feeling as "losing herself" to the therapist they saw after Rick's alcohol poisoning episode. The marriage therapist specialized in treating addiction. At first, Rick tried. He, too, seemed frightened by the incident. She could see it by the way he treated her; the kiss he gave her when she came home from work; the way he smelled, cigarette smoke and aftershave minus the alcohol. For two weeks, she'd searched for empty bottles and found none. After a month, she stopped looking. They went hiking, bowling, to movies and museums, had picnics in front of the fireplace, and he and Lucy sang duets, making them laugh so hard they cried.

Then came the call from Uncle Jack. Dad was acting strange. She'd reluctantly headed up north, leaving Lucy with Rick for one night because she had a birthday party that weekend for her best friend, Mary. Bad mistake, Charlie found out when she came home.

It was clear he'd started drinking again. He'd allowed Lucy to walk to school by herself. That night, he came home drunk and passed out on the couch. Then, around 2 a.m., he came into bed and tried to have sex with her. He'd called her a bitch when she pushed him away, and, of all the things he'd done, that felt the most demeaning.

I'm losing myself. Now she imagined Rick and Lucy having dinner at Booths Landing. He's drinking, ordering beers. What if he decided to take her, to head to New York City tonight? They could be near Milwaukee now with Lucy asking where they were going.

Charlie stood at the window and waited. The minutes passed slowly as her anxiety rose. Soon she was frantic, pacing from window to window, checking to see if they were out there. She gathered up her purse and keys, checking the television news to see if there were reports of accidents. But there were only warnings about a winter storm on its way, adding to her worries.

They were a half hour late. Did he take her to the dinky motel outside town where he was staying? Charlie grabbed her coat and keys, climbed in the truck, and drove through town. The empty streets were quiet with everyone at home, driven inside by today's first taste of winter. It felt strange, she mused, to have such a big storm predicted for early November. Even for Wisconsin. But the wind told her the weather forecasters were correct. It whipped angry swirls of leaves on the highway in front of her. She kept her eyes out for deer, wary of hitting one. They were especially active now, during rutting season. Ahead, flood lights announced the old sawmill and, shortly after, the one-story motel they'd called psychoville as kids. Rick's truck was parked in front. What the hell? Why did he bring Lucy to this dump? She'd only agreed to dinner.

When she got out of the car, Rick was walking on the sidewalk that ran from the motel office to the rooms. He stopped to light a cigarette.

"Where's Lucy?" Charlie ran over to him, seething with anger and fear, wanting to pound his chest with her fists.

"Hey." He acted like everything was fine, but she knew he'd been drinking by the way his eyes were lit and the cockeyed way his lips formed a smile.

"Where is she?"

"Calm down, she's in the room. We came back to sing some songs together. She asked me to."

"Which room?"

Charlie followed him down the sidewalk and waited while he opened the door. The smell of carpet mold was strong.

"You're kidding me," she said. "You brought her here?"

"Lucy," she called. Woody Woodpecker was yucking it up on the television screen. Charlie expected to see her on the bed watching the hyperactive bird, but she wasn't there. She opened the bathroom door, but still no Lucy.

"Where is she?" She was practically screaming. She lunged for him and grabbed his jacket.

"Where is she?"

Chapter 38

"She was right here on the bed when I left." Rick lifted up the cheap flowered bedspread as if expecting her to be hiding. Nothing.

"How long were you gone, Rick? And don't bullshit me." Charlie poked her finger into his chest for emphasis.

"Five, maybe ten minutes."

"What the hell? Where did you go?"

"I just went to bum a cigarette from the guy at the front desk." He ran his hand through his hair. "I locked the door."

Charlie scanned the room, the polyester bedspreads, sunken mattresses, photos of ducks on walls made of cheap paneling. "Where's her coat?"

"It's not here." Rick turned in a circle. "Jesus, she must have gone outside." Or been taken. Charlie didn't want to say it out loud.

She grabbed the phone on the nightstand between the two beds and dialed Larry's number.

"We can't find Lucy," she told him. "Please come. We're at the motel next to the old sawmill. I'll go look for her there."

"She couldn't have gotten far," he said. "I'll leave right now."

Hearing Larry's voice calmed her a notch. Lucy couldn't have gone far. She repeated it in her mind like a mantra.

Charlie ran outside, feeling a blast of cold air on her skin. *My little girl is out there and now it's freezing out.*

"I'm coming with you." Rick was close behind.

"No, you walk the other direction, away from town. That way we got both directions covered." She hated to think of Lucy going the other way. Or into the woods behind the motel. They loomed dark, sinister, the wind blowing the high branches in a frenzy. On the other hand, the woods would be warmer and safer than the open road, especially in a storm.

"Wait." Rick stopped, pointing his finger at an empty carry-out container on the ground. "The kitten."

"What kitten?"

"There was a stray hanging around the motel. Lucy was crazy about it, kept looking for it, even put some food out. Leftovers."

"Maybe she saw it. Maybe she was looking for it. Or followed it." That would be Lucy, always picking up strays.

"Maybe. I'm so sorry, Charlie." He looked defeated, no longer drunk. She almost felt bad for him.

"Let's just find her."

A familiar feeling hit Charlie with images—running to the house, Mom floating in the river, Ria lying in an iron lung. She pushed the memories aside.

As she hiked the few yards over to the sawmill, she scanned the side of the road for Lucy. She would have seen her on the way here if she'd been walking on the road, except she'd been looking for deer, not her daughter. Maybe Lucy was walking in the ditch that bordered the highway. If so, Charlie would have missed her.

Frantic. The word hit Charlie. She felt frantic. She forced herself to stay calm. Lucy was curious and loved kittens. She'd follow one. Charlie thought of those days they'd spy on Casper, long hours when she'd seen feral cats slink around the lumber yard, some days the only sign of life in the rundown landscape that began taking on the look of a dump with old appliances, tires, a couple of rusted-out cars, and a stained mattress or two. The yard was a breeding ground for feral cats. Everyone at school knew the stories of Falls River kids sneaking in to play with the kittens, being chased away by Old Man Raines. Charlie thought of Casper. The last thing she needed was to run into him.

The lumber yard was lit up by a floodlight positioned fifteen feet high on top of a pole. It had begun to snow, with soft, feathered flakes piling up on the cold ground. It was the kind of snowfall Lucy and Charlie loved— new snow, Lucy called it, the first snow of the season. Stacks of lumber loomed on the north side of the yard, left over from when the mill was in operation. Further north stood the sawmill, with darkened windows etched black with grime. On the south end of the yard was a trailer, an occasional home to workers when the mill was running, but abandoned now, its sides pockmarked with rusted-out holes and busted windows, with the door missing. The place gave Charlie the creeps. Ghosts pulsed from the darkened shadows beyond the stacks of logs. The eerie silence intensified by the falling snow felt ominous as she strained to hear any sign of Lucy.

How could her sweet girl be out here alone? She'd be so scared. Nerves were like raw wires in Charlie's chest. Her arms felt numb. She needed to find Lucy. She fought off a wave of dizziness. *Breathe.*

She called Lucy's name again and again, stopping to listen to the vast silence, hoping for an answer. God, she would do anything to find her. Anything. *Just help me this time.*

Then, a sound, barely perceptible, came from the direction of the trailer. Charlie ran over. Then she heard another sound. She strained to hear. It seemed to come from underneath. She crouched down and flattened herself on the ground. It was pitch dark, but she could see something moving. As her eyes adjusted, she could make out two glowing points of light. A raccoon? Shit, it was a kitten. She saw Lucy then. Lying on her side.

Relief spilled over her. "Lucy, are you okay?"

"I found the kitty. But I hurt my arm."

Army-crawling her way under the trailer, Charlie saw Lucy cradling a white kitten. "She's scared, Mom."

"Let me look at your arm." Charlie pushed up Lucy's coat sleeve on her left arm. Sensing freedom, the kitty wiggled out of Lucy's grasp and ran out from under the trailer.

"Oh no," Lucy cried.

"It's okay," Charlie told her. "We need to worry about your cut now. I'm going to help you out of here."

Dragging her as gently as she could from underneath the trailer, Charlie examined Lucy's hand and up her arm. There was blood everywhere. A gash traveled from her little hand to her forearm. Oh God. Now Charlie was shaking. She took off her scarf and wrapped it tight around the wound. Lights from a truck illuminated Lucy's face, her skin pale from the cold and blood loss. The truck was a black Ford. Larry. Thank God.

"I got her," Charlie yelled to him when he pulled up, stopped next to them, and hopped out of the truck.

She picked up Lucy. Cradled her. She was so light.

"She's hurt her arm."

"Larry, I cut my arm."

"We're gonna get you fixed up, little girl." He opened the passenger door, and Charlie laid her on the seat, sliding in next to her and placing Lucy's head on her lap.

"What happened?" Larry asked, behind the wheel now, shifting the truck into gear.

"She must have followed the kitten under the trailer. All I can think is she scraped her arm. There's so much blood."

"It was a white kitty, Larry," Lucy said, as if that explained everything.

Larry peeled out of the driveway and onto the highway.

"I'm going straight to the hospital."

Charlie thought of Rick. There was no time to find him and tell him she had found Lucy. Let him keep searching, she thought to herself. He would just have to figure out where they were on his own.

Chapter 39

At the hospital, two nurses took Lucy from Charlie's arms and placed her on a gurney.

"What happened?" One of the nurses pulled back the scarf she'd tied around the gash in Lucy's arm.

"She followed a kitten under a trailer. There were jagged pieces of metal under there. I think she must have got cut from trying to drag the kitten out." Her voice sounded reedy, rising into high-octave panic.

"Rusted?"

"It was hard to see. I think so." She gripped Lucy's leg, but the nurse gently pushed her away.

She fired off questions. "Is she up to date on her tetanus?"

"Yes, she got her shots in August last year before kindergarten. That would protect her from blood poisoning, right?"

"Still, we need to treat this with antibiotics. We'll clean up the wound."

"Any allergies to medications?"

"No."

"Any health issues we should be aware of?"

"No."

They began to wheel Lucy away in a whirl of hands, nurses listening to her heartbeat and taking her blood pressure and temperature. Her blonde hair was splayed out on the pillow. She looked so small.

Doc Cooper joined them and quickly examined Lucy. "She lost some blood. From the looks of it, she didn't hit an artery. We'll take her; you stay out here." They ran alongside Lucy like a crisis parade.

Larry pulled Charlie away from the gurney as they wheeled Lucy through the doors to the innards of the small hospital. "You take good care of her, doc," he told Doc Cooper. Doc was the one who'd informed them Ria was dying that day in his office. He'd allowed Charlie to see Ria even though she was too young for visiting.

She had sat with Ria for less than five minutes, and it was long enough to understand she wasn't going to get better. Even as young as Charlie was, she could feel it. The iron lung was loud like Mom's hair dryer, as it breathed for Ria. When she whispered in Ria's ear, "I miss you," her sister didn't move. Charlie smoothed back the hair on Ria's forehead. Felt her skin was hot. Like Lucy, she too had looked so small.

"Charlie." Larry was talking. "I called Jack in Florida. Told him about what happened to Lucy. He said he's praying for her. That's a first."

"Thanks, Larry." She thought about how she'd prayed to God earlier. What had she promised? Oh yeah, everything. Anything. Her hand shook when she pushed back her hair from her face. There was blood on her fingers.

"She's not Ria." Larry gripped Charlie's shoulders. She buried her head in her hands to stop herself from screaming, then, in slow motion, rested her forehead on his shoulder. He smelled like hay and fresh air.

They stood there for a moment. When she looked up, Rick walked into the waiting room.

"Hey, shithead." Larry's whole body tensed.

"How is she?" Rick ignored Larry.

"I don't know." Charlie wiped her face with the back of her coat sleeve. "She lost some blood. She's got a bad gash on her arm. It could get infected. She needs antibiotics."

"Thanks to you," Larry said. "I could kick your ass right here."

"Hit me, old man. Hit me. I don't care if you hurt me." Rick lifted his arms, palms up.

Larry looked stunned and skinny. He'd always been real skinny, and now he was kind of bent at the waist.

"You just better hope she's okay, mister."

"I got nothing left but hope." Rick shoved his hands in his pockets. He looked like he'd aged.

"You don't even got that, man," Larry said. "You lost yourself a beautiful family, all for drinking yourself half to death."

Charlie couldn't take any more of this. Her head throbbed. "Okay, you two."

Larry lunged at Rick—he was quick. The two men locked together, their arms on each other's shoulders, dancing a slow dance. Then Larry pulled his arm back, pushed it against Rick's face, and turned it like he was grinding a pie into his face.

Larry backed away. Rick's hands went up to his nose.

"Aw, shit, Larry, what'd you do that for?" Rick asked. Blood trickled out of his nose.

Larry rubbed his forearm. "I gotta sit down now."

They shuffled into the waiting area that smelled like burnt coffee and dirty socks.

"Larry, calm down, I don't need you getting hurt too." Though Charlie had felt a rush of satisfaction at Larry's pie-on-the-face end to their kerfuffle.

~

Time passed incrementally in the slow time travel unique to hospital waiting rooms. Charlie closed her eyes as she sat uncomfortably on a cheap, plastic chair.

Finally, Doc Cooper came out. "We stabilized her," he said. "She's sleeping now. We'll see how she does over the next twenty-four hours. We stitched up the cut on her arm. She's at risk for infection from the cut, but the antibiotics should prevent that."

"Is she going to be okay?" Charlie needed him to reassure her.

"The next twenty-four hours will tell us if her body resists infection."

"What about rabies? Is she at risk? There are tons of raccoons around that yard."

"She didn't get bit. We thoroughly checked, so that wouldn't be a factor."

Relieved, Charlie pushed air out of her lungs. "Can I see her now?" she managed to ask, willing away the lightheadedness homing in on her from holding her breath.

"Of course." The doctor's kind eyes had none of the defeat Charlie had seen the day Ria died. It was a good sign.

Then her knees felt like they were buckling under her. Rick tried to help her sit down, but she shrugged him off. Dizziness washed over her and the ground rolled under her feet like she was riding lake swells on a boat deck. With concentrated effort, she fought the feeling.

"Let's go see little Lucy," Larry said.

Chapter 40

Charlie walked with Larry to Lucy's room. Rick followed, now balancing an ice pack on his nose.

Lucy was hooked up to a monitor. She looked peaceful, with a bit of color in her cheeks. Charlie took her small hand in hers. Someone had put her coat on the chair, and Charlie smiled at the leaves sticking out of the pockets.

"Lucy, I'm here," she whispered. "With you." Where she should have been all along. Why was the factory so important? Why was getting the electricity going more important than Lucy's safety?

Lucy lay still, sleeping. Rick went around to the other side of the bed.

"I love you, baby." He touched her shoulder.

"You should have that nose looked at." Larry went over and studied it. "Come on, we're going to get you fixed up. Charlie's got this."

"You sure?" he asked her.

"Just go." She didn't want to look at him, see the hurt, feel sorry for him, and get sucked into his spiral.

"I'll be back."

They left Charlie and Lucy with the soft whisper of the machines, so quiet compared to the futile iron lung Ria had been imprisoned in. She sat for two hours while Lucy slept, held her hand, and watched the snow fall. Charlie must have dozed off. When she woke up, John stood next to her chair, holding two cups of coffee. "Hey, thanks for coming." She was relieved he was here and not surprised. Of course he would come. He was John, her old friend.

"How is she?"

"She seems better. She's been sleeping."

A nurse came in and began checking vitals.

"How about we go out in the hall?" John asked. "Do you good to get up for a few minutes." Charlie got up slowly, stiff from sitting for so long.

"I'll be right back, sweetie." Charlie kissed Lucy's cheek and studied her breathing one more time. Slow and steady.

John led her across the hall to an empty waiting area.

"I don't want to go too far," she told him.

"We'll stay right here then. You can almost see her." They stood by the window, looking at the pond that was the town skating rink in winter and fishing hole the rest of the year. It was snowing harder now. John handed her the coffee.

"How are you holding up?" he asked.

Charlie absently placed the coffee cup on the windowsill, too upset to drink it. "It's happening all over." She slipped back into the easy conversation she'd always had with him, before the awkwardness of the trip to Madison.

"What do you mean?" John asked. "Are you talking about Ria?"

"She died here." Charlie kept her eyes on the skating rink, watching Ria fall on the ice, then quickly get up, seeing her eight-year-old self clapping, encouraging her.

"I blame myself for her getting sick." The feeling was an old one, brought up like bile in the back of her throat. Guilt, shame.

"For her getting polio?" John asked. "How could that possibly be?"

"Remember that summer? Nineteen fifty-five."

"Sure, the newspaper called it the 'summer of fear,'" he said.

"The vaccine was already out there but we didn't get it in time. I think about that a lot—there was already a vaccine, for God's sake. She didn't have to die." Charlie was still looking at the rink, at Ria, a quick learner, skating around and around, the winter before she died. "Everyone was afraid. You remember." She turned back to face him. He was listening in that still way he had. It calmed her. She went on. "They closed all the parks. They canceled the county fair. A week or so before Ria got sick, I took her to get ice cream. She asked me to push her on the swing, across the street from the ice cream shop, at the park."

She took a sip of coffee. It smelled old and tasted bitter and burnt.

"I brought her there. So stupid. We were the only ones there. I pushed her on the swing. She was so happy she laughed out loud the whole time.

We could see the river from those swings. We could see the valley and the school. She said she could see the whole world."

~

She'd loved to swing high. It was why Charlie had given into her that day during the polio scare when she'd begged to ride the swings at the park. It was during the last week she was healthy.

A few days later, she got sick. They were at home, playing down by the river, skipping stones on the surface.

"You go first." Ria's smile showed her missing front teeth. A stripe of blackberry jam from breakfast marked her cheek. Charlie picked up one of the stones they'd collected from the field and flicked it sideways, so it skipped a few times before sinking into the summer calm water. Ria tossed hers and it landed just short of the water, in the muddy grass and cattails lining the bank. They skipped stones for the next half hour, until Ria sat down on the bench, her yellow romper covered in streaks of dirt and grass stains.

"My legs hurt." She rubbed her forehead where blonde curls glistened in the sunlight. She did look tired. On her cheeks were bright-red splotches Charlie had never seen before, and her eyes were half-closed. Maybe the heat was getting to her. Dad said you could get heatstroke from playing in the sun too long.

"Come on, Ria." Charlie grabbed the basket and reached for her hand. "Let's go back to the house."

They walked up the hill. By the time they got to the porch, Ria was complaining that her arms hurt. "Everything hurts," she said when Charlie sat her on the couch.

Mom was still in bed, so Charlie walked upstairs, her heart pounding in fear for Ria, who was crying now.

"Ria's not feeling so good," she told Mom. Her room was like an oven. The small fan did nothing to help.

"Probably just a cold coming on." Mom turned over so her back was to Charlie. Tears stung fast in the space behind her eyeballs. She felt so alone now. Dad was over in Fremont fishing.

"Mom, Ria is sick," Charlie yelled, fear and confusion urging her into the room. She tugged the white cotton sheet covering her mom. "Please."

"Okay, I'm coming."

It felt like hours before Mom finally got up. She was fully dressed in a blue sundress that hung on her slight frame.

Charlie grabbed her hand and hurried her downstairs, where Ria was on the couch, slumped on her side now from a seated position, her plump little legs askew. Mom put the back of her hand to Ria's forehead.

"She's burning up. Quick, let's get her to the hospital."

From the look in Mom's eyes and her sharp tone, Charlie knew she was scared.

It hadn't been just a cold.

~

A nurse passed them in the hallway head down, purpose in her step. "Later that night, Dad told us the county fair had been canceled. They were telling people to stay away from public places. I shouldn't have taken her there. I never told my parents."

Charlie closed her eyes to hide the vision from her memory, but all she could see was herself searching for Lucy, snow falling on the piles of logs, the abandoned trailer.

"I let Ria down. How could I let it happen again with Lucy?"

"You think your sister died because you took her to the park?" John pushed his hair back from his face. "You think it's your fault Rick left Lucy alone?"

She nodded. "I took Ria to the park. I knew about Rick. He's unreliable. None of this would have happened if I'd just . . ."

"If you just what, Charlie?" John stood perfectly still, then placed his hand on the side of her face and leaned in.

"Protected them." She blinked away tears and felt his warm hand on her face.

"You can't control everything, Charlie. Shit happens," John said.

She looked past him and saw herself alone now on the ice rink outside, skating under the light post.

He continued, "Ria died from polio. And I will tell you this: she died knowing her sister loved her."

"I miss you," Charlie said, leaning into him and planting her forehead on his shoulder.

He wrapped his arms around her and rubbed her back. "Me too."

Chapter 41

"I'm thirsty," Lucy said in a small voice. It was midnight. John was gone.

"Here, sweetie." Charlie held the cup of water for her and steadied the straw. The room was stuffy and hot. With the shades drawn, it felt like a cocoon.

"The kitten was so cute. She was skinny. I tried to bring her back to the motel, Mom. Do you know where she is?"

"Probably still roaming." Charlie placed her cheek next to Lucy's and held it there.

"Can we go back and get her?" She seemed unfazed.

"We'll see." She kissed Lucy's forehead.

"That means yes." Lucy grinned.

"It means we'll try."

Rick came into the room wearing a bandage on his nose.

"Daddy, I'm sorry I left the motel room. Are you mad?"

"No, Lucy, I'm just glad you're feeling better."

"What happened to your nose?"

"It was an accident," Rick said. "I made a mistake, a big one."

Lucy looked at Charlie. "Why are you crying, Mom?"

They sat together, the three of them, and talked about feral kittens, about New York and how they'd visit, and about the worsening storm. Lucy soon got tired and drifted off to sleep. Charlie needed to talk to Rick, even though he'd just screwed up royally and had a swollen nose. This was only the latest in a series of crises that had become their life together.

~

A couple of times during their marriage, Rick left home and would be gone for days. One of those times, when Charlie was pregnant with Lucy, she went to his friend Clark's house on a hunch that he would be there.

Charlie drove the thirty miles west from Milwaukee and pulled up to the house on a cold afternoon in spring. Rick's truck was parked in the driveway along with several other vehicles. A dreary sky hung low over winter-weary corn fields surrounding the house and barn. Everything was dirt colored, brown and gray, and even the grass was a dull mustard color. There were goats, fenced in next to the barn, standing deadly still, a look of expectation on their long-nosed faces, waiting for spring to really come.

Charlie pulled her tired, pregnant body out of the car, walked up to the front door, and knocked. A skinny hound dog trotted out from the back of the house and sniffed her coat. When no one answered her knock, she pushed the door open and stepped inside. Massaging the tightness in her belly, she continued into the kitchen, following the sound of voices and laughter. Around the table sat Rick, Clark, a guy she didn't know, and two women, one of whom was sitting on Rick's lap.

"What the hell?" Rick's hair was greasy, and he was unshaven, giving him a tired, seedy look.

"Hey, babe, what are you doing here?" he asked.

The woman got off his lap and walked out of the room, hunched over as if this posture would render her invisible. She was so young, college age, Charlie almost felt pity for her.

"Looking for you," she told him. "Or did you forget about me?"

How could he just leave for days? Especially when she needed him most?

~

With Lucy sleeping now, Charlie and Rick walked into the hallway.

"Do you remember the day I went out to Clark's farmhouse and found you there, drunk, with some girl sitting on your lap?"

"Come on, you're going to bring that up now?" Rick asked. "Is this when I have to answer for everything I've done wrong?" He ran his hand through his hair. "I guess I deserve it. But so you know, you can't make me feel any worse than I already feel."

"I brought it up because I was wondering if you remembered what you said to me that day. When I asked you if you forgot about me."

"Don't do this, Charlie." He ran his hand over his face, wincing when he touched his nose.

"I'll tell you what you said, Rick. You said, 'You are the only thing that keeps me from killing myself.'"

"I know I put a lot on you. But it wasn't just me. You never want to admit your part in this. Home for you wasn't with me. It was always here."

"Maybe." She supposed he was right. "But I stayed."

"I never wanted to hurt you," he said.

"I know," she said. "I loved you."

"And now?" he asked.

Charlie crossed her arms. "Now," she whispered, "I can't anymore."

"I'm sorry," he said.

Charlie nodded, turned around, and, without looking back, walked into Lucy's room, knowing this time was different. This time there was no question about it. She was leaving him. Staying because of her sense of loyalty to him was holding her back from what she was trying to accomplish. Maybe seeing how he'd put Lucy in such danger tonight had helped her finally realize she could not control what he did. She never could. She could only control what she did next. It was time to break away. She could feel it with every part of her brain and body. It was the same way she knew when the heated milk reached just the right consistency, set and ready to cut. At that moment, she always felt a little bit of fear of being wrong, but mostly she felt excitement for the next phase. The secret was knowing the right moment, and then calling it.

A clean break.

Chapter 42

Charlie was reluctant to leave Lucy, but she needed to check on the factory. Rick dozing in the chair next to Lucy's bed and hospital staff checking on her every half hour would keep her safe. One night to monitor her and she could come home.

As she drove to the house, the snow fell so fast and heavy that the windshield wipers couldn't keep up. She'd been in whiteouts before, and this felt like one, with snow piling up on the road in front of her and on both sides, no discernable demarcation between where the road ended and the corn fields began.

Her fifteen-minute drive stretched into forty before she finally pulled into the driveway. Larry had already plowed, though almost an inch of snow already covered the areas he'd cleared. As she hiked over to the factory, snow pelted her face. The temperature was dropping fast. Inside, she checked on the generator, relieved it was still running. If it broke now, there would be little time before the temperature inside the aging cellar would drop to levels that could ruin the whole batch of white cheddar along with all the cheese curds they'd packaged and stored in the refrigerators upstairs in the store.

Strong gusts of wind made it hard to walk back to the house, but an eerie quiet greeted her when she finally let herself inside. In the shower, Lucy's blood on her arms and hands changed the clear water to pink and spiraled down the drain. Despite the hot shower, her muscles screamed when she sat down at the kitchen table to eat a sandwich, and weariness took over. Pushing away thoughts of the hospital bills she was going to have to pay because they had no health insurance, Charlie stretched her arm out on the table and rested her head.

$\sim$

Mom was sitting at the kitchen table. "Please talk to me," Charlie pleaded with her. "I'm supposed to go to school."

Mom turned her head toward Charlie in slow motion, like she was underwater. She stared through her, searching for something. "You're not Victoria," she said.

"No, Mom. Ria's gone."

Her mother looked around the kitchen still searching, her eyes heavy-lidded and absent. She used to be so pretty, but now she looked like a different person. Her face and neck were strikingly thin. Mom got up, walked toward the door, and opened it, ignoring the blast of cold air.

"Don't go out there!" Charlie cried. Without looking back, her mom walked away into the frozen winter, wearing only her red robe. Charlie ran after her, desperate to catch up, but each time she got closer, Mom moved further away.

"Mom, Ria's gone," she shouted, and her voice echoed off the far shore of the river.

Above Charlie, a hawk circled.

"But I'm still here," she yelled, and the hawk swooped down, flying alongside her as she ran, getting nowhere.

~

"Charlie."

She pulled herself awake from the nightmare.

It was John. A light dusting of snow covered his shoulders.

Fear from the dream lingered.

"I'll get you some water."

"No, don't." Charlie stood up and placed her hands inside his open jacket. "Just hold me."

"Come here." He wrapped his arms around her, and she glued herself to his chest. He wore a soft sweater that smelled like pine needles. When he bent down and found her lips, his mouth was warm. They kissed.

"I need to tell you something." She led him into the living room.

"Okay." He looked worried.

"I told Rick it was over. I left him." Charlie stared at a photo on the bookcase next to the television set. John had taken it with her camera. On the rocks next to the Brule River, her younger self sat, half-turned toward him, messy curls framing her face with a questioning expression. It was the last time she'd seen John, back in college, before meeting Rick.

"You left him," John repeated, and suddenly it seemed more real.

"All those times I went back to him. The last time he told me he'd quit drinking, after Lucy turned four, lasted two months. Then he started again. Hiding it from me. Then he goes to the VA last month and stays for three days. I was stupid to think I could help him."

"You're not stupid," John said. "You tried."

"You're right." Charlie closed her eyes and felt odd. "I tried. It's weird. I feel nothing, no responsibility for him, no need to check on him. This is new."

"He'll find his way, or maybe he won't."

"Without me, either way," Charlie said, tired of talking about Rick. "Let's sit. I'm cold."

As they sat on the couch, John shook his coat off, reached over, and pulled the quilt off the back of the couch, placing it over both of them.

"When I came in, you were crying," John said, moving closer.

"I was dreaming about Mom walking into the river. I ran after her but couldn't reach her."

"Just keep telling yourself Lucy's okay. You made sure of that." John pulled her hair back and kissed her temple.

"Thank God," she murmured.

"You must have *someone* watching over you," John said. "I'd like to help with that."

She thought of how he'd come to the hospital, of the hawk gliding above her in her dream. "You are," she whispered.

Charlie looked into his eyes, the color of brown earth, as she slowly removed her sweater and unbuttoned and took off her blouse. "I'm ready," she told him.

He kissed her shoulder, then her breasts. She grabbed the bottom of his sweater, and they lifted it over his head. She traced the tattoo on his bicep, a hawk he'd gotten in high school. She had always liked it. She ran her hand down his chest, his firm stomach.

"I've wanted to do this for a long time," he whispered. "Since Brule River."

"Me too."

"Is this okay?" he asked.

She nodded. "Can't you feel my heart pounding?"

"Mine is too." He smiled and placed her hand on his chest.

"The way you look at me," she said.

"I've always looked at you this way."

Chapter 43

Brule River. Over the eight years since they had been there, it had taken on the feel of a dream—something she'd imagined, hoped for, and now visited in small bits and pieces of memory, like snapshots, separate frames of discontinuous time. The whole episode felt unreal—the canoe ride when John had guided them expertly through the river rapids, swimming in the river, that night in the back of the truck, watching the stars and searching for the Northern Lights.

It was the summer between junior and senior year in college. A group of them—Jenny, Pete, Faye, John, and others—had set up camp on the banks of the river up in Florence County in the Nicolet National Forest. Five tents, a campfire, and canoes were scattered about.

The second day, John announced he was going canoeing. "Want to come?"

Charlie stared at him, still trying to get used to the way he'd changed from chubby kid to handsome, square-jawed, and fit young man.

"Sure."

Later the group of eight dwindled to four, and then, by midnight, to two. They took John's truck to an isolated back country dirt road where the sky was wide, and they could see its entirety laid out like a big, blinking tarp—like it had been there, waiting to demonstrate just how beautiful the universe could be. They sat in the back of the pickup sipping beers.

"Remember in grade school, that first year I moved here?"

"I remember."

"You know how you were, like wounded. Your sister died, and you were trying to be strong, but I could tell you were so sad. And I was like an outsider. But you were nice. So, what I wanted to tell you is, thank you."

"For what?"

"You were never mean."

They laughed.

"That's all? I was never mean?"

"You were a good friend."

"Well, you and Jenny were the only ones who came around me."

"We needed each other."

"What do you want to do after college?" Charlie asked.

"I want to teach. Start a program where I take kids up the Boundary Waters. Teach them how to canoe long distances." Charlie noticed he didn't hesitate. He knew what he wanted.

"What do you want?" he asked.

"I've been thinking. I want to research infectious disease, work toward a cure for cancer and other diseases. Or maybe come back to Falls River to work with Dad, make cheese."

"So first, find a cure for cancer, then come home and work with your dad. Cool. Then we could be together." In the lights cast from the stars, Charlie could see his face, the way he looked at her.

～

"You looked at me like I was all you needed back then," Charlie said now.

"You're still that." He pushed himself up on his arms and focused his eyes on hers. "Don't go away this time."

She wrapped her legs around him, felt him close, as close as they'd been on that country road back in college. "Are you kidding me? I'm not going anywhere."

～

An hour later, a blast of wind whistled through the eaves and woke Charlie. Something wasn't right.

"Can you hear that?" she asked. John was half-asleep. She pushed herself up from his chest.

"It's the wind whistling through the holes in the window frames," John said. "This place definitely needs some work."

"Not that." She shot up from the couch. "I can't hear the generator." She pulled on her shirt and walked over to the window.

Through the trees and blowing snow, she could see the cheese factory. And through its north window, a mass of flames glowed inside—orange, yellow, red, alive with heat.

209

"It's on fire! What the hell?" She turned to John. He hopped over on one foot, trying to get his pants on.

"Oh my God, the factory, the trees," Charlie yelled.

"The generator must have blown up. Call the fire department."

She ran to the phone in the kitchen, stumbled over a footstool, caught her balance with the wall, felt around for the light switch, flipped it on, and grabbed the phone.

"It's dead," she yelled. "The lines are down."

John pulled on his coat. "I'm going over to Larry's. We'll get everyone."

Charlie ran outside, panic spreading between her shoulders. John caught up with her. He had somehow managed to grab her coat and boots. She was barefoot and held onto his arm for balance as she quickly plunged her feet into her boots.

"Do not go in there, Charlie." John wrapped her coat around her and held her shoulders. "Promise me."

"I won't," she promised, although she wanted to go in. She wanted to run into the factory and rescue Dad's notebooks, the new cheese presses, the rennet and cultures. She knew the vats were too heavy to lift on her own.

John didn't take time to brush off the snow piled up on the truck. He sped off fast, his tires plowing through drifts and snow flying off his windshield, creating a whirling cyclone of white.

Charlie stood in the driveway and watched the fire inside the old barn grow from flames licking at the windows on the first floor to a wild wall of fire engulfing the beams in the upper loft, visible through the second-story window. Black smoke spewed from the roof. Gusts of wind fanned the flames.

With the shattering of glass and a loud roar, the north wall collapsed, sending vibrations through the soles of her feet like an earthquake. Rafters hung suspended on the diagonal, offering themselves to the tinderbox below. Now the fire was exposed to the trees, and flames licked at the branches of the pines that towered over the factory. For the first time that evening, she was thankful for the snow piled in frosted clumps on the pine boughs, keeping the trees from catching fire. She knew that if they caught, the house would go too. Her face grew hot, and she smelled the barn burn, the wood timbers Dad used to shore up the structure in the early 1950s. He'd repurposed the entire barn, adding rooms, the aging cellar, the store, and the cheesemaking operation that took up the bulk of the space.

It hit her like a fist then—the cheese in the aging cellar was ruined, and the blocks on their pine boards were surely burning right now. Morgan Cheese was going up in smoke. Needing to do something besides just watch, she grabbed the snow shovel from the porch and began lifting up snow and throwing it at the side of the house. She hauled and tossed snow until her arms ached. Finally, sirens screamed in the distance, quiet at first, then louder. Relief was brief before smoke, black and noxious, burned her lungs and brought her to her knees in a spasm of coughing.

"Come on out of there." Larry helped her up from the ground in front of the burning frame. They ran into the house. When they got to the kitchen, Larry poured her a glass of water.

"Stay here." He gave her a worried look.

"I'm fine. You go; just be careful."

"We got this," he yelled, running outside, eager to help fight the fire. Charlie watched through the window, gulping down water and deep breaths of clean air. The driveway was crowded now with two fire trucks, a water truck, and several vans and pickup trucks. Volunteer firefighters shouted orders, dragged the hoses, and sprayed the barn from all angles, letting loose great walls of water pure and fierce until the fire was extinguished.

It took such a short time to wipe out everything Dad had built. In a few hours, the factory was gone. There was nothing left but a smoldering heap of charred, wet lumber.

Chapter 44

Charlie, John, Larry, and some of the other firefighters stayed up all night, watching to make sure the fire didn't reignite. When the sun rose, it shone a harsh light on the remains of the factory. With the help of John and Larry, Charlie surveyed the wreckage before leaving for the hospital to get Lucy. Where the office had been, Dad's desk was a shadow. Gone. Notebooks and everything. She was sad to lose them but not panicked because she'd memorized the most important recipes.

Nothing was left of the store. The wood shelves and everything on them—Karen's baskets, crackers, jam, maple syrup—were gone. In the factory, cheese presses were scattered about the floor, destroyed. Standing stalwart were the vats, covered in ashes. Bits and pieces that were tools of the trade were melted to the cement floor—her thermometers, skimmers, and curd knives. She picked up a tester and gripped it, black with soot. Overwhelmed, Charlie tossed it onto the floor.

A gaping hole had replaced the stairs to the aging cellar, where she could see the cheese was gone. The pine boards must have acted like kindling. This hit her hard.

"It's a total loss, I'm afraid," Larry said.

"At least we saved the trees." Charlie looked up at the tall pines singed in places but intact.

"And the house." John nodded at the house, still standing; the snow shovel she had used was abandoned where she'd left it. Snow was everywhere, trampled down by the boots of the volunteers, piled higher in the woods.

"What should I do? Holy stinking shit, will my bad luck never end?" She felt numb and overwhelmed. Everything they had built was destroyed.

"You can rebuild," Larry said.

"How? The place was not insured. So stupid. Dad had let it lapse, and I didn't renew. It was just one more thing on a long list."

She almost started laughing hysterically. This was so unbelievable. "Should I go back to Milwaukee?" Charlie asked herself quietly, but they heard her.

"That is a bad idea on so many levels," John said. He stood next to her. She was grateful for his unwavering presence.

"You can't walk away, Charlie," Larry said. "You were just getting started."

"Well, I need a new cheesemaking operation, and time, none of which I have right now. I have to go back to court in a few weeks, remember? Judge Flynn wants a progress report. Casper wants this land. We saved the trees for him." The irony wasn't lost on her. Casper Raines would get the land and the trees he wanted.

"I need to get Lucy," she said. John placed his hand on the back of her head.

"We'll take care of this," he said. "I'll get some guys over here, get an estimate for the cleanup."

"You guys are the last thing holding me together, so be careful here," she told them.

"Give our love to Lucy," Larry called as she walked to the truck, feeling pain in every joint.

Exhausted, Charlie started up the truck. On the radio, a reporter's serious tone caught her attention. She paused and listened. He was talking about last night's storm, how a freighter loaded with iron ore sank on Lake Superior near Sault Ste. Marie. Out on the lake, the storm had carried hurricane-force winds and swells up to thirty-five feet. The reporter said no one was rescued. All on board were feared lost. Charlie turned onto Cricket Road, shaken by the news. Having lost the factory in the storm, she felt a kinship with the men. What if the house had caught fire? What if she hadn't awakened in time? She'd lost property and inventory. The men on that freighter, the Edmund Fitzgerald, had lost so much more.

At the hospital parking lot, she turned off the truck and dug through her purse for the notes she'd taken when she'd talked to the nurse earlier. "Lucy's doing fine," the nurse had said. "We've moved her to a different room." Sure she'd shoved the note somewhere in her purse, she pushed aside her brush, wallet, and the roll of lifesavers, Lucy's new favorite candy. Shit, where was it? She dumped the purse out on the passenger seat. "Scheisse!" she yelled. Tears she'd held back since discovering the fire escalated into sobs. She gripped the steering wheel and cried. Bad things came in threes. Dad dying, Lucy getting hurt, the fire. That's three. That's enough. How many other things could go wrong? She slowly picked up the stuff from the passenger seat and placed it in her purse. Pulling herself together, she pushed the door open. She'd find Lucy without the note.

Chapter 45

"Mom!" Lucy's small body was dwarfed in an adult-sized wheelchair pushed by a nurse. "I got a ride."

"Nice wheels." Charlie was relieved to see her out of the hospital bed, smiling, with color in her cheeks.

"She didn't need one, but she insisted," the nurse said. Lucy jumped up and flung her arms around Charlie. It felt so good to hold her tight.

"She's doing fine, just needs to finish the antibiotics," the nurse told Charlie. "Her dad left a half hour ago. You take care, Charlie. Let me know if I can help out in any way."

"That's kind of you." Charlie was relieved Rick was gone.

The nurse turned to Lucy and gave her a pat on the cheek. "Now don't go chasing any more kittens, sweet pea."

In the car, Charlie explained what had happened in the fire.

"How'd they put it out?" Lucy asked.

"There were fire hoses and loads of firemen."

"Could it start again?"

"No way; it was a bad generator along with the snowstorm." Charlie tried to reassure her, knowing her questions were because of anxiety. Actually, she wasn't sure if the fire had been caused by the generator or the old wiring pointed out by Red, the electrician. Larry said it could have been a combination of both.

At home, John and Larry were still sorting through the wreckage. Charlie and Lucy waved to the guys and went into the house. From the windows upstairs, they watched them as Charlie ran a bath for Lucy.

"What happened to all the cheese?" Lucy sat in the bathtub in two inches of water, so her gauze-wrapped arm would stay dry.

"It burned in the fire." Charlie remained calm and downplayed the fire so Lucy wouldn't worry too much.

"How are we going to make cheese now?" Charlie saw the wheels start to turn, the focused stare, the barrage of questions. When she was anxious, Lucy had to fix things. She was like Charlie that way.

"I don't know." She soaped up her little body and rinsed her off, careful to avoid the gauze-covered sutures on her arm.

"I wonder."

"What, honey?"

"Can we make cheese in the kitchen like we did in Milwaukee?"

"Kitchen cheese." Charlie humored her, not letting on that she had no energy left to even contemplate her next steps.

"We don't need the living room either, Mom. All we do is watch TV in there."

"Hmm."

"Can we press the cheese in the living room?"

"Maybe."

"What about the basement?"

"What about it?" It was hard to follow what she was saying. All Charlie could think about was last night, John, making love, the fire, what she'd lost. At least Dad wasn't here to see the factory destroyed.

"We make the aging cellar down there. It's gross and dirty, but we can clean it. Mom?" Lucy's face was an inch from her own.

"What?"

"I said, can we give out samples of cheese at the Piggly Wiggly like the donut lady? The one with the big mole on her cheek Larry says looks like the state of Michigan? She gives out samples of chocolate cinnamon swirl donuts, the gooey ones, you know, Mom. Can we ask the Piggly Wiggly people, Mom, can we?"

"Sure, we can ask." It would be going through the motions. Even if they made the cheese at the house, they would still need equipment. It was so much to think about, her head hurt.

Lucy stood up in a cascade of water dripping off her small body. Charlie wrapped her in a towel, picked her up like she used to when she was younger, and carried her into her room. After Charlie helped her put on her pajamas, they got into Lucy's bed and snuggled.

Losing the cheese factory and her marriage felt like small potatoes compared to almost losing Lucy. Almost losing her—the thought sent Charlie's body shaking, first with a slight tremor, then violently, without volition. Was she going nuts? Careful not to wake Lucy, she slipped out of the bed and onto the floor, wrapped her arms around her legs, and lay there.

Chapter 46

Charlie spent the next few days taking care of Lucy and watching Larry and Daniel operate the backhoes, moving debris into dumpsters and cutting up the larger beams with chainsaws. She helped whenever possible, but Lucy was clingier than usual and followed her around everywhere. The doctor advised Charlie to keep her home for a week or so to heal.

After several days, the cement foundation was nearly empty. Larry and Daniel left after that and went up to the co-op. With the factory gone, Daniel had found another job milking at the co-op.

Charlie pulled out paints to pass the time. Lucy painted the kitten in all sorts of situations—huddled under a trailer, chasing fireflies on the edge of the woods, curled next to a snowman. They'd looked for the kitten one afternoon but had no luck finding her. Lucy insisted on naming her, painting her, and reminiscing about her like an old friend.

Charlie painted images of Dad and her younger self huddled over cheese vats exposed to a sky that was raining curds so cheese flowed through towns, woods, and cities, carrying people along in their current. Nostalgia had brought her to tears a few times that week, and she'd find herself staring out the window at the space where the factory had stood, thinking about the days when Larry delivered milk and they'd make cheese all day; thinking about how she'd help Dad stack cheese in the old, refrigerated coolers for tourists and townies; thinking about the times she'd roller-skated around the factory on the smooth cement floors.

When she wasn't painting with Lucy or helping clear out debris, she was making phone calls and pricing equipment. "I need over two thousand dollars to replace the equipment," Charlie told John on the phone. "What made me think I could do this?"

"Maybe I can help you. I got some savings."

"No, you have enough to worry about." She couldn't burden him with her debt. Most days after teaching and on weekends, he worked on his house.

Jake called several times from Chicago, telling her he'd help her rebuild, but she wasn't sure she wanted to. The last few months had been such a struggle. Bitterness had replaced her enthusiasm. As a woman, she'd had to fight harder just to get onto the playing field, and now she needed to build a whole new factory. It was mind-blowing. Finally, she stopped answering the phone, stopped going outside, stopped doing anything but taking care of Lucy. When, after a week, the doctor said Lucy could go back to school, Charlie was relieved. Lucy didn't need to see her this way. In the morning, Charlie dragged herself out of bed, got Lucy on the bus, and went back to bed. In the afternoon, she'd shuffle around the house for a while, then watch *I Love Lucy* reruns for a few hours before Lucy got home. Jenny called several times to offer her moral support, but as a new mom she sounded overwhelmed and tired.

Nights were the hardest. She couldn't sleep, and the darkness intensified her ruminations about failure, stuck on a loop that started with Ria and Mom and moved on to embarrassment about her failed marriage, to fears that whatever she did would end in destruction and that, if she tried to rebuild the factory, something would happen to sabotage her efforts. Why try? Underneath it all was the voice that screamed, "You're becoming your mother!"

After two weeks of this malaise, Charlie became antsy and bored. She needed to pull herself out of this funk. She told herself to get moving. Get busy. She was determined to accomplish something and decided a good place to start was upstairs in Dad's room, organizing his clothes and personal belongings. She cried when she folded his white cotton pants and shirts, piled his suspenders in a box, and stripped the sheets from his bed. She was glad Lucy had a playdate with a friend after school today. She taped up the box and decided to tackle the closet in the living room. Downstairs, she hauled out several boxes of photographs and memorabilia saved from when she was in elementary school: old report cards, Mother's Day drawings, pictures she and Ria had made of Christmas trees and snowmen, and several of her old notebooks.

She found a photo of Mom sitting in a chair with Charlie standing next to her, laughing. Mom was looking at her with so much love, it took her breath away. Curious, Charlie searched through other boxes of photos with urgency. She'd always wondered if Mom had ever been happy here in Falls River.

One box held a series of photos of Dad and Mom and their friends. One photo was from a New Year's party from 1950 with Walter and Ruth, Larry, Uncle Jack, and other people she didn't recognize. Everyone, even Mom, looked so young and happy. Charlie studied her face for any traces of melancholy and found none. Her mother had a wide smile, standing next to Dad, her hair in victory curls, wearing a New Year's hat. Another photo showed Dad, Mom, and their friends the Vandercooks at what looked like a picnic on the river. Another showed Mom and Mrs. Vandercook bundled up in winter clothing, wearing ice skates and standing near the rink piled high on all sides with snow. Charlie had known Mom and Mrs. Vandercook were friends, but, from the number of photos of them together, it appeared they'd been close.

She dug further into the box of photos. In an envelope marked "Victoria" was a series of pictures from when Ria was a baby. Charlie was shocked: Mom looked so different. She was thin, and, when there was a smile, it was strained.

Charlie rummaged through the depths of the closet and pulled out an old Sears box covered in dust. She opened it and gasped.

Folded carefully, smelling musty, was Mom's robe.

It was the robe she'd worn the morning she walked into the river.

Chapter 47

It was four months after Charlie's time raccoon hunting with Larry and seven months after Ria died. She woke up, swung her legs around the side of the bed, and could tell before her feet hit the floor that it was colder than usual. Strange. Normally on Saturday mornings, she slept late, but not this late, and why was it so cold? Dad always woke early and built fires in the kitchen stove and the fireplace in the front room. By the time Charlie woke up, the heat would have warmed her room next to the kitchen. Not today. Today she blew out two quick puffs and could see her breath. She put on a sweater and wool pants over her long underwear.

Charlie hurried into the kitchen and yelled for Dad. The house was eerily quiet. At the window above the sink, she noticed frost had formed on the inside edges, but she could see out to the river and beyond to the frozen hills on the other side. A feeling something bad had happened caused a tingling sensation in her extremities. Mom had been getting worse with every passing day.

Charlie struggled into her coat and boots and ran outside, calling for Dad, for Mom. No one answered. Her sense of dread increased. She'd had this feeling for the past month. Whenever she'd tried to talk about it, her mother just stared past her and would not even respond or would say, "Ask your dad," or, if she was in bed, just roll aside, putting her back to Charlie. She had stopped eating, and Dad said he was taking her to the Mayo Clinic in Rochester.

Charlie ran down to the river. There, the strong current that flowed in the middle section had pushed chunks of ice against the shore. The thawing and refreezing had created an arctic landscape of haphazard, jumbled ice plates with jagged ridges that looked like miniature mountain peaks. Charlie knew not to walk out on it. She'd heard plenty of stories about some poor, hapless ice fisherman or stupid kid falling through the ice.

She scanned the river, looking north, then south. Where were they? Something was desperately wrong. Images of Mom flashed through her mind: Mom sitting on the couch, pulling at the edges of her blanket; at the kitchen table, pushing her fork around her plate, not really eating.

Sobs escaped from Charlie as she ran south along the river's edge, the bitter wind stinging her cheeks. Finally, she saw him. Dad was crawling on his hands and knees on the uneven ice along the shore.

She saw Mom then, floating in water and ice chunks not far from where Dad kneeled, her body covered in a red robe, the one she wore all the time.

"Mom," she screamed, her own voice deep and raw, a sound she didn't recognize.

"Charlie," Dad yelled as he grasped Mom's arm and yanked her toward him. She looked frozen. Unresponsive. "Get help. Have the switchboard call the ambulance."

Charlie stared at Mom, unable to move her legs to run and get help like Dad wanted. A low moan came from somewhere inside her.

"Charlie, go," Dad yelled.

She turned and ran, her cries of "help" echoing in the bleak morning stillness. She slipped on the ice-crusted grass and fell to her knees. Snot streamed out her nose. If I don't make it in time, she thought, Mom will die. She dragged herself up and sprinted the final yards to the front porch. Inside, she picked up the phone with shaking hands and yelled to the operator that they needed an ambulance. Just as she placed the receiver in its cradle, the door flew open. Dad carried Mom to the living room couch, the same one Ria had laid on before she went to the hospital. Water dripped from her tangled hair. Dad covered her with the handmade blanket she'd knitted herself. It was strange how peaceful she looked—her colorless lips, her wide, unseeing eyes. Dad sat next to her and held her for a long time while Charlie sat on the floor with her hands wrapped around her knees and watched, shivering.

For some reason, her mind turned to the stories Mom had told her about her name, how she had named her after Charlotte Bronte, her favorite author. Charlie had looked up the Bronte sisters in the encyclopedia at school and was surprised to read that Charlotte had lost her sisters to tuberculosis and her mother to cancer when she was a young girl. This realization only added to her fear.

Charlie looked over at Mom. Dad had pulled the blanket around her face, so she could only see her nose and a part of her cheeks. Her skin was white, as white as the snow-covered ice on the river.

When the ambulance came, they checked Mom's pulse and couldn't find one. Foam oozed from her mouth. Charlie screamed her name over and over, begging her to wake up, but she lay limp on the couch. When the EMTs moved to pick up Mom, Dad pushed them out of the way. "I'll do it." He slid his arms under her and lifted her from the couch as drops of water fell off her tangled hair and her robe onto the living room floor, like tears from the river.

~

Now Charlie ran her hand over the robe. It was still soft. She considered what had led Mom to the river that night. After having sunk into her own wide sadness, Charlie had a better understanding of how Mom must have felt when depression took away all her energy, leaving her exhausted, unable to cope.

A sudden, loud noise echoed in the silence, its low essence booming through the stillness. There was no denying it was a gunshot, which wasn't unusual in this community of hunters. Was Raines lurking around? Stiff from sitting so long, Charlie got up from the couch and walked to the front door. Down by the river was a man with a rifle. What the heck? Someone was hunting on their property. Ignoring the voice in her head telling her it wasn't safe to follow a gunshot, she grabbed her down jacket and pulled on her boots.

Chapter 48

Charlie opened the door and stepped onto the porch. Mounds of snow surrounded what remained of the cheese factory: a pile of Lannon stone, some bricks, pipes Larry was saving for a guy he knew who made sculptures from junk metal. There was a dumpster nearly full of cheesemaking equipment and charred pine boards from the aging cellar. In the driveway sat Dad's truck, her Volkswagen, and Daniel's old Chevy truck that wouldn't start. Crossing the yard, she followed a trail someone, probably Larry, had cleared to the river. A few feet from the river, she stopped. Wind rustled through the bare tree branches. The current rushed with the wind, heading north to Green Bay.

"Hey," someone yelled. She recognized the voice. When she looked down the path to the north, she saw him: Casper Raines, just a few yards from her. He was holding a rifle.

Charlie stood her ground as he approached her, keeping her eyes on the rifle, which he held under his arm, pointing downward. Was he going to shoot her? She saw the way he'd looked at her in court, like he despised her. What reason could he possibly have for showing up here? She was beginning to think he was a stalker. She wanted him to leave her alone.

"What are you doing here?" Charlie scanned the area. The midafternoon light was dull and the air held an expectant feeling. More snow was on the way. "I've seen you on our property before. For all I know, you burned down the factory."

Casper walked closer to her. "Are you kidding me?" He looked genuinely surprised. "I was visiting my dad that night."

"I hope you can prove that."

"I signed in. He'd had a fall. They all know I was there."

"So, what are you doing here now?"

"I'm hunting. Walking. Trying to clear my head."

"Don't hunt on our land."

"Your land." He snickered. "This land should be mine. My dad sold it to your dad for five lousy bucks."

This surprised her. She had found the article about the sale of Benny's woods in the newspaper when she went to Madison, but there was no mention of price. Still, she believed him. Shit. It made sense. It explained why he was trying to get the land back, why he was sizing up the trees that day she saw him.

"Why did he do that?" She was determined to figure out the nature of their fathers' connection. "I know they were in the war together."

"My dad told me he got your pop out of a jam in the war, saved his ass," Casper said. "It's why your dad never did anything when my dad beat the shit out of me. You were there; you saw it."

Casper shifted his rifle from his right arm to under his left arm. It dawned on her. He'd seen her that day at the old sawmill.

"I did," she admitted. "You were holding something in your hand." His dad was yelling at him about it. The next moment, he was lying in the dirt, his dad kicking his head with his boot. She winced at the memory.

"I had his car keys. I was trying to keep him from driving because he was drunk," he said.

"We ran and got my dad."

"I remember thinking, Mr. Mayer will help me. He'll stop Dad from beating me up. But your dad didn't call the cops, didn't take me to the hospital. Now that was screwed up. I had a concussion, bruised ribs." Casper closed his eyes for a quick second, opened them, then looked up.

It was snowing, light flakes that hung suspended in the cold air.

"My dad told me he regretted not helping you," she said. "Just before he died."

Casper was quiet for a few seconds. He stared past her at the river. His eyes narrowed. "Really?" The tone of his voice softened.

"He said, 'I should have helped that boy.'" Maybe hearing this would nudge Casper off his monotonous circle of revenge seeking. Though it was a small reckoning for all the abuse he'd endured.

"A little late. Don't you think? There was more after that day you saw. I couldn't concentrate, couldn't finish school. I dropped out."

In his expression, she saw a scared kid who had suffered. Like her. But unlike her, no one had helped him.

"Ah, hell, he's dead now," Casper told her. "He ain't hurting no one anymore."

"He died?"

"This morning."

"I'm sorry for your loss."

Casper nodded to her and in the gesture, she saw the glimpse of what could become a fragile truce.

"I'll head out now." He turned around and gave her a backhanded wave as he walked in the direction of his home.

She stood there for a moment, thinking about how crazy it all was. She was scared of Casper, but from what she could tell, he had spent a good chunk of his life being scared of his own father. She checked behind her and saw truck lights in the driveway near the house. She pulled her hood up against the harsh wind blowing down from Canada.

Chapter 49

When Charlie got back to the house, John was standing on the porch.

"Hey, what are you doing out here?" he asked. "It's freezing."

"Casper was out there." As they stepped inside, she unzipped her coat, took it off, and hung it up on the peg near the door. "He told me his dad died."

"Hmm. Maybe he'll sell everything and leave now," John said. "I heard he lost his license for a year for selling bad milk."

"One year, huh? They went easy on him." She didn't care. She just wanted to put the whole Casper episode behind her. "There was something different about him today. We actually talked. About how his dad owned Benny's woods. After Benny left, Old Man Raines sold the land to Dad for five bucks."

"So that's why he was sizing up the woods back in July," John said.

"Yup, I think so." Charlie took off her boots. "Thanks for coming over." After she said it, she realized how lame it sounded. What she'd really wanted to say was how much she'd missed him. But she was emotionally exhausted.

"I was worried." John placed his hands on his hips and tilted his head.

She stepped into the living room. He followed her. She became aware her hair was a rat's nest of knots, her jeans dirty with dust, and her breath probably smelled like gummy bears, the last thing she'd eaten. They stood in front of the couch, where boxes from the attic sat, spilling out photographs.

"So, what's going on?" he asked. "You haven't answered the phone. Are you okay?"

He clenched his jaw, stuffing his hands in his pockets.

"I'm working on it." Admitting she wasn't okay made her throat tight.

"Tell me what's going on."

"It's everything. Losing Dad. Being so scared when Lucy got hurt. It's Rick, the cheese factory, the fire, not having money."

"It's a lot."

"I loved it, though," she said. "That feeling of being on my own, not having to worry about anyone but Lucy."

"And now?"

"I'm just trying to process everything, and I don't talk about it, ever, but sometimes I get overwhelmed and kind of stuck. It's happened before, like after I had Lucy." Mired in the muck, as Mom used to say.

She continued. "After Mom died, it was hard. But I was a kid. I didn't really process it. Then after Lucy was born, I realized what I had lost." Like the river during a hard rain, her grief rose until it flooded her. "Dad's dying really hit me. I think about all the things he'll miss. All the things Mom missed." Charlie pushed her hair back from her face with both hands. "I don't want Lucy to have to go through that. I want to be there—when she graduates from high school, when she gets married, when she has her first child."

"I want to say you will." His tone was soft, full of empathy.

She nodded. He'd never lie just to make her feel better. She knew there were no guarantees.

John looked around the living room and took his hands out of his pockets. She'd never seen him like this. Then she realized he was holding back tears. "What's with all the boxes? Are you leaving?" He looked up at the ceiling, studying it like a book.

"Leaving?" Was she leaving? Suddenly the thought terrified her—more than rebuilding, more than the risk of failing again. She'd been so obsessed with being independent. She saw all the things she'd miss if she resisted this pull. Toward him. She stepped closer. He lowered his head but didn't touch her. They were so close his coat brushed her hand, and she opened her fingers and reached for it.

"You think you have to go through this alone, Charlie?"

Alone is all I know. She tugged him closer to her. Being alone was okay, but being lonely was getting old. "I don't want to," she said. There, she said it. John reached for her and finally pulled her close. Their bodies came together, their kisses tender. When they pulled apart, he was smiling.

"I was afraid to call," she said. "You've been so busy. I didn't want to burden you. It felt selfish."

"You're in the middle of a shitstorm. I get it." He shook off his coat and tossed it on the couch. "But we can, I don't know . . . dig out together."

She leaned against him, feeling better, the shakiness gone. He rested his arm on her shoulders.

"So, what *is* all this?"

"Old pictures, photos of my mom." She showed him a stack she'd set aside.

He took a long time looking at each photograph. "I like this one." It was the photograph of Mom ice-skating with Mrs. Vandercook. John inspected it, holding it close to his face. "Wow, it's Mrs. Vandercook."

"They were friends," Charlie said.

"You ever talk to her about your mom?"

"I want to. At Dad's funeral lunch, she told me to come and see her, but I haven't with everything going on."

"You should. Maybe she can help you understand what happened with your mom."

Charlie spread out the pile of pictures on the table in front of the couch.

"Wow, look at this one." John picked up the photo of Mom hanging wash on the line.

"I remember that day so vividly." Charlie stood up. "It was summer 1955, shortly before Ria got sick. We were hanging wash, and Dad came and told us the story of how they'd met. They danced. The flowered skirt she was wearing drifted around her legs. He held her hand high, like this." She lifted her right hand, and she turned it this way and that, positioning it just as she'd remembered.

"Like this?" John stood up and took her hand, placing his other hand on her back.

He put his head close to hers.

"They danced the Lindy Hop, real slow, and I could see how much they loved each other," Charlie said, not thinking of Mom and Dad anymore.

Chapter 50

Mrs. Vandercook lived in a small cottage on Main Street twenty miles west of Falls River in Westfield. Charlie remembered her as a vivacious woman older than Mom, quick to laugh, chatting to customers as she sold cheese at the market in the front section of the Vandercook family's cheese factory just outside Falls River. Back then, stepping into the Vandercook factory was thrilling. The market was the entry point, and just ten feet beyond were the cheese vats where her husband and two sons could be seen making cheese six days a week. They'd built the large factory in Westfield when their gouda became so popular they'd needed more room to mass produce and distribute. Mrs. Vandercook's husband, Zeke, died four years earlier, but her sons, Russell and Joseph, still ran the business. Dad and Zeke had been good friends. Dad had learned much about making cheese from Zeke. They'd joke about being competitors, stealing each other's recipes, but really they were two of a kind—both were a unique combination of scientist, artist, and chef.

Charlie knocked. Mrs. Vandercook opened the door right away, as if she'd been waiting on the other side.

"Dear, so good to see you. Come in. I've put out some cookies and made some tea, just like when your mum would come over, and we needed a bit of home. Dutch Windmill cookies and English tea."

"You know I loved your cookies, Mrs. Vandercook," Charlie said. The Dutch speculaas cookies, made with a handful of spices—ginger, nutmeg, cinnamon, cardamom—were the best antidote to anything that had ailed Charlie growing up. Mom had purchased a windmill cutout and learned how to make the cookies from Mrs. Vandercook. She had fuzzy memories of baking the savory treats with Mom. Happy memories.

Mrs. Vandercook guided Charlie into her kitchen, a bright room with a linoleum floor and metal chairs around a table covered in a white lace tablecloth. The teacups were Delft Blue porcelain from the family's native Holland. Charlie sat down and looked out the window at a complex of bird feeders. A cardinal, stark red against the white snow, fed on nuts and seeds at a feeder in the shape of a barn.

"Now, tell me how you've been." Mrs. Vandercook's blue eyes were hooded under droopy lids. Her face had more wrinkles than before, but she still wore her hair in an elegant French twist and dressed in one of her usual flowered house dresses.

"Oh, you know, ups and downs."

"Dear, I said this to your mum years ago and I'll say it to you now, give it to me straight."

Charlie warmed to her kind-hearted, motherly tone. "It's been one road-block after another—getting the cheese factory up and running again."

"I heard about the fire," she said. "Let me know if I can help in any way."

"Thank you, I will." Charlie paused as she poured some tea into her cup. "Getting the money to finance the startup was hard. I got an investor, but I don't want to ask him for money to build a new factory."

Mrs. Vandercook leaned in closer. "Don't you give up, dear. Keep going. They said I couldn't do it after Zeke died. I've been doing this for a long time. I can sure do it without him, though I do miss him terribly."

Charlie smiled, feeling better; she wasn't the only one to take over a family cheese factory. "I found some pictures of you and Mom and had some questions."

"What do you want to know?"

"I remember so little about Mom, only bits and pieces." Charlie plowed ahead and asked something she'd been wondering about for a long time. "What was she like when she first came here?"

"Oh, she was sweet, quiet. We bonded because we were both from Europe. So many were in those days. It wasn't easy for either of us. Zeke and I left Holland just as the Nazis were taking over. A horrible time. As you know, your mum was what they called an English war bride. These girls who met American servicemen, fell in love, and came to America."

"Did she ever talk about London?"

"Oh, yes. She missed it. Her parents, her brother especially. He died in the bombings, you know." She took a sip of tea. "I do believe she loved your father deeply, and she was happy at first even though she was home-sick. We had parties. We'd go bowling, a group of us, and ice-skating.

Gradually she became more comfortable here. But remember, she'd been through the blitz in London, the war; she'd left her family. "

"You left everything too, though, right?"

"I left a country occupied by the Germans. We were lucky to get out."

"When did things change for her?"

Mrs. Vandercook squinted as if she was looking into her memories. "So, when she became pregnant with you, she felt really nostalgic. She was scared to have the baby here. That's why she went back to London to have you. Your dad was worried. I was worried. She had such melancholy, you see. And it was getting worse. Your dad decided the best thing to do was to send her back to her mum. Then, after you were born, she became so sick. That's why she stayed there so long with you. Six months."

"What was wrong with her? I'd never heard exactly why we'd stayed in England after I was born."

"I believe it was the melancholy."

"How was she after she came back?"

"She was better, more herself. She helped in the cheese factory. We'd have our tea afternoons, every week."

"Mom kept the books for Dad around that time. I saw her handwriting in the accounting ledgers."

"She set up the store, really had fun with it," Mrs. Vandercook explained. "She bought the coolers for the cheese, even added a few things made locally like the maple syrup. You'd play at her feet, color pictures as you got older. Then off to help your dad in the factory not long after you started walking."

Charlie was stunned by the revelation that Mom was so involved in the store. It made sense, though; she'd been a cheesemonger.

"She worked in the store about eight years or so. I remember because it was around the time we moved."

"When she became pregnant with Ria," Charlie said.

"Something really changed in her then," Mrs. Vandercook said. "Of course, after Victoria died, well, she just could not see her way out of her grief. But you know, when she was in England, the doctors said the melancholy was related to having children."

"Wait, what? The doctor told her that?" This was something she hadn't considered.

"A doctor in London told your mum this happens to some women. That there really was no cure for it but to get busy."

"I saw some pictures of Mom after Ria was born. She did not look good."

"She really had trouble. Some women have an easy time of it. Not your mum. But we had moved up here to Westfield by then and didn't see each other as much. When I saw your mum at Victoria's funeral, I was beside myself with worry for her. I think the isolation got to her, everyone keeping to themselves, scared they were going to get sick with polio. And then, after Victoria died, she was even more isolated. Poor thing. You were the light of her life, dear. Here, I found this note she wrote to me. I want you to have it."

Mrs. Vandercook pushed herself up. She opened a drawer near the sink, pulled out a small letter, and handed it to Charlie. Mom's neat writing filled two sides of a thank-you card.

Dear Berta,

Thank you for helping me after Victoria died. You have always been like a sister to me. What would I do without you? My dear Victoria, I will never understand why she died. I blame myself. Now I am hanging on by a thread. Some days I am unable to get out of bed. I'm so weepy. Then that morning you stopped in and brought me tea and cookies. What a gem you are.

I am worried about Charlotte. She wants to take care of me. Karl keeps her busy in the cheese factory. She is such a special girl, though, so smart. I know she'll be fine.

You are the best friend I could ask for. Always there for me.

Your immigrant sister,

Evelyn

"Wow. I didn't realize she blamed herself," Charlie said. Another revelation.

"We do that, don't we, dear?" Mrs. Vandercook said. "I blamed myself for not visiting her more often."

"Mom got sick after both pregnancies. That had to be part of it." With this realization, the last missing piece of the puzzle fell into place. It finally all made sense. Mom was sick and Charlie knew now it was more than her brother dying in the war or being away from her home in England. It was more than her grief after Ria's death or the depression after her children were born, although these were the most important pieces. The pieces only made sense if you looked at the whole puzzle.

The older woman's gaze shifted to a squirrel on the bird feeder, digging for seeds. "Then she started taking those pills. I told her, 'Evelyn, you don't want to become like Marilyn Monroe.' But she was too far gone by then."

"She needed help, but more than what we could give her."

"We had the war. Then we had polio." Mrs. Vandercook tsked and shook her head. "So much suffering. And your father, he tried everything. Even offered to send her back to England. Told her he'd sell off some of those woods he owned to pay for her to go to Mayo in Rochester. Only she never did make it there."

"Dad was going to sell off some of the woods?" Charlie was shocked. Dad had always held such reverence for the old forest. Mrs. Vandercook was full of revelations. Thank goodness she'd come to see her today. She felt a rush of warmth toward her, so she got up, came around the table, and hugged her shoulders.

"Thank you so much, Mrs. V. You've helped me more than you could ever know."

"I'm happy to, dear. Your mum was my best friend."

~

Back home, Charlie sat at her kitchen table. Lucy would be home from school soon. She stared at the painting of Ria at the carnival with the cheese curds pouring from the sky like rain. Lucy had taped it to the refrigerator, claiming it was a masterpiece.

Charlie took a sip of beer. Think. She knew there had to be a way out of this mess, a way to rebuild the factory. Talking to Mrs. Vandercook had given her clarity. Understanding more about the reason for her mom's death brought a relief that was palpable, like a weight had been lifted. Maybe she should think about this differently—as a beginning, not an ending. She could change things. She'd been thinking a lot about how hard it was for her being a woman on her own. Maybe she could teach young women the science of making cheese. It would be a way to give back. Ha! She would be fulfilling her promise to God when Lucy went missing. *I'll do anything.* She could make sure women were schooled in the business aspects of cheesemaking too: design the factory to accommodate testing of new recipes, buy a vat for smaller test batches.

Dad had always wanted to build a new factory. He claimed the old one was just temporary housing. But how would she do it? Maybe she *could* sell some of the trees. Learning that Dad had considered it changed everything. She wouldn't be dishonoring her father's memory. This would help her dad live on. It's not like Charlie was going to sell the whole forest. Just a small portion of it. Like how the Menominee people managed their forest on the reservation. She'd heard the pride in John's telling of how the tribe allowed swaths of trees in their massive forest to grow old before they cut them down for lumber, strategically leaving others to thrive, grow, and mature. She'd learned these lessons from John and Karen, and she recalled that her Dad had talked about how the Menominee's practices had become a model for sustainable forest management.

She got up and pried off the tape that affixed the cheese curd painting to the refrigerator. She carefully smoothed its curled corners flat on the kitchen table. What was it about cheese curds falling from the sky that had always fascinated her? It wasn't the first time she'd painted curds raining down. The first time was when she was about twelve years old. Dad was on a cheese curd kick, and they had made them all day. It was summer. They intended to sell them at the county fair. Best sellers, he called them. *Easy to make, easy to sell.* What if, she wondered. What if she switched to making cheese curds for a while and sold them in bulk to grocery stores? Could she sell them at Packers games? There had to be a market. Quick and easy. People loved cheese curds. Between the cheese curds, selling a small portion of the trees, and investment from Jake, she could pull this off. But there was one thing she desperately needed.

She picked up the phone and dialed Mrs. Vandercook. She started the conversation by thanking her again for the tea and chat. "And I have a favor to ask of you," Charlie told her.

"Of course, dear, anything," she said.

"Would you let me use your factory at night? Just for a few months, until we rebuild? You know I'd keep it clean, be done by the time the guys get started in the morning." Charlie held her breath, hoping for her help, praying she'd say yes.

"Why, of course," she said. "What a wonderful idea. We'd be happy to help."

"And one more thing," Charlie said. "Can I get that windmill cookie recipe from you? I've been craving them."

Chapter 51

December rolled in and Uncle Jack was back. Tanned and relaxed, he oozed calm, and Charlie felt good just looking at him. He and Karen had offered to come back to Wisconsin after the factory fire, but Charlie had insisted she could handle the cleanup. They were here now, though, and Charlie was relieved.

"I had an idea," she told Uncle Jack as they surveyed the area where the factory had stood.

"Personally, I think it's a good one," John said. He was measuring the foundation dimensions of the factory's footprint.

Charlie nodded, grateful for John's support. "I want to rebuild right here, and here's my idea. What if I sold off some of the woods back there? I know Dad loved those woods, and I hate to do it, but I think I could bring myself to sell if it means being able to stay and rebuild."

Uncle Jack said nothing. He walked to the edge of the woods, surveying the trees. Charlie followed him. As she began to worry he didn't like the plan, he turned around and faced her. "I was wondering if you were going to consider selling some of the trees. You've got an old forest here; you'll get good money, and you don't need to sell all of it."

"Exactly what I was thinking! I called Jenny's father-in-law last night and got an idea of how much I'd get. I figure I can pay off the loan to Jake *and* pay off Casper. There's enough to at least pay for materials to rebuild this place."

"Labor would be cheap, at least for John and me," Uncle Jack said.

"Count me in," John said. "I have all summer off, and I can get a crew of high school students to help with construction."

"That's perfect, we should be ready to build in summer." Charlie smiled at him. She clapped her hands together, barely able to contain her excitement. "And the best news is Jenny's father-in-law made me an offer. He's interested in the trees for his high-end line of cabinets."

"You already got an offer?" Uncle Jack asked.

"It's a good one. He was here at the crack of dawn and took a look at the trees. I'm sure being Charlotte's godmother helped expedite the process." Charlie felt a wave of warmth spread through her when she thought of baby Charlotte. "I just have to convince Judge Flynn to give me a little more time again. They can't do the cutting and hauling until late spring."

"Gives us some time to draw up the plans, order materials," Uncle Jack said. "We can start right now."

Charlie spread out a few sheets of Lucy's drawing paper on the picnic table. The three of them stood around it and watched as Uncle Jack sketched out a rough outline of what would be the new factory. She looked over at the woods and thought about how happiness sometimes arrived as overwhelming joy. But other times, it was a gentle nudge that faded unnoticed unless it was labeled, nurtured, and allowed to grow.

Chapter 52

"This is taking too long," Charlie told Daniel. She hadn't quite mastered making test batches of cheese in her father's kitchen. Using the stove to heat and then transfer everything to the bathtub for draining was arduous, messy, and bad for her back. Until the new factory was built, she was making cheese curds in bulk at the Vandercook cheese factory five nights a week. She'd be happy when the new factory was done. The plans were complete, and she had gotten bids for electricity and plumbing.

"I got this." Daniel took the thermometer out of her hand. "You go."

"Okay." She lifted the apron off. "Just keep an eye on it."

"Until it's just shy of Jell-O," Daniel said. "You taught me this, remember? And after shoveling cow manure the past few weeks, I know what I'd rather be doing, so I got a good reason to do this right."

"That's the best thing I've heard all morning." Also, it was the most he'd talked to her since he started. He was that quiet. "And remember, Walter's coming to tutor you after court."

Two hours later at the courthouse, she watched the judge review the documents she'd provided. His expression was serious, lips compressed. Was that good or did it mean she hadn't provided enough proof they were on the right track? Jake was sitting next to her this time. The two of them had worked hard on the documents outlining Morgan Cheese's financial status. There were invoice orders for curds from the Milwaukee Cheese Market, the Falls River Co-op, and several grocery stores, including a large order from Tom O'Hearn. There were earnings projections going out two years. Maybe it was too much. Maybe they were reaching too far. Before they had overdue bills, and now they were building a new factory.

Walter cleared his throat. He was here for moral support, looking much healthier than the last time they'd come to court. Despite having Walter and Jake by her side, Charlie knew it was up to her to lay out her case. She glanced over at Casper Raines, who looked hungover and weak from whatever binge he'd been on the night before. She felt a little sorry for him, regretting she hadn't insisted Dad call the cops the day his dad beat him up. Maybe they wouldn't be here if she had.

Then she caught herself. Wasn't this what she'd been doing all her life? Thinking she had control over what was out of her control. Thinking things were her fault. It was time to put aside what she couldn't control and focus on what was within her power to change.

She shook her legs and her hands, took a deep breath, and exhaled. She'd come so far and was so close. Shit. The judge was talking to her.

"Pardon me?"

"I said it looks like you were able to start making cheese again. After the fire."

"Yes, your honor. I'm working nights at a friend's factory."

"And now it seems you are asking for more time."

She covered her right hand over her left to quiet the shaking as she nodded her head.

"Charlie, I don't know what kind of a cheesemaker you are, but I do know this . . ."

Her jaw ached. In fact, her teeth had started to hurt from the constant grinding. She felt like he was talking in slow motion. Here it comes. He'll drop the boom, tell her it's over, liquidate whatever assets she has left, which consist of the house and the land. Well, she wouldn't let him do that.

"A fighter."

"Pardon?" She'd missed the boom he'd lowered, something between *I do know this* and *fighter.*

"You are a fighter. I understand you lost your sister and your mom when you were very young. You lost your dad, suffered huge losses in the fire. But you picked right up and put together this plan that includes selling off some of your woods, the partnership with Jake Rasmusson. He must have a lot of faith in you and your work."

"I do, your honor." Jake stood up.

"We all do." It was Uncle Jack. Charlie twisted around and saw Karen sitting next to Uncle Jack, Jenny, and Michael from the Rosewood Co-op. Next to them were Larry and John. Jenny waved her hand, Larry waved his cap, and John nodded.

"I'm going to give you another six months." Judge Flynn closed his file and nodded at her. "You showed me more than enough."

~

More than enough. She thought of Larry telling her the same thing. It was at Mom's funeral lunch. She was in line to get food in front of Larry, placing ham on her plate, when she heard Dad's voice. He was talking to Walter. "The coroner ruled her death 'misadventure.' Can you believe it?"

Misadventure? Like a mistake? she wondered.

Larry, scooping potato salad onto his plate, heard it too. She could tell because he jerked his head toward Charlie when Dad spoke. She pretended she didn't hear. She didn't care what the coroner or anybody else said; she was angry at her mom, for deciding this life—Dad, her, the house, Falls River—wasn't enough.

"What's it like to be enough?" she asked Larry, placing a handful of potato chips on her plate even though she wasn't hungry.

Larry set down his own plate, piled high with ham, German potato salad, and bean casserole. He bent down, so they were eye to eye. "Look at me, Charlie. You are more than enough, little girl. Every time I see your face, I think, Did God send me an angel or something?"

"Really?"

She was skeptical but willing to consider it because she had always trusted Larry.

"You better believe it." Larry rubbed his eyes with the back of his hand. "Your mom was just too fragile for this life. Too darn fragile."

"You mean like she could break easy?" She'd watched the way Mom took on life's tasks, large and small, as if they were so hard; even pinning up wash on the clothesline seemed hard for her. Maybe he was right. Mom was fragile. In her young mind, fragile seemed like a good word to describe her mom.

"Some people are like that," Larry said. "Some people bend with the wind and some break. Not you. You're a strong one. You can bend."

"How do you know?"

"I can tell." He stood up with a grunt and picked up his plate. "Look how you draw so good, look at how you help your dad in the factory. You knew a clean break the very first time you seen it. Look at how you took such good care of your sister when your mom was sick."

She considered this and arched her back a bit. Yes, she was a pretty good artist, and could read cheese pretty well, but taking care of Ria?

"Not that good," she said.

Larry stared straight ahead and for a moment she thought he hadn't heard her. He was rubbing his eyes again. She picked up a roll and some pads of butter. Larry cleared his throat a few times, then looked down at her.

"Good enough."

~

Now the judge was saying the same.

"This is good enough, more than enough to convince me, Charlie Sobczak. I'm giving you more time to pay your debt to Raines Dairy. Don't make me regret it."

Chapter 53

After two weeks of subzero temps, the ice rink was frozen solid by Christmas Eve. The warming hut was open, and Christmas music blared from a speaker attached to a solitary light pole illuminating the area. They'd arrived early so Charlie could teach Lucy how to skate, before the rest of the group arrived. Charlie held onto Lucy, hunched over, her arms wrapped around her waist.

"Like this, Mom?" Her skates wobbled at first until her ankles steadied.

"You got it. Now, push off." Charlie showed her how to glide on the skate blades, then gradually let go. She watched her daughter take off on her own. Her low center of gravity helped her find her balance as she plunked her skates on the ice in small steps. Soon, she managed a few longer glides.

A dim memory of Dad materialized. It became clearer and sharper as Charlie concentrated hard on retrieving it. She must have been Lucy's age, and they were skating. Dad was holding her hands and skating backward. *Steady, take it one step at a time. You're doing it. See how strong you are.* Dad's hands were bare, and he held onto Charlie's in their oversized knitted mittens, then let go, slipping off to the side. Charlie took off on her own, exhilarated. After a few glides, the tip of her skate caught on a gouge in the ice, and she fell, the belly flop knocking the wind out of her. *Get up,* her dad called. *You go right back to it.*

"I'm skating!" Lucy yelled. She was in the middle of the rink, and the glow of the hospital lights shone behind her, beyond snow piles rimming the rink.

"You're a natural," Charlie yelled. "Look how strong you are!" Lucy's little arms swung side to side across her body like a hockey player as she propelled herself forward. She wore a new, hand-knitted, multicolored, striped stocking hat with matching mittens from Karen. Charlie caught up to her, turned around, and skated backward in front of Lucy. They skated that way across to the other side of the rink. At the far bank, Lucy crashed into Charlie's legs and they both fell onto the snowbank, lying on their backs, laughing.

"Hey, there's the Big Dipper." Charlie pointed to the handle and large bowl. "Follow the star at the tip of the dipper." Charlie snuggled in close to Lucy, tracing the sky. "There. That's the North Star. Sea captains use it to navigate."

"What does navigate mean?"

"Um, it means to figure out where you're going, and how to get there."

"Like if I was in the woods and got lost, I could look at the North Star and find my way home." Lucy cupped her mittened hand in front of one eye and peered into it like a telescope.

"Hey, you two." Larry walked over, thermos in one hand, a bucket in the other. "I brought hot chocolate and a surprise for you, little lady."

"Yay!" Lucy stood up, climbed down the snowbank, and waddled gingerly over to him. Charlie followed, and they peered into the bucket he placed on the ground next to a picnic table in front of the small warming house.

A long nose, big eyes, and cute ears poked out of the bucket. "It's a baby goat!" Lucy cried. "It's so cute."

"You got her a goat?" Charlie asked, aghast. Who gave someone a goat for Christmas?

"Merry Christmas," Larry said. "I figured it'll be good for her to learn to take care of it."

"I love it," Lucy said. "Thanks, Larry. Hey, Uncle Jack and Karen." Lucy waved her arms above her head. "We're over here. Larry got me a goat." She reached into the bucket and with Larry's help lifted the little black-and-white kid into her arms.

"Cool! I want to see it. And I want to show you the shells I brought you from Key West." Karen was wearing a huge down jacket and furry boots. Three men walked behind them. Charlie squinted. Yes. It was Walter, Jake, and Wyatt, who was carrying skates and hockey sticks. Jake waved to everyone as he guided Walter along the snow-packed path.

"I know how to skate now," Lucy announced in a loud voice to Hadley, who arrived with his parents, Michael and Christine. They played with the goat until Lucy handed it over to Karen and went back out on the ice with

Hadley. Jenny arrived holding Charlotte, who was wrapped up in a down sleeping bag. Pete was close behind, carrying a cooler and blankets. Uncle Jack unpacked mulled wine and snacks. A light snow fell with quiet magic, and the kids began to yell the obvious: "It's snowing."

Charlie thought about how close she'd come to being stuck in her grief after Ria and Mom died. She understood now what had, over the years, filled in the spaces her mother had left. It was these people. It was standing next to Dad and Uncle Jack at the vat, knowing she was loved. It was Larry telling her she was good enough, Walter teaching her about fear. It was Jenny with her easy friendship, her fierce loyalty, her enduring humor. It was Karen showing her how to mother even as she grieved for what her mother could not give.

She thought about Rick less often now. He'd called last night, told her about the rap groups he'd attended. These were groups run by vets where they talked freely about the war. He said it was helping, that it took some of the edge off his anger.

Larry, Jake, and Walter started singing "White Christmas," screwing up the words, stopping to argue about the lyrics and eat the Dutch windmill cookies Charlie and Lucy had made that morning. Wyatt and Pete raced each other onto the ice and Uncle Jack held Charlotte, looking smitten, telling her detailed stories about dolphins and manatees and the best bait to use when fishing for grouper in the Florida Keys.

Jenny walked over and plopped her arm on Charlie's shoulder. "Merry Christmas, friend. Let's hope your luck is better next year."

A truck pulled into the parking lot, windshield wipers brushing light snow into the wind. John and Daniel got out of the cab.

"It's looking better already," Charlie told Jenny, and together they watched the skaters circling around the rink, with Elvis singing he'd be home for Christmas and Charlie thinking this was good.

Good to be home.

Acknowledgments

I am indebted to University of Wisconsin Press director Dennis Lloyd and author Dr. Ann Garvin for supporting this story and challenging me to delve deeper into the novel's historical context of the incredibly eventful years of the 1950s through the 1970s. I am truly grateful to Jacqulyn Teoh, Janie Chan, Adam Mehring, Jennifer Conn, and everyone at the University of Wisconsin Press for the expertise and care they gave to the process of preparing this novel for publication. For her careful and intuitive editing, I want to acknowledge and thank Sheila McMahon, senior project editor at UW Press. A big thanks to Kim Suhr for her help with early drafts, and her skillful editing support throughout this journey. I appreciate all the thoughtful feedback from Robert Vaughan and fellow Thursday night and Friday morning roundtable members at Red Oak Writing. I also owe a huge thanks to Tim Storm for his insightful guidance on story development.

The idea for this novel came from a visit with a friend to a cheese factory in northern Wisconsin, near Gillett, in 1977, when I tasted fresh cheese curds for the first time and gained a fascination for the art and science of cheesemaking. During my research, I approached several Wisconsin cheesemakers. I am extremely grateful to Marieke Penterman of Marieke Gouda, whose female college interns sat in on our interview and who was the inspiration for Charlie's decision to teach young women how to make cheese. Thank you to Julie Hook of Hook's Cheese Company for sharing her expertise about the technical aspects of cheesemaking and to Dean Sommer, cheese and food technologist at the UW–Madison Center for Dairy Research, for patiently helping me understand phage, the contributions of Alice Evans, cheesemaking equipment in the 1970s, and other technical issues. Thanks also to the Widmer family (Widmer's Cheese Cellars), the Stettler family (Decatur Dairy), and Brian Knox from Hoard's Dairyman Farm Creamery, all of whom kindly answered my random questions about cheesemaking. In addition to interviews with cheesemakers, I used countless resources, and some of my favorites were *The Master Cheesemakers of Wisconsin*, by James Norton and Becca Dilley; Gordan Edgar's book *Cheddar*; and Jeanne Carpenter's *Cheese Underground* blog.

For helping me understand Menominee Indian history and culture, I owe sincere thanks to Marin Webster Denning, educator, and Dr. Bryan Rindfleisch, associate professor of history, at Marquette University. For information about termination and the fight to restore the Menominee tribe's sovereignty, I relied on Ada Deer's inspiring book, *Making a Difference: My Fight for Native Rights and Social Justice*. Some of the other excellent resources I used were *Little Hawk and the Lone Wolf*, by Raymond C. Kaquatosh; *Freedom with Reservation: The Menominee Struggle to Save Their Land and People*, edited by Deborah Shames; Marti Matyska's PhD dissertation, "Culturally Responsive Curriculum and Pedagogy for Students of the Menominee Indian School District"; and many historical documents about the creation of the Menominee Indian School District.

For historical information about second-wave feminism, I turned to the book *Moving the Mountain: The Women's Movement in America since 1960*, by Flora Davis. To understand the historical context of the first-wavers, I looked to Genevieve McBride's *On Wisconsin Women: Working for Their Rights from Settlement to Suffrage*. For information on the Vietnam War, I relied on stories such as Tim O'Brien's *The Things They Carried*, and research articles about post-traumatic stress and healing for Vietnam veterans.

My heartfelt thanks to Wisconsin author Jerry Apps for his insights about what it was like to contract polio as a child. I recommend his book *Limping through Life: A Farm Boy's Polio Memoir* for more information on this important topic. Special thanks to my husband, Michael Fleissner, for his guidance on legal issues covered in the book, and to my brother, Mark Wimmer, who taught me about the intricacies of raccoon hunting and shared his memories of our grandpa's sawmill. Thanks to Dr. Robert Ninneman for answering my questions about heart disease; Diane Verkuylen-Murphy, who shared her mother's Dutch windmill cookie recipe; friends Kate Wimmer, Maureen Terry-Jestes, Lori Lindquist, Peg Edquist, Barb Monnat, the Wimmer Women, Park Avenue Book Club, and Michael Jon for listening and sharing their thoughts about the novel; and Sue-Ellen Gray, who designed my author website. Finally, I am grateful to Terri Feely for her wisdom and for always encouraging me to keep on writing.

Any mistakes related to any aspect or topic in the novel are mine alone and not the fault of the amazing people who shared their expertise with me.

MARY WIMMER, PHD, is a writer, school psychologist, and educator. She is the author of *Reaching Shore*, first-place winner of the Midwest Independent Publishers Association–Young Adult Fiction Award. She is also the author of two nonfiction books about school refusal and truancy published by the National Association of School Psychologists. Her short story "Floe" was awarded second place for fiction in the Wisconsin Writers Association 2021 Jade Ring contest. She lives in southeastern Wisconsin.